ABOUT TIME

ABOUT TIME

EILEEN PHYALL

Eileen Phyall

Copyright © 2024 by Eileen Phyall

The right of Eileen Phyall to be identified as author of this work has been asserted by the author in accordance with sections 77 and 78 of the Copyright Designs and Patents Act 1988.

All rights reserved. No part of this book may be reproduced in any manner whatsoever without written permission except in the case of brief quotations embodied in critical articles and reviews.

This is a work of fiction. Names, characters, businesses, places, events, and incidents are either products of the author's imagination or used in a fictitious manner. Any resemblance to actual persons, living or dead, or actual events is purely coincidental.

First Printing, 2024
ISBN 9781399988179

For Joyce Judge

CONTENTS

Dedication v

Chapter 1   1
Chapter 2   6
Chapter 3   16
Chapter 4   25
Chapter 5   29
Chapter 6   40
Chapter 7   49
Chapter 8   56
Chapter 9   65
Chapter 10   71
Chapter 11   80
Chapter 12   91
Chapter 13   102

Chapter 14	112
Chapter 15	118
Chapter 16	123
Chapter 17	132
Chapter 18	141
Chapter 19	147
Chapter 20	152
Chapter 21	159
Chapter 22	171
Chapter 23	176
Chapter 24	181
Chapter 25	191
Chapter 26	196
Chapter 27	203
Chapter 28	212
Chapter 29	220
Chapter 30	224
Chapter 31	230
Chapter 32	241
Chapter 33	248
Chapter 34	255

Chapter 35	258
Chapter 36	265
Chapter 37	271
Chapter 38	275
Chapter 39	279
Chapter 40	285
Chapter 41	294
Chapter 42	298
Chapter 43	304
Chapter 44	306
Acknowledgements	309
About The Author	310

Chapter 1

I would have stayed in the pub if I'd known what awaited me. Thursday evening at The Swan was quiz night; it was a boon for five penniless students. We often claimed one of the cash prizes and the drinks were half price. I looked forward to it, but tonight I was in an odd mood. I didn't feel part of things. My friends were all talking at once, planning the strategy. Confident we'd win again. I could hear Cyndi Lauper singing *'Time After Time'* over the speakers. It was still my favourite, even though it had been out of the charts for three years. Three years ago, I was eighteen, still trying to decide which university I wanted to go to.

"Come on Imogen, you look miles away," Caro's voice interrupted my thoughts. "We need you to do the science as well as the history parts of the quiz. Harry isn't coming. I'll get you a pint."

"I don't want any more drink. My head aches, I think I'll go home." Caro looked at me eyebrows raised. "But how will we win the history without your brain?"

"Sorry Caro I don't feel right, Sarah's good at history too."

She touched my arm. "You must be bad if you're missing

the quiz. She called over to George. "Change of plan, Imogen's going home."

George followed me to the door. "Imogen, are you okay?" he asked. "You've been working too hard."

"I think I just need an early night."

"Are you all right to walk home by yourself?"

I assured him I was, he kissed my cheek saying he would see me soon.

I glanced back. He was still there, looking concerned, I waved, and he went inside. It didn't take long to get to my flat. I didn't understand my mood and the need to be alone.

Usually, I would enjoy the company and have a little too much to drink, leaving inhibitions behind as the evening wore on.

Once in my room, I pressed the light switch. Nothing happened. I tried again. Perhaps the bulb had blown. I stumbled to the table and pushed the switch on the lamp, again no light. I guessed a fuse had blown. The streetlight outside the window cast a glow across the room.

I had a large, scented candle on the shelf, but where were the matches? I cursed the fact that my flat was electric only. My head really was aching now.

A car drove by casting a light across the room. As it rippled along the wall, I could see the outline of a door. Strange, there was no door there. The house was old, had there been one previously that had been blocked up? Walking over to the wall, I banged my knee on a chair. I felt along where I had seen the outline. Nothing. Was it imagination? I felt a handle, as I turned it the door opened inwards, and I fell through the opening.

Once inside the musty smell made me hold my breath. The smoke from the large fireplace billowed into the room and stung my eyes. Through the gloom, I could see a man sitting at a desk. Was he real? It felt as if I'd stumbled into a museum setting. My head was throbbing, and I could hear my pulse beating in my ears. He looked up.

"You're late," he said brusquely.

I swallowed. "What did you say?"

"You're late, I was expecting you over an hour ago."

"Me?"

"What is this? Are you stupid?" He sighed deeply. "They told me they were sending someone who would know what to do and they've managed to get hold of an imbecile."

"Now look here. I don't know what's going on. I've come through a door, which I have never seen before. I am totally confused but there is no excuse for your rudeness."

I turned, determined to go back into my room, but the door had disappeared. I walked over feeling along the wall, trying to find it.

"You'll not find the door if that's what you are looking for. It served its purpose."

"What do you mean?"

"It allowed you in. That's all it needed to do."

"So I can't go back?"

"Not yet. Not until it's time?"

"When will that be? All I want is a match to light my candle. How long have you been here? I want to go back to my room now."

I could hear my voice sounded a little wobbly, this was all too creepy. If I'd had more than two drinks, I'd have blamed it on the beer. I pinched myself, it hurt. I was definitely not asleep.

I took a deep breath and walked closer to the desk. The man wore a dark jacket over a white frilly shirt. There was a silver inkpot beside him. He dipped his pen into the pot wiping the excess ink on the side. He wrote something, I could hear the pen scratching on the paper. I felt in my pocket for a tissue. He looked up, staring at me. "Well, do you know the answer?"

"I don't know the question. What are you asking me?"

He sighed again. "If you don't know the question, why did you come here?"

"I didn't come by choice," I said.

"Do you know about electric light?"

"Yes of course I do, everyone knows about it."

"This chap Swann is talking about using it to light homes, and they are saying it will harm people's eyes, especially women."

I looked at him, at his odd clothes and wondered what was happening. Was this a joke? Electric light harming people, I looked around the room. There were candles on the walls. I could see no other light fittings, no light bulbs. An oil lamp flickered on the desk.

"What year is it?" I asked him.

"The year of Our Lord eighteen hundred and seventy-eight."

That explained his question. It made more sense. If finding myself over a hundred years in the past could make sense. What had happened when I came through that doorway? I had felt no sense of going backwards. My mind was doing summersaults.

"That was about the time when electricity was installed at Cragside in Northumberland. If I remember correctly, Edison claimed he had invented the electric light but eventually he and Swann worked together to produce light bulbs." I was thinking aloud. I'd been to Cragside when I was at school and had found the story fascinating.

"Is it dangerous to sight? That's what the learned society wants to know, should we support it?"

"Oh yes of course you should, otherwise Britain will miss out on one of the most important inventions of the century."

"Thank you, so you did know. Now I suppose you want to go back to your own time." He reached behind him and pulled a black cloak around his shoulders.

I nodded, "I do."

"I'll do my best. You need to leave by that door, the one on the right will send you into the past." He pointed across to the left of the fireplace before bending his head back down to write. My journey back was of no interest to him at all.

I walked across the room; I could see no door in the wooden panels.

"Think of a door, think hard." His voice seemed to come from far away. "You have to work at it."

I looked at the panels trying to imagine one opening. This time I did have a feeling of something moving, whether it was time or me, I couldn't tell.

Chapter 2

I opened my eyes; it wasn't quite light. I was very thirsty, and my bladder was complaining. I swung my legs out of the bed. Well, I tried to. I moved the duvet, but my legs didn't follow. They were so sore and my back hurt. I was completely awake now. I remembered the night before going into the other room but not coming back. Perhaps travelling through time, for that is what I seemed to have done, had made me stiff.

I realised I needed to hurry to the bathroom. I could feel a slight dampness between my legs. I opened the bedroom door. Where was I? I could see a bathroom at the end of a small corridor. I made it just in time.

I took a few steps to the sink. As I washed my hands, I looked into the mirror. It was not my face looking back. What was happening? I could feel hair across my eyes so lifted my hand to brush it out of the way. The hand in the mirror did the same, but it was old, scrawny and wrinkled with brown age spots on the back. I looked down at my hand, to my horror I saw that it was the one reflected in the mirror. Did that mean the lined pale face looking back at me was mine too? I leaned forward to get a better look. The mirror reflected every move I made. It was me. How could it be? I thought hard about the night before. I could only remember being in that other room. What had he said?

"I'll do my best." If this was his best, I couldn't think of anything worse. Was this how I'd look when I was old, how awful. All those lines and for the first time I registered the short grey hair. He'd said he'd send me forward in time, but why was I in this old body? Had going through time barriers had this devastating effect on me? I looked again at my hands. How could I face anyone? Tears traced along the lines on my cheeks.

I made my way painfully along the corridor to the bedroom. I was feeling chilly, there must be some warm clothes somewhere. My jeans and sweatshirt were in a pile behind the door. I quickly put them on. The jeans were loose on my scrawny frame, but they were more inviting than the frumpy skirt hanging on the back of the chair.

There was a buzzing sound and the flat device by the bed lit up. 'Call from Lilly,' I read. There was a green square and a red one. I touched the green. A woman's voice said. "Mum, where are you? You said you'd come for coffee with us this morning. Are you up yet?"

"Who is this?"

The voice sounding cross, said, "it's Lilly, Mum. You promised you'd meet us."

Mum, I thought, I'm no one's mum.

"Are you dressed?"

"Yes I am."

"Drive round then, we'll wait for you. Remember we said we'd have breakfast at Bernie's."

"Drive, I can't drive."

"Of course you can. Oh Mum, do you mean you don't feel up to driving? We'll come round and get you."

Before I could ask who 'We' were, the light went out. I picked it up. It was metallic with a glass front. It buzzed again and words came up on the screen.

C u in 5.

I pressed the button on the bottom.

Sender's name Alicia appeared. Who was Alicia?

I went back to the bathroom and combed my hair. I started to feel a bit better but not for long, as looking at that face made me feel sick. There was a toothbrush in a glass and some toothpaste, I didn't fancy using someone else's toothbrush. I looked to see if I could find a new one without success. I did need to clean my teeth, my mouth tasted awful. In the end, I ran the brush under the hot tap for several minutes before cleaning my teeth.

There was a loud jangling of a doorbell. I went to the end of the corridor and opened the door. A girl about eleven years old stood there grinning.

"Mum's parking," she said. "You know how bad she is at finding a space, so I came straight up."

"Alicia?"

She threw herself at me, wrapped her arms around me.

"Oh Grannie, it's so good to see you. This term seemed to last forever."

"It's good to see you too," I said, slightly out of breath after the bear hug.

She came in. "Like your new outfit Gran, don't know what Mum will make of it though. I'm supposed to hurry you up, shall I get your coat and boots?"

I nodded. Alicia went to a cupboard and got out a padded dark blue coat and a pair of black boots. I sat on the chair by the door to pull on the boots, while she chatted away telling me how awful school had been.

The doorbell rang. Alicia opened the door. A tall blond woman stood there.

"Alicia, stop talking for a minute, you'll exhaust your grannie. Hello Mum, do you feel better now?" She came over and gave me a kiss that didn't quite reach my cheek.

"You didn't sound too good when I phoned. You did say you wanted to help choose Alicia's dress."

"Oh yes Grannie, please do come."

"I'm not sure where my purse is. Could you help me look for it Alicia?"

"Of course I will. It should be in the kitchen where you normally put it. I'll get it for you."

She came back into the hall holding a small bag. I thanked her and looked inside. "There doesn't seem to be much money here, will we be near a bank?"

The woman who said she was my daughter, sighed loudly. "Mother, I keep telling you, money is not needed, you can do everything contactless. You know all the banks have shut."

I looked at her, not understanding. "Contactless?"

"With your card." She took the bag from me. "Here's your card, you can do everything with it. You do know that." She sounded exasperated. Her lips were a thin line.

"Okay," I said feeling confused. "But how do you pay your bills if the banks are shut?"

Alicia said. "By internet banking Gran, do you remember

I've shown you how to do it? Your passwords are on the back of the kitchen calendar."

"Oh yes of course," I said, not wanting to annoy Lilly who looked as if she regretted coming for me.

"Come on then let's go."

Lilly locked the door for me using the keys that were hanging on the wall. She handed them to me. "Here, put them safely in your bag. We won't have time to come back up with you." As we got in the lift that was along the hallway, I turned back to look for the number of the flat. I would need to know where to return. It all looked so strange to me. It certainly wasn't my student flat. Nicer and tidier, but not where I wanted to be.

The lift went down to a car park and Lilly walked quickly over to her car. Once we were inside, she pressed a button and the car started to reverse out of the space. We were soon going along the road in what seemed to be a silent car. I'd never been interested in cars but this one amazed me. It needed little input from Lilly. When we arrived at our destination Lilly pressed the button again and the car reversed into a space.

"How does it do that?" I asked in surprise, "and why can't I hear the engine?"

Lilly sighed, "the car is electric, I have had a self-parking car for years, you should be used to it by now."

I thought it best to keep quiet.

We got out of the car and walked over to an escalator. I was expecting a shopping centre, but I could see no shops. There were large buildings that looked like department stores. When we got close, I could see that they were gyms, and the windows were full of stylised sports clothing and equipment. The rest of the buildings seemed to be coffee shops or restaurants.

I asked Alicia where she was thinking of going to choose her dress.

"Here, Grannie, we will choose it while we are waiting for our food." She pointed towards a large coffee shop full of people sitting in comfortable armchairs.

Lilly found us a table and asked me if I wanted my usual. I said yes, not wanting to ask more questions. Alicia took from her bag what looked like a larger version of the phone I had.

"I'll just scroll through the ones I like," she said, and within seconds, pictures of pretty dresses appeared on the screen. She was soon showing me the three she liked best.

"Are you sure you want to buy the dress?" Alicia asked.

"It's more than you would normally spend on me." She seemed very happy; how could I have said no? She turned to her mother, and they agreed that she would order two, to see which looked best.

"So, you're not going to a shop to try it on?" I asked.

Lilly gave me a withering look. "Do you see any shops?"

"Well, no I did wonder about that."

"It's all internet shopping now, Grannie. Will you put your card on my tablet so that they can charge you please? Remember they will refund the one we don't keep."

I handed the bankcard over to her as our food came.

Mine was an avocado sliced into a fan with scrambled eggs. There was a piece of hard looking toast on the side plate. When I bit into it, I liked the flavour, but Lilly saw me looking at it.

"What's the matter, don't you like sourdough anymore?"

"It's nice, but unusual."

"It's what you always have," she said between gritted teeth.

I asked her what she'd called it, everything was bewildering.

"Mum please concentrate. This is why you're having the test for Alzheimer's tomorrow. I'm worried about you; you can't remember anything. You really shouldn't be living on your own." Her face softened, "I'm sorry to be irritable with you. I'm just so worried. You seem much worse today." She looked as if she might cry.

"I'm sorry. I'm just having a bad day." I felt for her, but I couldn't help. I remembered nothing about the life I'd lived in this body.

Alicia squeezed my hand. "Sometimes if you don't sleep well, it can be difficult to remember things."

I thought how lovely she was and wondered if I really would have a granddaughter like her one-day. Then the terrible thought struck me, what if this was it? What if I never return to my own time. This life was nearly over, my joints ached so much, and I was to have an Alzheimer's test tomorrow.

It sounded as if Lilly was going to put me into care, which would be even worse. I sat thinking of my friends wondering if anyone was missing me. I had taken over this old body. Was mine still back there in my own familiar place, or lost in time somewhere? How could I get back?

I was aware of them looking at me.

"Mum you've gone dreadfully pale shall we get you home? Do you have indigestion?"

"No not indigestion but I don't feel quite right," I replied.

It was true I didn't feel well at all. The waitress was called, and Lilly's card tapped on to a small machine.

"I feel I'd like to walk a little," I said.

Alicia offered to come with me while Lilly finished her large mug of coffee.

"Take care, don't go far," she said as we set off. My bones creaked as I moved at a fraction of my normal pace.

Alicia chattered away delighted at the thought of her new dress.

"I'll come round tomorrow to give you a twirl." I nodded, finding it difficult to concentrate on her chatter. A thousand questions were whirling around my head. We walked until we reached the end of the paved area.

"We should make our way back, so Mother doesn't start to worry," Alicia said. We walked slowly back, passing people in doorways, so many beggars.

"It never used to be like this."

"Dad says it's because the welfare system lets people down."

We were almost back at the coffee shop when I spotted him. Huddled up in his big black cloak, he looked cold. As we passed by, he looked up.

"Got any change, love?"

"Come on Grannie," Alicia tugged my arm.

I felt in my coat pocket, there were a few coins. I fetched them out and bent down to give them to him. "How did we get here?" I whispered.

"Something went wrong. I need to help you."

"Too right. How are you going to fix it?"

"I need a roof over my head to do so."

"Come to mine." I realised I didn't know where I lived.

I turned to Alicia to ask her my address, but she had disappeared into the coffee shop, calling for her mother. I had to act quickly.

I remembered the house keys. The key ring had a label with the address written on it. I tore it off and gave it to him.

"Come later." He nodded.

Lilly was at my elbow, grabbing me. "What are you doing, these people are off their heads on drugs."

"I felt sorry for him, he's known better times," I said.

"Look at the quality of his cloak."

"Most probably stolen," she said rudely, pulling me away.

We returned to my flat. I sat in silence in the car, while Lilly lectured me on the dangers of talking to strangers.

"I thought I recognised him, I'm sure I knew him years ago," I said.

"Well, I don't want you talking to him now. You should be ashamed of frightening Alicia like that."

"I sorry I frightened you Alicia, but poor man, think how awful it would be to have nothing and be without a roof over your head."

"Don't say things like that to Alicia." Lilly's face creased in an angry frown.

When I get back to normal, I vowed to myself, I'll treat my mother with respect when she gets old. When did it become okay for daughters to tell their mothers what they should do and think?

I suppose because people are living longer until they are very old, I thought. What a horrible state to be in, I really want to be out of here. I will make sure I will never have anyone control me when I am old.

I thought, but I am old, and she thinks I'm senile. She wants to put me into care. I really don't want to stay around for that. He'd better turn up later and sort things out. Why did this happen to me?

They both came to the flat with me. Lilly turned to go as soon as I put the keys in the lock.

"Hang on Mum. I'll put the kettle on and make you a drink Grannie," Alicia said. She gave me a big hug. Lilly waited in the doorway, tapping her foot. Don't forget I'll be round tomorrow afternoon," said Alicia, then they rushed off to continue their day.

Chapter 3

Sitting in the chair I didn't know which ached most, my head or my back. I wondered if there were any painkillers in this flat. I stood up, and despite the pain I hurried to the bathroom not wanting a repeat of the morning's embarrassment. Once my bladder was empty, I looked in the mirrored cabinet. Again, I didn't recognise the lined face that looked back at me, dark smudges under the eyes and lipstick had run into the lines around the mouth.

It was no good disassociating myself from the person looking out, whether I liked it or not it was me. I was feeling the pain and tiredness very acutely. I opened the cabinet door and looked inside; the shelves were stacked with packets of pills. I saw one labelled paracetamol and codeine. *Two to be taken when needed.* I filled a glass with water and downed the pills making a mental note to examine the other packets when the pain had gone.

I sat back in the chair to enjoy the drink Alicia had made for me now that the pain was subsiding. The tablets were strong, they worked quickly but made me feel muzzy. I felt myself dozing. I didn't try to stop, what else was I to do in this old body?

A persistent knocking on the door awoke me, it took me a few minutes to realise where I was. I got up and groggily made my way to the entrance hall. When I opened the door, an old man stood there. I was disappointed I hoped it might have been my man in the cloak.

"Had you forgotten I was coming round?" He stepped into the hall and leaned towards me.

Oh no he's about to kiss me, I thought. I stepped back, forgetting how narrow the hall was and banged my head against the wall. I would have fallen but he reached out and held me, drawing me to him. I managed to turn my head so that he kissed my cheek.

"What is it, Imogen? Come and sit down, you don't look well."

Once I was sitting, he went into the small kitchen.

"What are you doing?" I asked.

"Making you a cup of tea and a sandwich. You look faint, I bet you've forgotten to eat again."

"I had a late breakfast with Alicia and Lilly," I said indignantly.

"It's nearly five o'clock. Good, there is some cake in the tin. I'll cut us both a piece."

He obviously knew his way around and seemed kind. I looked across at the photographs that were on the mantelpiece. There was one of him and the person in the mirror. Both smiling and looking happy, so I should know him. There was a card next to it. I got up and looked, written inside in a scrawling hand was, *To my beautiful Imogen, all my love, forever Brian.*

So, was this Brian in my kitchen? It was unlikely there would be more than one man in the life of someone so old.

I decided that he must be Brian.

He reappeared carrying a tray containing two mugs of tea, a plate of sandwiches and two slices of cake. He put the tray down on a small table, pushing books, which were there on the floor. I started to pick them up and place them carefully in a stack.

"Oh, you and your books," he said condescendingly.

"Books should be treated with care."

"Yes, but humans are more important." He passed me a mug of tea.

I took a sip and pulled a face. "No sugar," I said.

"You don't take sugar."

"I would like some sugar."

He went back into the kitchen. I could hear doors opening and shutting. He came back with a bag of brown sugar. "This is all I can find."

I put a large spoonful into the mug and took another sip.

"That's better, thanks."

"I take it you don't feel up to coming out tonight."

"No, sorry, I don't. My back's painful, I'd rather be alone if you don't mind."

He looked hurt and stood up. "I'll go then."

I was being mean. There was no need to be unkind. "No, please don't go yet. Stay for a while, tell me what you have been doing."

He launched into a tale about his day and reminded me that we were going for lunch the next day.

"Lilly's arranged for me to have an assessment so I wouldn't be able to have lunch."

He frowned. "Why does she think she can organise your life? She wants to get you into care. She sees our relationship as a threat to her inheritance. It's true your memory's not so good, but you're quite capable. If you let me move in, we can manage very well together. I love looking after you."

I started to understand my daughter's concern. He might be genuine, but this short meeting with him made me feel uneasy. Was he as controlling as he seemed?

My head started to ache badly again. When I said it hurt, he offered to get me some pills, he knew where everything was it seemed.

"I've taken some, I need to lie down."

"I'll go as soon as I've washed the pots and cleared up."

"No, please leave them." He ignored me and started to clear up. I raised my voice.

"Leave things, I'll do it later." He looked shocked and stopped.

"Okay I'll see you tomorrow then."

"No," I said. "I'll call tomorrow and let you know how I feel."

I got up and saw him to the door. I turned my face so that he kissed me on the cheek again. I had difficulty not rubbing my cheek dry. I felt a bit sorry for him but couldn't cope with his company any longer. I'd hoped I hadn't ruined things for my future self.

Back in the room, two books caught my eye. My name was on the cover. I picked one up. Inside the first page stated.

An exciting novel. Imogen Hadley's career in medical

research and her love of psychology have informed her writing, giving her books an exciting and unusual slant. Writing fiction in her maiden name is a retirement project. Her books continue to surprise and delight her readers.

It sounded quite good. Very different to the senile person Lilly believed me to be. I started to read the first chapter of the book. I decided to take it to bed. First, I thought I must look at the rest of the pills in the bathroom. I took all the packets out, five different pills to be taken in the morning and six at night. Wow is this what happens when you get old? I read the leaflets in the packets, several of the pills were for pain relief and arthritis but two were for high blood pressure.

The question was should I take them? They were prescribed for this old body, which from today's experience needed some pain relief. I decided to take the evening pills.

I popped them out of the strips and took them to the bedroom with a glass of water. I didn't want to take them too soon in case my mysterious co-traveller turned up. So many questions were rushing around my head. The brain I had was mine, the body was most possibly mine but a much older version. If I got back to my right time, would I rejoin my young body? It would be horrendous if I took this one back with me. That would be a worst-case scenario. How had this body joined my brain? Where was the brain that belonged to this body? Had that joined my younger body? Oh, how my head ached. What of my future? Was this it, would I go senile? I lay down on the bed, it was less painful.

I awoke. Has it all been a bad dream? One look at my hands told me it was real. At least this time I knew where I was. Not comforting, I wanted to be back in my own time.

It was four o'clock. Again, unwanted thoughts raced around my head. I could remember everything that had happened yesterday but nothing before that, nothing from this life. My memories were of when I was in my last year of university. I knew I would have to face questioning later that day. Having complete memories of my youth and teens would not convince anyone my mental state was sound. I didn't even know what year it was. I guess I could roughly work it out from the age I seemed to be. At least fifty years older than I should be, I shuddered. Why was Lilly having me tested? Surely, no one could make me move from this very pleasant flat, could they? Whatever happened I needed to do the best I could for my future self.

Was this my future self though, or was it another version on another wavelength? Nothing to do with the self I'd left behind. I remember my tutor believed there could be many versions of ourselves, all slightly different according to how we were treated and how we chose to behave.

"Yes, but this is me," I said aloud. I was aware of being in a different time zone but could do nothing about it. Why was I in an old body though? One answer I guess was so that the normality of the time was not disturbed. Everyone would expect to see me as I now appeared. If my younger self had suddenly been in this situation, it would have rocked the equilibrium.

Again though, why was I here? Could it be to help my future self? If so, I was making a poor job of it.

I must have slept again. I woke in daylight to the buzzing of the device that seemed to be a phone. The screen lit up 'Lilly' under her name was a date. 26.09.34

"Mum please be ready at ten," said the voice. "The psychological testing assistant is coming to see you at ten fifteen."

I started to say I didn't want to be tested but she had gone. At least I knew the date now.

I sat up, my body felt even stiffer this morning. The pills were still by the bed, the water tasted stale, but I took the painkillers. I then rushed to the bathroom. Old age, I thought, is pain and a leaky bladder. Other people thinking they have the right to take control of you make it even worse. I would be more considerate to old people when I managed to get back to normal.

When I was drying myself after showering, I looked down at my sagging belly and a healed scar which ran horizontally across. I wondered what had happened there. The whole body seemed to have lost tone and muscle; it was a long time since it had been to the gym. I resolved never to stop. I didn't want to end up like this. I did notice that the heat of the shower helped to lessen the pain and stiffness. Once I was dry, I did a few stretches, feeling my muscles complain as I did.

In the kitchen I found bread and butter, so I made myself some toast. I had barely finished eating it when the doorbell rang. It was Lilly. I must have looked okay, she nodded and smiled at me. I offered her a drink and she said she would wait until the tester came. She told me to do my best, the doctor had pulled strings to get this sorted for us. I didn't say that I hadn't wanted it. It was for her not me.

A young man came to do the testing.

"Hello I'm Jason," he said. "I'm here to have a chat and make sure you're safe and happy living here on your own." He noticed my frown, "I know you might not have requested this. It is very important your wishes are respected, but we need to see what help you might need to ensure this is the best life you can live. May I have a look around your lovely flat?"

"That will be fine won't it Mum?" Lilly said. I was silent, he glanced at me and went into the kitchen.

"We help mum with the shopping and there's a laundry service here."

"Yes, I can see you're well stocked," he said looking in the cupboards. He then went through to the bathroom. While he was looking around, Lilly made coffee for us all.

The next bit was the formal test. He sat asking me questions, recording my answers. I knew my name, but not the name of the prime minister. I had no idea of the answers to so many of the questions he asked. He then gave me a sheet of paper with simple arithmetic problems and spelling type questions. They were easy. I had no problem with them, as I handed the paper back, he raised his eyebrows.

"Oh, you've completed them, that was quick." He compared the answers to his sheet.

"How do you feel about living on your own, cooking and cleaning for yourself?" he asked.

"It gives me no problems at all."

"You have a cleaner twice a week," Lilly reminded me sharply.

When we had finished, Jason said he needed to talk to his manager. "Your case is complex because your memory is very bad, but your cognitive skills are exceptionally good."

"I'm concerned about Mum living alone. Being good at arithmetic doesn't make her safe," Lilly's voice was shrill. Jason asked me to show him how I turned on the cooker and took some things out of the fridge asking me about the sell by date and when it was safe to eat things. I fumbled a bit with the cooker.

"It's different to what I had before," I said without thinking. I had no problem with the sell by dates.

"I recommend you attend a memory clinic to help remember necessary things Imogen, but I have no qualms about you living alone." He said I should accept help from Lilly with shopping and decision-making. I could see that Lilly wasn't satisfied. I knew there was nothing wrong with my memory but of course, I had no knowledge of many things that were everyday occurrences. If I couldn't go back, there was a great deal I would need to know. I was happy to have help with shopping and maybe cooking but decision-making. No way did I want that bossy Lilly making decisions for me even if she did mean well. Lilly showed Jason out, he said he would be in touch soon. Lilly said she had to be going and Alicia would be round later with whichever dress she had chosen to show me.

"You do remember about the dress, Mother?"

"Of course I do," I said.

When I returned to the kitchen, I found a roast chicken dinner on a plate Lilly had left for me. I realised I was hungry and heated it up in the microwave. It was delicious.

Chapter 4

At two o'clock exactly, an excited Alicia was at the door. She had both dresses so I could help her choose. This girl was lovely, she restored my confidence by treating me normally. She tried the dresses on. They were both pretty, I preferred the blue one. She threw her arms around me.

"Good I do too, is it alright if I have that one then?"

"Of course," I said, she was delightful, and I was sorry that the other Imogen had missed this. I guessed she had many moments like this she cherished. I decided I would write a note about the dress so she would know what had happened in her absence.

She stayed for a while chatting excitedly about the party she was going to the next week. As she left, she gave me a big hug and said she would see me soon, which left me thinking that old age did have some compensations.

After Alicia left, I looked at the rest of the photos that were around the flat. They showed versions of me at various ages. One was of me in my cap and gown with George and my mum, obviously taken on my graduation day. There was another in a swimsuit by a very blue sea. I guessed it was taken somewhere abroad. There was one of me in a wedding dress with a tall handsome man. On the walls were several of babies and small children. Were they all mine? Surely not, it was interesting to see the ageing process. There were younger versions of Lilly. As I looked at them, I felt sad. The person that had placed them around the room was desperately trying to hang on to her life. Apart from the photos, there weren't many ornaments. The drawers were tidy, too tidy. Had this flat been a recent move? It was difficult to understand much about the woman that lived here. She seemed tidy, not like me then. What had happened? My head started to throb again, I felt tired. I needed to sit down. I dozed again, I wasn't used to the strength of the pills, and they made me sleepy.

I woke up in the chair, my back hurting and my hands painful. I was beginning to despair. It seemed I was stuck in this time, in this body. How was I going to cope?

I rubbed my eyes; someone was in the other chair. How had he got into the room? Had I not shut the door after Alicia left?

It was him. The man in the cloak. He looked at me.

"I have ways," he said. "You hadn't left the door open. I think I have found a way for us to return."

"Will I leave this body behind? I'm rather sick of being old."

"Hopefully, it would be inconvenient for you to appear like that."

"Hopefully? Is that the best you can do?"

"It is. Will you take the chance?"

I felt angry. "It's not much of a choice, is it?"

"Nevertheless," he said in his old-fashioned way. "You may choose to stay."

"Like this, with most of my life gone."

"None of us know where life will take us, indeed nor when it will end. Age is not always an indication."

"Thanks."

"I need to say though, I'm not sure your advice about electricity was good, looking at how the world seems now."

"Well, it's a pity I was brought out of my time to answer your question then. There would have been nothing you and your learned society could have done to stop progression. It would have happened."

"Hmm. Progression I suppose it could be called that."

"Yes, in your time ordinary people were treated appallingly by ones of your class. Boys still sent up chimneys for instance."

"I don't see much improvement. Everyone is looking at electronic devices, having no time for each other. Electricity has a lot to answer for it seems to me."

"Possibly," I said. I was getting impatient. I didn't want to argue about a social structure about fifty years ahead of my knowledge. I wanted to be at home, preferably with a glass of wine, and no one making decisions about my mental health.

The phone pinged. I looked at it and there was a message from Alicia reminding me I needed to put my phone on the white disc to charge it up. I smiled, not just my memory then, she had done it just before she'd left.

"You need to remember to do this each evening, Grannie, so you can keep in contact with me," she'd said before she left the flat.

I could get used to this phone. Alicia had shown me it had a torch, and a thing called an app, which predicted the weather. The only mobile phones I'd ever seen were in the hands of businessmen on trains. Large black bricks into which they shouted. His voice interrupted my thoughts.

"You can't take it with you. You must ensure you take nothing with you, or it will upset the time factor."

"Just make sure that we go back, if we go any further forward, I will be dead."

He nodded. I wondered how it was he hadn't aged. The light was dim when I'd seen him behind the desk. Was he the same person? He looked the same, but he seemed less austere and perhaps younger. As I looked at his face, I thought again I knew him from somewhere, where was it? He looked different now. He wasn't behind that huge desk and the light was good here. I gave myself a shake of course he was the same person. I realised I was staring at him. What was it about his eyes?

As I stared, the room seemed to get larger, no not larger. The walls were moving, fading, less substantial. Then they were gone. I could hear the music of that song, what was it? *Time After Time*.

I was sitting on grass - damp grass, someone was saying to me.

"You look as if you've had too much wine already." I tried to get up and everything swayed, moved. I fell back down.

"You see I was right," the voice continued.

"You're always right." I could hear my voice slurring. Then everything went black.

Chapter 5

I was propped up; something was sticking in my back. I was against a picnic hamper, a large one made of cane and one of the corners was sharp.

"Oh, you're back with us." His voice was posh and condescending. I started to remember as I looked at my hands, oh what a relief they weren't wrinkled. It took a couple of seconds for me to register my left hand was weighed down with a large diamond ring. When did that happen? Where was I now? My poor head was spinning; it felt as if I'd had too much to drink.

"You look rather worse for wear old girl," said the voice. "I go to all the trouble to bring you here for a picnic to propose to you and you drink the champers so fast you pass out. Hardly touched the salmon tartlets I persuaded the cook to make."

"Propose?" I said. Who was this? Had I agreed to marry him? I must have. I had a ring on my finger. I didn't much like the sound of him, why would I want to marry him?

"Sorry I can't remember, but I have to finish my degree before I make any decisions about marriage." The ring was heavy on my finger. I was struggling to gain time, to work out where I was and what was happening. What had I missed while I was in that old body?

"What are you talking about? Did you bang your head when you fell? What do you mean you can't remember, it's been decided for years, once I was made junior partner we would get engaged."

"Who decided? Sorry I need time to think."

"Your old man is keen enough; he and father have drawn up the pre-nuptials."

"What?"

'Don't look so surprised we get married and the two firms merge, your father needs it to happen to stop his business going down the drain, you know that."

"So, am I the sacrifice?"

"Oh Issy, how can you say that? Anyway, you were all over me earlier when you'd had a little drink. Your reputation is shot if we don't marry. James saw us and he is bound to talk."

Me, all over him? I shuddered at the thought. He pulled me to him and stuck his tongue in my mouth, his kiss wet and unwelcome.

"Come on, we'll go and tell Ma and Pa the glad news then I'll take you home."

He pulled me to my feet, my head throbbed, I found a pair of discarded shoes and put them on. They were flimsy and not suited to grass, but they fitted.

I shivered, the sun had lost its power, and my dress was thin cotton. He put a jacket round my shoulders. Not a complete cad then.

I looked at the glasses and the remains of the food and

started to clear it up thinking we would need to take it with us.

He pulled me away telling me to leave it. One of the servants would come and sort things out later. Servants, who had servants, obviously he did. Is that why I had agreed to marry him because he was rich? It was an unwelcome thought. I didn't like to think that I would put money before happiness. I'm sure he called me Issy, oh my head throbbed. What on earth was happening?

We walked slowly, me struggling in those silly shoes. He led the way past a lake to a driveway lined by tall pines. At the end of the drive was a large house, the type my mum used to drag me round when she belonged to the National Trust. We didn't go up the stone staircase to the imposing front door but made our way to the side door. Oh, good I thought, he must work here. I started to panic a bit when I thought his family owned this pile. We went through a tiled hallway.

"Go into the lavatory and wash your face, I'll see if the cook has any aspirin for that headache of yours. Smooth your dress down too, it looks as if you've tumbled in the grass."

"I thought you said I had by you," I said crossly.

He ignored my comment and flung the door open. It wasn't a large room but quite grand, very old fashioned. Over the large white sink was a gas heater. The toilet was one of those with a high flush, a gaudily painted bowl and large wooded seat. I sat down for a few minutes trying to understand what was happening. I had a pee then saw there was no toilet roll. A packet of sheets of what was like tracing paper was on the shelf. It was shiny and harsh. I decided I'd use my tissue, didn't want to scratch delicate parts. Except when I looked, I had no pockets, no tissue. My knickers were satin I noticed as I pulled them up and a lot bigger than my normal ones. They were pretty but a bit strange.

I looked in the mirror, the face looking back at me wasn't mine. It wasn't such a shock as the old, lined face I'd seen before. It wasn't mine. I hadn't had time to think about whose body I was in. I was so glad I wasn't ancient and lined. However, this wasn't my face. I felt sick.

There was a sharp knock on the door.

"Are you coming out?" I couldn't go into melt down now. I wouldn't give him the satisfaction, and I didn't think it would do any good.

I washed as instructed and smoothed my dress. There were no fluffy towels as I'd expected, just a roller towel made of material like my gran's tea towels from years ago. Bit mean then, despite the trappings of grandeur.

He was waiting for me in the hall with a glass and two tablets. I gulped them down while he leaned over and re-adjusted my hair with pins.

"There you look a little better now. Let's go and speak to the parents."

His father was in his study.

"Oh Lionel, there you are. A little late your mother is anxious to go up to dress for dinner. Hello my dear." This last remark was addressed to me.

"Come along then."

Lionel that was his name, at least I didn't have to ask him now. That would have been embarrassing. He took my arm, and we followed his father along a carpeted corridor, which led into a large sitting room. A woman was seated at the far end with two little dogs at her feet. Lionel drew me over to her. He bent down and kissed her cheek. We stood by her side and his father stood in front of the fire, hand behind his back.

"Well, my boy?"

"Father, mother, Isobel and I are engaged to be married. She has done me the honour of agreeing to be my wife."

Isobel? Am I Isobel? Who the hell is she and where am I? More to the point, when is this? Everything has the feel of an Agatha Christie play I'd seen recently. Is someone about to be killed?

His mother was looking at me. She sniffed, not as you sniff if you have a cold or feel emotional. A sniff like there is something unpleasant in the room.

She annoyed me. I could sense she didn't like me. Even when seated, it was clear that she was slim to the point of thinness. Her pale hair was scraped into a simple bun at the base of her neck. A long pearl necklace matched the studs, which adorned her ears. I thought, they were not cultivated pearls, but real. Her elegance would have been hard to match. I felt more tousled than ever.

"Vivienne and I are delighted," his father said, coming over and kissing me on the cheek. She clearly wasn't.

"I hope the wedding will be soon, it will be good to have some little feet pattering about this empty house."

I realised with horror he was talking babies. He must have noticed my face.

"We need an heir as soon as possible my dear, can't have my cousin inheriting if anything were to happen to Lionel, can we? How gross, what a thing to say. His mother at last spoke.

"Frederick, you're scaring the poor girl. Give her a chance

to enjoy getting married. My dear I think we need to talk to my dressmaker about suitable clothes for you. We can't have Lionel's future bride going around like a scarecrow, can we?" She looked me up and down. "As I said last week dear, you need to think about losing some weight too. Shed that puppy fat, it's no longer fashionable."

I drew breath thinking how rude. There is no way I'm going to put up with her comments. I started to say that I was more than capable of choosing my own clothes, but she butted in saying.

"It really doesn't look that way dear."

The dear was so false. Lionel pinched my arm. He actually pinched it.

"Well, we need to be off, Isobel has to get home to see her father before it gets late, he goes to bed early."

"Get James to take her, dinner's ready."

As soon as we got out of the room, I turned to him.

"Your mother is unbelievably rude, and you pinched me. How dare you?" I showed him my arm. It had a small blue bruise.

He bent and to my disgust kissed my arm.

"That won't make anything better. She obviously doesn't like me." I pulled away from him.

"I'm sorry I hurt you, but mother must be humoured. I could see you were about to upset her."

"Upset her, what about me?"

"My dear you will have to learn the order of things. Nothing works in this house unless mother is happy."

"Then the sooner I am out of it the better."

He shook his head; said he couldn't understand me. "You

know how things are," He said, reaching out and stroking my arm. "She brought money to this place when she married my father."

I was desperately trying to take the heavy ring off my finger, but it refused to budge. I felt close to tears, it seemed as if I was in just as bad a situation as before.

"I just want to go home," I muttered.

We walked back along the carpeted hallway, past huge pictures on the walls, presumably of his ancestors. They all looked arrogant, looking down their long noses at me.

We stopped by a book-lined room, the library. Normally I would have been delighted to be close to so many books. Now, I thought, nothing is normal. He strode over to an ornate bell push and within minutes, a girl appeared.

"Tell James he is needed to take Miss Isobel home." She nodded and disappeared again.

"Let's hope you will be in a better mood when I next see you." He bent his head and again pushed his tongue into my mouth. I resisted the urge to bite, but it was very strong, especially when I felt his hand slowly moving up my leg. His fingers were on the edge of my knickers, I tried to push him away, but he had pinned me to the edge of the bookshelf.

"Don't be modest, we are engaged now. This is allowed."

"Not by me it isn't."

"That isn't what you said earlier, you seemed keen enough then."

I didn't believe him. He was the sort of man that thought unless a woman was actually screaming and running away, she wanted his fumbling.

There was a discrete cough, in the doorway stood a man.

"Ah James, take Miss Isobel home."

"Good night my dear, sleep well. I must dress for dinner."

He turned on his heel and went back down the hall.

I walked towards the man he had called James. It was him. He looked different without his cloak.

"What's happening, where are we or when are we?"

"I believe it's the nineteen twenties, the exact year escapes me I'm afraid."

We were walking along the other corridor now, the one that led to the side entrance.

'It's not only the exact year that's escaped you, is it? Your sense of time is not very good to say the least."

"We did go a little too far back, but at least you will be comfortable this time, it seems you won't be short of money."

"Money? I want my life back. Has it escaped you that I'm in someone else's body?"

"Mm, it does happen. It could be much worse. You might have been one of the servants, having to get up at five and working hard all day."

"Oh, that would be so much better." I said sarcastically. "I've had to put up with that oaf and his mother. One trying to force me to have sex with him and the other being unbearably rude. Oh yes, I should count my blessings, and it seems I'm to marry him. How much worse could it get?"

He looked at me. "Much worse, you could be the girl he's forced himself on for months. She had no power to say no. She's been thrown out for being pregnant with his child."

"What and I'm expected to marry him? What a pig, give me a break, get me out of here."

"At the moment I am the chauffeur, and I am taking you

home to your father's house. I will do my best to get us closer to your time."

I sighed. "Please do, I have essays to finish."

"Unless I succeed, you will have to marry the man. Women don't have much say. You would be ruined, your life not a lot better than the maids."

We drew up at a large house, not as large as the one I'd left, but substantial.

He rang the doorbell before he left me, telling me to try to sleep.

A maid answered the door and ushered me into the dining room. "Dinner is ready, Miss. Mr Phillips is waiting for you."

The man seated at one end of the large table looked up and said, "Isobel you're late, I was about to start without you." I apologised, I felt obliged to. I sat at the other end of the table where a place was set. I looked at all the cutlery, remembering from somewhere, I should start on the outside. He rang the bell at his side and dinner was served. We ate almost in silence until he saw the ring.

"Oh, my dear you have done it. Well done, your future is secure now."

He left his plate and came round to me, planting a kiss on my cheek.

"I'm not happy," I said.

"I know my dear, but it's for the best, you will grow to love him, that's how it works. You will be marrying into an important family. It will give you a good life."

I felt too tired to argue, I couldn't imagine a life with Lionel being good in any way. I was close to tears again. I could eat no more food.

A maid appeared and started to clear the table and I made my excuses and went up the wide staircase.

When I got to the top, I opened several doors, before I found one that I thought must be mine. I laid back on the large bed, wishing I was back in my narrow one at home.

There was a tap on the door, and a slim young woman looked in.

"Scuse me Miss, are you thinking of sleeping in here tonight?"

"I was but I don't have to."

"It's just that your own bed is made and this one being the guest room isn't. I can soon do it for you Miss, if you would like me to?" She looked tired and I felt stupid. What was her name? I'd heard the man that was my father saying it earlier, when she brought in the dinner. "That will do Lottie," he'd said.

"I'm sorry Lottie my head aches, I'm not feeling myself."

"Would you like me to run you a bath, Miss?"

"Please," I said, thinking I could follow her to my room.

I walked alongside her down the landing. The room was at the end. She opened the door for me, and it took me all my time not to gasp. It was a large room decorated in pale blue wallpaper. The carpet was a slightly darker shade. The silver tasselled bedcover was the same pattern and colour as the wallpaper. The effect was stunning. There was a cane chair over which was draped a long blue silky robe. Huge wardrobes completely covered one wall. There was a dressing table with a large triple mirror under one of the windows.

The curtains round the windows were the same delicate shade as the walls, with birds of paradise embossed in silver flying across the material. Later when I examined the wallpaper, I could see the same birds. Smaller this time, blue with a silver shadow, so they seemed to be flying out of the wall.

While I was standing staring, Lottie walked across the room and opened the door at the far end. I could see the bathroom's black and white tiled floor and the claw feet of the bath. Within minutes, I could hear water flowing. I called out to her.

"Thanks, I can manage now."

She had put white fluffy towels on the chair beside the bath and there was beautifully scented soap by the taps.

I sank into the hot water. It had been years since I'd had a bath, my flat had a shower. It was blissful. I could feel the pain across my shoulders and my head easing.

When I returned to the bedroom, I found satin pyjamas laid out on the bed and the cover turned down.

Gratefully, I got into bed. There was a slight tap on the door and in came Lottie carrying a glass of hot milk, two aspirin and homemade biscuits on a tray. She put them down then went into the bathroom and I could hear her tidying up and cleaning the bath. I must have slept the minute I finished the milk.

Chapter 6

I was awoken by the curtains being drawn. Sunlight poured into the room. I was almost afraid to open my eyes. Where would I be? I was still in the blue room. Lottie had put a tray of tea on the bedside table.

"Shall I put your green dress out, Miss?"

I sat up and drained the cup. "Yes please."

The bed was so comfortable I was reluctant to get up. I kept my head on the soft pillows thinking, this might not be such a bad life. I certainly wouldn't want to swap places with Lottie, I wondered what time she had to get up.

Once out of bed, I sorted through drawers of undies trying to decide which to wear. The clothes I'd worn yesterday had disappeared. I guessed Lottie had removed them for washing. There was a tap on the door. It was Lottie. "Oh dear, you haven't got your stockings on yet, Miss, I was wondering if you wanted me to fix your hair?"

"Thanks Lottie, I'll just pin it up."

Stockings, I hadn't thought of them. I was used to wearing jeans or thick tights in the winter. Thank goodness for Lottie. She left the room and I found stockings and suspender belts in another draw. Hoping I was now dressed properly I made my way down the stairs to the dining room. There was no one there. No sign of breakfast. My nose led me to the conservatory. A table was set for one, a coffee pot and toast were already there. Another girl wearing a maid's uniform came in and started to pour me a coffee.

"Mr Phillip's left Miss, he said to let you sleep in this morning. Do you want your usual Miss? I wondered briefly what usual was?

"Just toast and coffee thanks." Oh God, what was this one's name? I heard a voice, calling "Rose," from along the corridor.

She smiled at me and hurried off. When I'd finished, I sat there for a while wondering what I was supposed to do. Rose came back into the room.

"James is here with the car. He said Madam, Mrs Miles, is expecting you to go to her dressmaker with her today. He said it was arranged yesterday."

Her voice rose at the end of the sentence as if she was querying this. Madam must often have expectations that others rush to fulfil. I thanked Rose, and made my way to the front door, no one was there. Feeling stupid I made my way to the side entrance, but there wasn't one, so I carried on. James was standing by the back door, finishing a large cup of something, talking to Lottie.

He looked across at me.

"Morning Miss. Are you ready?"

"I guess," I said rather rudely, after all it wasn't his fault. Well in a way it was, he was the one that had brought me here, even if it was by mistake.

"If you could get Miss Isobel's bag and coat Lottie?"

He handed her the cup and gestured that we return to the front of the house.

As we walked round, I asked him through gritted teeth what was happening.

"You are to accompany Mrs Miles to her dressmaker, to be measured for clothes for your engagement party and your trousseau."

"I am not going to marry her son. He is a pig." I clenched my hands into fists. I could feel my cheeks redden. James told me in a very measured tone that someone, whether it was Isobel, or me, would marry him and she would need clothes.

"As you are literally in her shoes at the moment you must go through with it or you will upset time," he said.

"What about my time? That's upsetting and nobody seems to care. Including you."

"You need to keep calm; I am doing my best to return you. Fighting against time will not help."

I took a deep breath. There could be worse ways of existing and thought of Lottie clearing up after me. I wondered about him; he was a servant now.

"What do you think about cars and driving?" It was a long way from when I'd first seen him by candlelight. To my surprise he smiled, "I love it, so much simpler than sitting at my desk making decisions." I warmed to him then, he seemed a real person.

He opened the car door for me, I automatically looked for the seat belt but there wasn't one. I sat back and Lottie appeared with a coat, shoes, and handbag.

"I thought you'd want matching shoes Miss," she said.

We drove back to pick up Mrs Miles, when we stopped at

the iron gates I started to get out of the car. James asked me what I was doing.

"I'm going to open the gates of course." I said.

"No, you mustn't. You must remember your place. Never do anything a servant can do."

I felt uncomfortable. "But in reality, you are an Honoured Fellow of a scientific society, not a servant."

"Here I am a servant called James, not my real name of course."

"What is your real name?"

"You will find out in due course."

"What? How long is this to go on for?"

"As long as it takes."

We had arrived and Mrs Miles was making her way down the steps, he opened the car door for her, and she got in without a word of thanks.

"To my dressmaker James," She commanded.

"The one on the high street Madam?"

"No, you fool, Chester Road."

I was impressed how he'd found out where to go.

We drove in silence until we reached Chez Marianne.

Madame herself came to speak to us, in what I was sure was a false French accent.

"Ah ere we have ze new bride, oui?"

"Yes, she wants a dress for her engagement party first, then we need to think about the trousseau."

"Oui, Madame."

Mrs Miles pushed me towards the elegant woman who, if anything was even slimmer than she was.

"Do what you can with her, she's a bit dowdy I'm afraid."

I was affronted but remembered what James had said and kept quiet.

Mrs Miles sat herself down in a Louis IVX chair, gold and plush and I'm sure as much of a sham as Madame, who called out, "Elise."

A girl appeared who took me behind a heavy tasselled curtain and proceeded to divest me of my dress, another older woman dressed in black then came through with a tape measure. She measured and Elise noted down the numbers that she called out. It seemed to take an age. I put my clothes back on and Elise fussed with my hair. I went back into the salon to find Madame and Mrs Miles discussing fabrics and colours. They had settled on a beautiful pale green floaty material; it was lovely and soft to touch. She draped it around me.

"Voila, parfait," she said. I looked in the mirror, she was right. I would have liked to disagree but everything about me was saying. *'Let me have this dress.'*

"We will have shoes in the same material, it needs to be ready in two weeks for a fitting. You can give us your plans for her trousseau then too."

I said that I thought the material was perfect, but didn't we need to discuss the style? They both looked at me as if I were stupid.

"That," said Mrs Miles, "has been discussed whilst you were being measured. Madame knows exactly what you need."

I looked at them. "Do I get a say?"

She again looked down her nose at me.

"No, why on earth would you think that? It's a pity your bosom is so large, but Madame can sort that out with the correct undergarments."

I started to feel indignant, my breasts were quite normal and why shouldn't I have a say in the dress design. I thought I wouldn't be the one wearing it at the engagement party, so it really didn't matter. How arrogant though.

These clothes were beautiful. I had seen similar dresses from this period in an exhibition at the V and A. They were exquisite. I thought of my normal clothes, mostly tee shirts and jeans. Mrs M would be shocked.

They had obviously been discussing the wedding dress too.

"As soon as you get those drawings from Monsieur Worth, I wish to be informed," she said as we left.

As if by magic James was outside, waiting with the car. Looking around I saw no yellow lines, no parking restrictions, indeed very few cars. Life was simple if you had money. He drove us to a hotel further along the road. We had a light lunch, a clear soup and salad - chosen by Mrs Miles for both of us.

"We do need to concentrate on your diet my dear, to rid you of that chubbiness."

Isobel was the same size as me. I'd never thought of myself as chubby, but I suppose when compared with Mrs M I was positively plump.

"But I've been measured for the dress," I said.

"That's all in-hand we expect you to lose an inch all over for a start. By the time your wedding dress is ready, with a little work you should be presentable."

I had thought modern brides were stupid to starve themselves so that they would look slim on their big day, but being told by your future mother-in-law it was mandatory. That was another thing. I would never feel sorry for my real self again.

The next day I was taken to the hairdresser, I thought to have my unruly locks trimmed. I was pleased James came to pick me up on his own. I asked him about our return to my time once I was in the car.

"I think at the moment you should concentrate on doing as well as you can here," he answered.

This threw me into a panic. "What's happened? Why are you saying that?"

He muttered; it was difficult to hear him. "The machinery's not responding well. I don't want to risk anything. Just try to relax and enjoy this life for a while." Relax, I was the opposite of relaxed, my fingernails were making red marks in my palms, and I could feel my stomach churning.

"Enjoy it, it's awful having this woman dictate to me how I look and what I can eat. Now she has decided I must have my hair cut a certain way."

"It's not easy for me either. In fact, when was life ever easy? Remember it's imperative you do as the person whose body you are inhabiting would do."

He got out of the car and came round to open the door for me.

"I will pick you up when you are finished here, to take you to luncheon with Mrs Miles."

"I don't want you picking me up and I don't want to have lunch with her."

I turned around, the door of the salon was open, and a girl was standing there waiting for me to enter. I watched the car drive off, trying to control my breathing before I went inside.

The girl took my coat and bag. A young man came up to me.

"So lovely to have you here, I'm Claude and I'm looking after you today."

I was ushered to my seat and the girl placed a satin cover around me. Claude came towards me with a pair of scissors, he was annoyingly snipping them in the air. He then put them down and removed my ribbon and pins as my hair tumbled down, he ran his fingers through it.

"Such beautiful curls it seems a shame to lose them."

"Lose them?"

"Yes, Mrs Miles is insistent that you have the new look. So today it is 'the shingle' for you."

Before I could protest, he was cutting through my locks.

"Hang on a minute. I'm not sure about this." It was as if I hadn't spoken. I daren't move, he might snip my ears. He led me to the basin and the girl washed my hair in expensive smelling shampoo. Back at the mirror I looked in dismay at my shorn locks. Claude fetched his scissors and trimmed again. How much shorter was it to be? I kept reminding myself that this was not me. Then as he styled the finish, I began to think it didn't look too bad. He finally stood back and held a mirror up so I could see the back.

I gave a faint smile. I smiled at my reflection. Isobel looked so like me; I was getting used to the face in the mirror.

"I think you are in shock at the moment, but you will find it easy to manage. It will make you less dependent on someone else doing your hair. Give you freedom. That's what all the young women are saying."

I thanked him and the girl fetched my bag and coat I reached in to get a purse, but he stopped me.

"It is paid for, on Madam's account," he said. "Your car is waiting for you."

I walked out feeling strange. James was there, holding the car door open.

"I'd rather walk." I said.

"No, get in, you don't imagine Mrs Miles lunches at the same place two days running, do you?" So, I did as I was told, why not? I was getting used to being pushed around. We drove for about fifteen minutes to a country hotel. She was waiting for me.

"I've ordered," she said. "Well, you do look different, better than I'd hoped. Once that weight is off you will look the part."

"What part is that?" I knew I was being rude.

"Why the wife of an important man in the city. I know you resent me my dear but one day you will thank me. As one gets older, it becomes clearer how important appearance is. Now come along, our table is ready."

Chapter 7

I was relieved to find out I didn't have to see Mrs Miles for the next few days.

"Tomorrow afternoon you are having tea with two friends," Lottie told me.

"You know more about what I am doing than I do, I appear to have lost my diary."

"It's part of my duties, Miss. Your diary is on your desk in the library as usual if you want to check." I found the diary in the library. It was as Lottie said on a desk. My desk it seemed. I sat down and started to read it.

The people I was to have tea with were Edith and Sophie. At least I now knew their names. We were having tea here, it said at three pm.

The dressmaker and hairdresser appointments weren't in the diary. I was right in thinking that Mrs Miles had just decided that they would happen, knowing she would be obeyed.

I looked back in the diary, several days had Lionel written against them.

Comments on the facing pages said things like. *He seemed to like me, and danced with me most of the evening.* One read. *Having supper with Lionel, met his parents, his fathers a sweetie, bit scared of his mother though.*

Looking further back in the comments I saw she'd met Lionel through their fathers doing business together. She went along to a dinner expecting it to be boring and Lionel was there, representing his father.

Comments for weeks after said, *can't stop thinking of Lionel.*

Then more recently she had written. *I'm not so sure about him, he does expect to get his own way all the time.*

For many weeks though she seemed to have dates with him, very proper ones with family or friends present. Her comments seemed to waver between thinking she was in love with him to being upset about how he had behaved.

In the most recent entry, she wrote she thought he was going to propose and that left her feeling confused. *Father says his business needs an input of money to keep it afloat. If I marry Lionel, he's sure his father will invest in the business.*

I do love him. But I'm not sure...

What wasn't she sure about? I suppose if I was here much longer I would find out. The diary had his name at six-thirty in two days' time. I fervently hoped that she would be back by then.

Would she know she'd been measured for a dress and her engagement party was being planned? More importantly, what would she think of her hair? I found myself wondering what Lionel would think. It might be enough that his mother had decided on the style.

Although I didn't really want to see him again, I was intrigued.

Edith and Sophie were due to arrive the next afternoon, surely that would tell me a little more about the girl whose body I inhabited.

Lottie woke me as usual. My neck felt cold, then I remembered about my hair or my lack of it.

When I went through to the bathroom and looked in the mirror I gave a little scream. My shorn locks were all standing up on end. Lottie came rushing in. She hid her smile behind her hand.

"Not to worry, Miss, I can soon sort that out for you. They say this style is easy, but it does take a bit of looking after."

"And a bit of getting used to. I wish I had my hair back."

"Don't fret. It will be fine." I had my bath and damped my hair.

When I came back into the bedroom, she had laid some clothes out for me. I got dressed then she was back.

"Just sit at the dressing table and I'll do your hair for you Miss."

There were benefits. I'd never had anyone sort my hair out before.

After lunch, I went to the library again and spent some time looking at the books. Most of them were old leather-bound, dusty, boring. Then I found a whole row of Jane Austin. I was about to sit and read when Lottie appeared.

"It's almost two thirty Miss, I've put out your rose pink dress I thought you'd want to wear that."

I realised I was expected to change. I thanked her and started to make my way upstairs.

"Would you like tea served in the conservatory? It's such a lovely day."

I said I would. The rose dress was very pretty, and a pleasure to wear. Lottie came and sorted my hair out again, saying, "you look very nice, Miss."

I went through to the conservatory and shortly Rose brought a young woman in to join me.

"Miss Edith."

I stood up, not sure what the protocol was, but she came over to me and air kissed both sides of my cheeks. She stepped back.

"Your hair looks fantastic. I thought you weren't going to have the bob."

"Mrs Miles insisted."

"It suits you, shows off your cheekbones. Since when did you ever do what that horrid woman wanted though?" Before I had time to explain, Rose led Sophie into the room.

Sophie came over greeting us both then stepped back letting out a shriek. I wondered what was wrong. She grabbed my hand. "He did it, he did it."

I was about to ask what did he do, when I realised she had seen the ring? I guess it was so big it was difficult to miss.

"Oh yes and your hair, you look wonderful."

"I was so taken by your hair I completely missed the ring. I don't know how that happened." Edith took my hand and turned it to the light making the diamond flash. They both examined the ring, saying it was quite perfect and kissed me again.

Edith said. "You decided then?"

I looked at her.

"Last time we came you were unsure about him. You thought he'd been making eyes at one of the servants."

"Oh that," I said, not sure how to continue.

"Well," said Sophie. "That sort of thing happens; my mother says you must turn a blind eye. Security is important and he is rich. I'm sure he loves you, but men can be fickle. If you have the ring, it means he is yours. Oh, it's so exciting."

"Have you set the date?" asked Edith.

"No," I said. It will be soon; his mother has ordered my dress from Paris."

"How wonderful," Sophie breathed. "A Paris wedding dress. What about an engagement party?"

"The invitations are in the post. Mrs Miles has seen to all that," I told her. "Now tell me all your news."

Sophie spent ages talking about Jonathon. She hoped that he would pop the question soon. She said he had hinted several times recently.

"I think he might be waiting until my birthday. That's not too long. We'll be able to compare rings. I do hope he gets me one as lovely as yours."

When I turned to Edith asking how she was, her eyes filled with tears. Her father had disapproved of her boyfriend; he had banned her from seeing him. She felt wretched.

"Do you love him?" I asked.

"How can you ask that? You know we love each other, but father won't hear of it."

"I'm so sorry Edith, surely you should follow your heart?"

"It's all right for you Issy, he doesn't have enough money to keep us. I need father's support."

I started to say can't you get a job? I stopped realising that there wouldn't be many respectable jobs for women at this time. Sophie put her arm around Edith.

"Chin up. It's not the time to be unhappy Edith. I'm sure someone else will turn up soon. Someone rich and handsome like Jonathan who will sweep you off your feet. You might meet someone at Issy's engagement party. Are any single men invited?"

I was surprised how insensitive she was. I felt uncomfortable.

"I hope your father will come round when he realises how unhappy you are Edith," I said.

"Highly unlikely. Father's word is law. He doesn't change his mind."

There was an awkward pause, and Sophie made a great fuss of looking at the ring again. It was beautiful and I was getting used to the weight of it on my finger.

I heard the rattle of the tea trolley. "Well timed," I thought, as Rose came into the room. She set the small table and put tiered plates of wafer-thin sandwiches down, then two plates with cakes, meringues and scones.

Lottie followed with a large tray containing the teapot and a hot water jug, delicate cups, saucers and tea plates.

"Cook says there are some meringues without cream, for you Miss Isobel, as instructed by Mrs Miles."

"How thoughtful," said Sophie.

"What a cheek, she's not in charge of you yet," Edith said, when the two maids had left.

"I don't intend she will ever be. She has put me on a strict diet so that I will fit into my wedding dress when it arrives."

"That's ridiculous, they will make it too big so that it can be taken in if necessary, surely. That's what they did with my sister." Edith sounded indignant. At last, it felt like I had someone on my side.

Sophie was working her way through the delicious sandwiches. "It won't hurt to lose a few pounds, so you look good on the day."

I handed her a cup of tea stifling a desire to spill some of it on her to remove the smugness from her face.

I buttered a scone, topped it with jam and cream. It tasted wonderful. I had a meringue, the largest one, full of cream. I finished with a slice of Victoria sponge. I felt I had scored a victory, but soon my stomach was very uncomfortable. I might have to give dinner a miss I thought.

We spent the rest of the afternoon talking about clothes and my haircut. Edith had hers in a similar style, but Sophie said she would never cut hers. I looked at her long dark red hair curling around her face, escaping from the bun low down on her neck. I agreed that it would be difficult to imagine her with short hair. The maids came to clear away the tea things, which seemed to be the signal for Sophie and Edith to go home. I breathed a sigh of relief when another hurdle was overcome.

Chapter 8

Friday evening came and I was both dreading it and intrigued. The diary said drinks and dinner with Lionel, Harry and Frances. I spent time reading the comments pages and found that Harry was Lionel's older brother. I guessed that Frances was his wife.

I didn't have to worry about what to wear. Rose helped me to decide between three beautiful dresses. I had the comforting thought that Lionel would behave himself if his brother and wife were there. It was of course the first time I'd seen him since that first awful afternoon.

He came to collect me, asking me to do a twirl after he had exclaimed about my hair. He said I looked very nice and was looking forward to showing his fiancée off to his brother. I said I thought we'd met before. Which was a stupid thing to say. He said of course we had but now I was his fiancée, as if that made me a different person, which of course I was.

We drew up at his parent's house, I had forgotten how big it was, well not so much forgotten as not taken it all in. I was in shock when I'd been there before. We went to the front entrance. I was determined not to be overawed. I failed as soon as the door was opened.

"Thank you, Jenkins," Lionel said as he handed over his coat. I was wearing a lovely, fringed shawl, which I kept around my shoulders. It made my neck feel less naked.

I was soon glad I hadn't relinquished the shawl in the hall. The room we were in was cold. The sun probably never penetrated the bricks of this old building. I was served a sherry. I hated sherry but sipped it nervously. In this situation, any alcohol was welcome. I asked Lionel how his week had been, he started to talk about some deals he'd done. He seemed very pleased with himself.

When the door opened and his brother came in, I could see the resemblance between them. Harry came over and pecked me on the cheek.

"My word you do look up to the minute, it suits you," he said. "Frances is powdering her nose, and saying hello to Ma and Pa, she'll be here in a minute."

I didn't know if I'd met Frances before.

It seems I hadn't, she came sweeping into the room and looked me up and down.

"So, we meet at last Isobel. You're not as fat as Ma in law says. I should have known though; everyone is fatter than her."

I didn't know what to say. Perhaps that was just as well, I could have been very rude. I remembered James's warning. Even so, this was rudeness to a fine art. Here was a woman who didn't want to be outshone by anyone else. Not that I thought for one moment there was any fear of me doing that.

She looked amazing. Lionel went over to her, kissed her cheek saying. "You look wonderful, Frances, how do you do it? More beautiful every time I see you."

She gave him a half smile while her husband glowered at his brother.

I was soon glowering too as Lionel whispered to her.

"Now be kind to my little country mouse Franny dear. Ma hasn't quite got her up to scratch yet."

The bastard. I was so angry; what did they all think I was? I felt my eyes filling with hot tears. Why did he behave as if he was doing me a great favour?

Mrs Miles came into the room before I could say anything.

"Ah Frances you've met Isobel, isn't she a pretty little thing? Has good childbearing hips don't you think?"

There was a gasp. I thought, because she was being rude about me. Frances swung round to face her mother-in-law. "That's so unkind, it's not my fault. You need to talk to your precious son about why we don't give you an heir."

She started to walk towards the door. Harry came over to her, tried to put an arm around her, but she pushed him off.

"This family is too much."

"Now look here this is supposed to be a family party to welcome Isobel. Not one to air dirty laundry. Vivienne you really should be more careful, you know babies are sensitive ground here. Frances, please stay."

Lionel's father spoke quietly and kindly, but he expected to be obeyed.

I wondered what was going on. Frances sat down and Harry stood behind her chair. Lionel bent down and asked me if I was all right.

I sniffed and said I needed to blow my nose.

"Come on then we'll walk to the cloakroom together," he said in a gentle voice putting his arm under my elbow.

"Don't be long, come straight into the dining room," his mother's voice rang out.

"She seems to be the only one that's not upset," I commented.

"Ma is as tough as nails, always had to be. Pa has led her such a dance over the years."

"Really? I find that hard to believe he seems the kinder one."

"He's quietened down now but always had an eye for a pretty girl and never thought to hide it. They had to pay off several maids in the past."

I was quiet, thinking of those poor girls. If I understood what he was saying, there would have been babies whose parentage wasn't acknowledged and girls on the street, with a few pounds in their pockets if they were lucky.

"Is that the problem with Harry and Frances then?"

He looked at me. "You are naïve, aren't you? I thought it stuck out a mile."

"What does?"

"Harry has always batted to the left." I looked at him bemused.

"He prefers boys, always has done. Sent down from school because of it. Of course, Pa had it all hushed up. I got stick though; we were at the same school. He's two years older. Once he ignominiously left - was removed - they all took it out on me, called me Nancy boy and queer. I wasn't but I was quiet and shy, always been in my brother's shadow. I eventually learned to develop a thick skin but it took a long time.

"I guess he doesn't fancy Frances then?"

"Shouldn't think they've been successful at it from her hints. Shame she's lovely."

"I noticed you thought so. So, you take after your father then, an eye for a pretty girl?"

"Well, I spotted you didn't I?"

"You know what I mean, I don't want to end up like your mother."

He did a mock salute. "Honest Gov. I'm a reformed character. Your love has transformed me."

He took this as an opportunity to kiss me, grabbing hold of my bottom and squeezing hard. He pulled me to him; he left me in no doubt of his manhood as he pushed against me.

"See I'm no Nancy boy. I'd have you against the library wall quick as a flash."

I couldn't help laughing. "Well not that quick I hope."

"My, my, that's more like it. I thought you'd turned into a prude now that you have my ring on your finger." His hands were straying up my leg now I was getting uncomfortable.

"Hey, you two lovebirds Ma is getting arsy about the length of time you are taking." Harry's voice saved me.

We made our way to the dining room, hand in hand. I did feel kindlier towards him even if I didn't want his hand in my knickers.

Lionel took me home himself even though he seemed to have had a lot to drink. I was hoping to see James and ask him how he was getting on. I wanted to go back to my real home.

Luxury could feel good for a while, but it was boring. I found myself longing for student conversation and pizza.

As the car drew up, the front door was opened, which stopped Lionel doing more than kissing me good night.

"Do you want a nightcap Miss?" Lottie asked as I wearily climbed the stairs I nodded gratefully. I'd had more than a little to drink. It had helped me through a long boring evening. The three men seemed to talk business constantly. When at last the port came and Vivienne stood and told us to withdraw, I was pleased to do so and sat quietly listening to her and Frances talking about arranging my engagement party. Such a fuss about small details. I was so bored I could feel my eyelids drooping.

I dreamt that night about being at a society gathering and calling napkins, serviettes. I guess I must have read somewhere that it was not the thing to do.

When I awoke, I was hot, and my head was aching. The horrors of getting things wrong were still in my brain.

I sat in the chair in my room wearing the satin robe, feeling not very pretty myself.

My face felt stiff and dry. I hadn't taken off my makeup the night before. When I looked in the mirror I saw great black smudges under my eyes, I hoped it was mascara. It certainly mirrored how I felt.

There was no tea by my bed, when Rose tapped at the door I asked where Lottie was? I needed my tea and some aspirin; they didn't seem to have anything stronger. I wondered when paracetamol became a common drug. They didn't seem to know about it when I asked for some a few days before.

"Lottie's poorly Miss, I've come to look after you."

"Oh, thank you Rose, I need my tea and some headache pills."

She came back after a while with them and offered to massage my head and face. I guess she took one look at me and summed up how I felt. I lay back on the chaise-longue and she worked such magic, I could feel the headache lifting and the creams she used soaked into my parched skin.

I murmured how wonderful it was and asked her how she knew such skill. She told me that when she was younger my mother had a French maid who had taught her. She said my poor mother had suffered badly. I asked her if she knew my mother well. She gave me a strange look and said,

"I was just a maid Miss."

I didn't like to ask any more questions. I noticed that she put the jar of cream back into one of the drawers. I made a note to use it again later.

Once I was dressed, I saw that the morning had almost gone. I ordered coffee and toast to be served in the library.

"In the library? Your father wouldn't approve."

I repeated in the library and went down the stairs to wait for it to appear.

I sat down and the man who was my father put his head around the door. I had forgotten it was Saturday, he was home.

"It's a little late for toast my dear. Do you have to have it in here?"

"Yes, I do." I was fed up with people telling me how to behave. "Rose said my mother had terrible headaches. What happened to her?"

He looked at me then turned on his heel.

"You know we don't talk about that," he said abruptly.

Well of course I didn't know, it was silly of me I don't even know when she died it could have just been a year ago and I would know about that if I were really Isobel. Rose came in with my coffee and toast.

"Cook sent her new marmalade, she hopes you like it."

I thanked her a bit grumpily, thinking she must have moaned about me being in the library for him to know.

"You all right now Miss? Do you want me to draw the blinds?"

I nodded then asked her what year my mother had died. I knew I was taking a chance but wasn't prepared for her look of astonishment or her answer.

"She's not dead, Miss, not that I know of."

"Where is she then?"

"They put her in that special nursing home after she tried to run away."

"Run away?"

"There was talk about her being too friendly with someone at Mrs Mile's stables."

"I didn't know that."

"No Miss, you were far too small, and we were all told never to talk about it. However, since you asked, it didn't seem right not to tell you. You clung to her skirts when they took her away and cried for days."

"Who looked after me?"

"You had a nursemaid, but we all had a soft spot for you, Miss."

"So everyone knows but me?"

"Well Lottie, she's fairly new isn't she, but the rest of us do." She frowned and looked worried.

"We was all told we would lose our jobs with no references if ever we talked of it, please don't say I've told you."

"I won't but I would like to know where she is."

"Please Miss, leave it alone, it won't do no good to start looking now. Please don't tell of me or I'll never get another job."

"I won't you can rest assured of that, but Rose thank you."

She bobbed a little curtsey and left the room. I thought about what she had told me and what Lionel had said the night before, so many secrets. Were all rich families like this, I wondered?

I wondered how old Rose was. She looked as if she was in her late forties. She could be older; her face was lined and tired. I hadn't asked her anything about herself. From what she had just told me she had obviously worked for the family for over twenty years. Did she have a family of her own? I knew very little about this period, I'd read that ordinary people struggled after the First World War. Many women who'd lost their men became the breadwinners of the family, and injured men had little compensation. I supposed that being in service was better than being destitute. Was she one of these women? I was still sitting thinking about the history I didn't know, and the huge difference between the rich and poor, when Rose came back in and asked if I wanted my soup in the conservatory.

Chapter 9

The next two weeks flew by, and I got into a pleasant routine, gradually learning more about the family I was about to join and the one I was in. I found that Mrs Miles, although a pain in the neck, was bearable if not crossed and Lionel and my father were only around at weekends. By asking questions I found there were only two nursing homes that took mentally ill people, I assumed that's where Isobel's mother had been put away. There was also a forbidding building in the middle of gloomy grounds called a lunatic asylum, but I doubted that she would be there.

I decided that I would investigate. I couldn't visit as I had no transport, but I could phone and ask questions. I wasn't sure how the telephone worked. I'd seen old films with phones like this. I asked Rose for the telephone directory, she looked at me like she didn't know what I meant. I explained that I wanted to find a number.

"Oh, you just pick up the phone and dial 0 and ask the operator when she answers, she will find it for you and put you through. I've never done it myself, but I've seen it done," she said.

I tried it out by asking for the Miles house first. A pleasant young woman told me the number and asked if I would like her to put me through. I said no but asked if I could dial the number myself later.

"Oh no Miss," she said. "Just dial 0 and ask for the number and the operator will put you through."

I thought what a performance but asked her if she could find me the number of the nursing home. She did so and put me through, after a few rings a voice answered. "Meadowlands Nursing Home."

I asked if they had a patient called Mrs Phillips, there was a slight pause, then I was told no one of that name was there. I asked if there had been a Mrs Phillips there in the past twenty years. She told me she couldn't possibly say without looking at the records. I told her I would wait while she did so. After a minute the operator's voice came on the line.

"Caller, is this call still active?"

Was she listening in? I told her yes it was and waited a little longer. I could hear the rustling of pages. Finally, the person said, "sorry I can't find anyone of that name. Is there anything else I can help you with?"

I asked her if they took patients with mental health problems. There was a long pause, then she said they took people that were disturbed and confused and asked if I had someone who needed care. I told her no and thanked her for her time. I had a similar response from the other place, when I phoned, no Mrs Phillips. Where had she gone then?

My severe diet as dictated by Mrs Miles was working, I made sure each day I walked briskly, which stopped me thinking about food, and I started to like the change in my shape.

The afternoon of my final fitting had arrived, Madame fussed over me saying how *très bonne* I looked. I had gone down a bra size, so the first task was to find one that fitted.

Once suitably clad in underwear the dress was put over my head. It was beautiful, the bodice clung to my new shape, the skirt fell in layers of gossamer green. I loved it. I gave a little twirl in front of the large mirror and the skirt flew out.

It needed no alteration and as soon as I had taken it off with the help of Elise, it was packed in tissue and placed in a large box. The shoes fitted and were a perfect match. There was also a headband in the same colour edged with silver. I was beginning to look forward to the engagement party.

Mrs Miles was meeting a friend for afternoon tea, so my boxes and I were to be sent back with James.

Once I was in the car we drove a little way, then he pulled up.

"What are you doing?" He sounded angry.

"What do you mean, I'm doing as I was told? I have my dress; they are pleased with me because I've stuck to my diet and lost weight, and I've been nice to Lionel. I've been stuck here for weeks doing as you told me, and you seem no further on with getting me back."

"I'm talking about you asking questions about nursing homes and places for the insane."

"I asked questions originally so I was aware of family history, so I wouldn't be caught out. Surely that was the right thing to do?"

"Yes, but you are interfering with things that have nothing to do with you. You mustn't change things, you'll upset the structure of time."

"So you keep saying. I should think that the structure, as you call it, is a bit random by us being here. How easy do you think it is to not know anything?" I am angry now. "None of this is my choice. I don't care about the structure of time. Quite frankly, if you ask me, it's been completely fucked up by you and the people you represent. Please just get me home."

He said nothing, he looked at me blankly, I couldn't tell what he was thinking. He started the car and we continued to drive. I could see his eyes in the mirror. His look was one of concern. I calmed down a little. I had been excited to think I was going to be wearing the beautiful dress in the box next to me. I was also scared of what might happen if I did or said the wrong thing. His voice interrupted my thoughts.

"Don't worry about the party, you will be fine, everyone will be pleased for you. You only have to smile and agree with them. It's the rest of the time I worry about, I know you are used to researching but you need to leave this alone, it will help no one."

"What if this poor woman has been locked away for no other reason than she is depressed? Why is it a secret?"

"You have to remember that people with problems were treated differently, there was little understanding of the way the brain worked."

"But it seems wrong, how can Isobel have no knowledge of what's happened to her mother? Surely, she'd want to know."

He wasn't listening, he continued to drive. We drew up to the front door, he had to remind me not to carry the boxes out myself.

The day of the engagement party arrived. A few days before Mrs Miles informed me, absolutely everyone had accepted their invitations. It was the first time I had seen her happy. Lady something was coming with the honourable Harriet. In addition, Lord Brice's younger brother was going to grace us with his presence. She rolled off a list of names that meant nothing to me.

I got up late and had Rose give me a massage that relaxed me and calmed my nerves. At lunch, for once, I was glad to only eat the small amount I was allowed. My nerves kicked in again. I knew I would look good, the clothes would do that for me but would I sound right. The names on the list were intimidating.

I sat in the library looking at an old book. On the flyleaf was an inscription '*To Rachel with love Frank*'. I knew this was Isobel's mother's name, but father was not called Frank. Was it a brother? Or could it be a lover? Had I unearthed a piece of the puzzle?

The phone shrilled out, Lottie came in, answered it, and looked at me.

"It's for you Miss." I picked up the receiver. There was a lot of noise on the line, but I could make out a voice saying, "Imogen look at the records for St Mark's."

The line went dead. The person called me Imogen, my real name. St Mark's was the name of the lunatic asylum. Perhaps the woman I'd been looking for was in there?

I picked up the book I'd been looking at, it was the story of Iseult and Abelard, and unrequited love.

I felt quite strange with so many thoughts rushing around my head. The sad, sad story of a young woman married to an older man who falls in love with Abelard. The strange telephone call using my correct name. If I stayed here, I would be entering a marriage to a man that I didn't even like. Would that be a repeat of what happened to Rachel, Isobel's mother? What was I going to do?

I decided to put the book back and go and lie on my bed for a while to calm down. I walked over to the bookcase, reached up to the gap and put my hand right through the shelf. The books flew up into the air and turned into one enormous volume the pages flipping over becoming larger. I was lifted off my feet. Swirling now in the centre of the book as the pages turned. I watched things around me change, scenes flashed before my eyes, buildings giving way to hills and fields.

Chapter 10

Everything stopped. I was in what looked like a barn but there was no wall, only a roof. The floor was filthy. I could smell manure, a cow bellowed, and a few scrawny chickens ran past me. A man appeared dressed in what looked like sacking.

"Get that there cow milked," he yelled. I turned to look behind me and saw he was talking to me. I was wearing a dirty faded long blue garment. My hair was in plaits and my feet were sore from the wooden shoes that I was wearing.

"Did you 'ear me, woman?" He shouted again. I heard but had no idea what to do. I sat down on the seat next to the animal and pushed a wooden bucket under the teats, I could see milk dripping from them. I remembered seeing a television programme about farming. It had explained to milk a cow the teats should be pulled not squeezed. In desperation I pulled, warm, creamy milk flowed into the bucket. I felt such relief. Goodness knows where I was this time. I seemed to have gone back centuries. A small boy came up with a container and dipped it in the frothing milk. I pushed him away as he guzzled down what he had managed to steal.

A woman in a similar garment to mine, only more ragged

if that were possible came and took the bucket. I pushed another bucket in place but the milk flow was easing

"Ger on w'i it." The man was back. "Yo gone stupid or somat?"

I stood up - tripped over the bucket – hit my head hard on something and landed face down in mud, cow shit and milk. Everything started to lose focus again. Spinning totally out of control, I saw scenes flash by me as if they were illustrations in a book of English history. I was slip-sliding, wavering between time. I was terrified. The spinning sensation was stronger. I wished I hadn't eaten. My ears hurt, all I could hear was someone shouting and my pulse beating. Should it be that fast? Why had I said I didn't care about the structure of time?

I found myself back in my own room feeling very sick, I'd not felt this bad since I went to France on the hovercraft. I looked around the room. My room, my own room, I was back. It all looked normal. I saw my candle had burnt down and there was just a mess of wax left. How much time had I missed? I had no idea I looked at the wall and felt all over it. No door, no handle. Had it all been a dream?

I decided to get myself an anti-nausea pill. The cupboard door was open, I picked up the box of pills; but when I looked at my hand there was nothing there. Going to the sink to get some water, I found I couldn't turn on the tap. Confused, I decided to ask George for help. His flat was on the landing below mine. I was on the stairs when I saw George come out of his room. I called out to him. He didn't hear me. I called again, quickening my pace trying to catch up with him. He just carried on walking. Once outside I closed up to him and touched his arm but still he ignored me. I stopped, had I upset him? He could be moody if he thought someone had slighted him, but he'd never ignored me like this before. I decided to follow him and ask what was wrong. He walked to the convenience store at the end of the street. I followed him in. The lights were bright. I could see his shadow at the end of one of the rows. I could pick up a packet of fruit sweets while I was there, that would give me an excuse to be at the till. As I looked at the display, I noticed there was no shadow of my arm when I reached out. I moved a little to where George had stood. Still no shadow. Giving myself a shake I thought what does it matter, I'm here to speak to George. I moved around to the till. The girl completely ignored me. How rude.

"What's with everyone ignoring me?" I asked as she started to serve the man behind me. I saw the headlines on his paper. *Pictures of Charles and Diana's trip. Why everyone loves her.* I wanted to pay for the sweets, but there were none in my hand. Confused, I turned and bumped into George. Well, I just fell straight through him and the drinks display. Then I was spinning again. Oh no, I thought I was safely back. What was happening? I could see the shelves in the shop coming back, then fading again. I was slip-sliding in and out of my own time. Then there was no shop, no pavement. I felt sick again, I could hear angry voices.

I was back in the sitting room of Isobel's house, it was still slightly out of focus. The curtains were moving as if there was a breeze. Mrs Miles was sitting on the sofa reaching out to me with her mouth open, goodness knows what vitriol spewing out. Her dogs were excitedly yapping at her feet. I took a step towards her half expecting my feet to go through the thick carpet and find myself spinning off again.

I could hear angry voices from all sides. I started to ask her what was wrong.

I had never seen her face red before, she was usually so pale. "What's wrong?" I asked.

"You have such a cheek; you know perfectly well what's wrong." A voice behind me was speaking. I turned to see who it was. I was looking at myself, no Isobel. She had tears in her eyes. Traces of black mascara were running down her cheeks.

Isobel? Who was I then?

I looked down. I was wearing a maid's uniform. Rose was standing by the door looking upset. Lionel was saying that everyone should calm down. That didn't go down well with his mother. She started to say someone should call for the police.

Lionel said, "it's found now, Lottie has it and I'm sure she can explain."

In a high-pitched voice that sounded as if she was about to have hysterics. Isobel asked, "why are you being so calm? It's there on her finger, how did it get there unless she meant to steal it? Tell me, why is she wearing my ring?"

"Give the girl a chance to explain Issy." He looked across at me as if to say you'd better have an explanation. He strode across the room. "You had better give me the ring now Lottie."

With some difficulty, I pulled it off my finger. I noticed it had made a deep mark, so I covered it with my other hand.

"If you please Miss?" I remembered how Lottie had spoken to me when I was Isobel. "If you please Miss." I couldn't continue I was terrified they would send me to prison thinking I'd tried to steal the ring. Oh God, when did they stop hanging people for stealing?

"Speak girl, why do you have the ring?"

I stood there not able to answer.

Mrs Miles was straight in for the kill. "She obviously was trying to steal it, she'd get so much money for it, it would be worth the risk."

I was indignant and forgot my lowly place in society. "How dare you, I'm not a thief."

"What are you then?" This time it was Isobel asking the question.

I took a deep breath. "Honest, that's what I am. Would I be here now if I was going to steal the ring?"

"If you please Madam," Rose was speaking now. "I know what happened, Lottie found the ring in Miss Isobel's clothes when she took them down to the laundry. Lottie tried to return the ring but Miss Isobel told her to get out of the room because she wanted to sleep. I was there, I heard her. She put it on her finger because she was scared she'd lose it. She was in a dreadful state about it Madam. She wasn't thinking straight."

Mrs Miles said that if she wanted servants' opinions, she'd ask for them, but Lionel thanked Rose and turned to Isobel. "You must admit that you were worse for wear after the party. I expect James had to pour you indoors last night."

Isobel gave him a look that would have frozen milk.

"I did tell her to get out this morning. I had such a bad head."

"We have to think of what would have happened to the ring if she hadn't found it."

"Yes, Lionel I know that and I'm glad I've got it safely back, but I still can't understand why she walked in here wearing it as if it belonged to her. She must have heard me crying I'd lost it."

"I'm sorry Miss, like Rose says I was in a state. I started to worry bout whether it was my fault that it was in the clothes, you normally put it on your dressing table."

"You walked in here bold as brass wearing that ring." Mrs Miles didn't want an amicable ending. "You should be sacked at the very least. I think the police should have been called."

Isobel's father walked into the room. She ran over to him.

"Oh father, my ring has been found."

"That's good then, I said it would be. Who found it?"

"Lottie," she said.

"Good that's sorted then. Take better care of it in future, Lionel can't afford to buy another like that. Come on all of you, Frederick and I are fed up with waiting for our luncheon."

Mrs Miles rose from the sofa, as she went out she looked at me. "I will be watching you," she said as she swept out of the room.

I felt like collapsing on the chair but thought that would too be a crime in my position.

I felt an arm around my shoulders. It was Rose.

"That was close my girl, don't know what you was thinking, putting her ring on your finger. He might fancy you but wouldn't save you if things turned bad."

I thanked her for helping me and she told me to get a move on as we had to serve the food.

I had a great desire to pour soup down the front of Mrs

Mile's expensive dress. As it was my hand was trembling so much, I was glad I didn't have to serve her.

When they had finished eating, we cleared everything away, then the kitchen girl washed the dishes while cook dished up food. My relief that we had a break until four o'clock was short-lived.

"You haven't finished the laundry, there's a great pile of clean washing to be ironed," Rose told me. I couldn't believe it when I saw the iron. How was I supposed to iron with a museum piece?

I was working hard, and the kitchen girl came to help me. I hadn't even known of her existence when I was Isobel. As I finished, James appeared at the door.

"What did you do?" he said when I went outside to speak to him.

"I told him about the gap I'd seen in the library."

"Why did you go through?"

"You weren't doing anything to help me were you?"

"Yes but look what's happened now. You were nearly arrested. I couldn't have helped you then."

I'd had such a terrible time; I was exhausted and now he was moaning at me. My back was aching from the ironing and having to stand for so long in the sitting room. Overcome, I started to weep.

"I've had enough, no, more than enough. I was called a thief by that awful woman."

"You messed things up, you went through the time gap. Now look what's happened?"

I was angry and I brushed my tears away. "I know, don't you think I know, it's me it happened to. It was awful. I had to milk a cow and now this. My back is about to break and all you must do is drive spoiled people around."

To my surprise, he bent down and kissed me, to my further surprise I enjoyed it.

"You look rather adorable in that outfit, especially with your hair tumbling down. I think it needs to be pinned up though, before you get into any more trouble. They expect their servants to look smart."

"Hmm. You try looking smart when ironing with this antiquated equipment."

"Yes, they're not big on modern equipment," he said, looking through the window at the dolly tub and rubbing board. "Of course, all Isobel's clothes must be washed very carefully. They are delicate as you know. You wore them."

I felt tearful again, I hadn't known when I was well off.

"I'd better go," he said. "You need to get on with your work. You will need to change into your evening uniform soon."

He vanished, leaving me more bewildered than I'd been before. I finished the ironing, desperately hoping that no one would notice how inferior the finish was to when the real Lottie had done it. I returned to the kitchen, hot and sweaty. Sure enough, cook started to scold me.

"Get changed," she said. "You can't serve dinner like that."

I climbed the flights of steps up to the attic rooms. Rose was there.

"Come on," she said. "You're late." I obviously shared a bedroom with her. The room was small with scarcely enough space for two narrow beds. She had kindly put my afternoon uniform on the bed for me. I saw that I only had to change the apron and cap for a frillier version of each. She watched me, then sighed.

"Take off your sleeve protectors," she said, pulling at the white edges of the dress. She spent the time it took to climb down the stairs to grumble at me, saying she didn't know where my sense had gone. She was clearly worried I would be sacked.

"That Mrs Miles doesn't like you, don't give her any chances."

Chapter 11

The silver had been polished in the morning, so we started to set the table. I followed Rose's lead. When we had finished, she stood back clearly taking pleasure in the gleaming crystal and silver. We returned to the kitchen where we sat for a while drinking tea. I watched cook with admiration as she made dinner over the old gas range. My only skill was with a microwave.

By the end of the evening, my feet, my back and my knees hurt. I had taken it all for granted when I was in Isobel's shoes. Never gave a thought to all the hard work. What would these people think of TV dinners? Not much, I expect.

All I could think of was my bed as I cleared away the debris. Finally, everything was back in its place, and I made my way wearily up the stairs. I was stopped on the first landing by Mr Phillips who took a firm hold of my arm.

"You look tired Lottie. Come to my room, you can have a soak in my bath."

I was shocked. "I don't think so sir. Rose would notice I wasn't in the bedroom with her."

"She knows better than to say anything, come on."

I pleaded that I was too tired, wondering if this was a

common occurrence, the elderly owner of the house forcing the maid to spend the night with him? His grip on my arm tightened

"Come on, don't forget, I saved your bacon this morning, all that hullabaloo over you wearing Isobel's ring. If I hadn't intervened, you'd be out on your ear, miss." He let go of my arm.

"Don't forget who pays your wages. Your sick mother wouldn't be happy if you were thrown out."

I walked along the corridor with him. It didn't seem as if I had much choice. Once I'd had a soak in the bath, I didn't ache so but I dreaded what was coming next.

I climbed out of the bath, and he wrapped me in a large towel, told me to sit down then he bent down and massaged my feet. I hate to say this, but it was bliss. My head was recoiling in horror and distaste, but my feet were loving it.

He left the bathroom and came back with a large robe, which he draped round my now dry body, he led me back to the bedroom. He got into bed and patted the mattress beside him.

"Come on, you've done this before, don't act like a virgin."

I sat down and looked at him, he didn't seem as if he was ready for action. I lay down beside him and he put his arm around me, one hand on my breast. Then to my surprise and delight, he fell asleep. I waited for a while too scared to move in case I woke him. Eventually I slipped out of the bed, gathered up my clothes from the bathroom and, wearing the robe, crept out of the room and up to the attic.

Rose stirred. "He's up to his old tricks then?" she said sleepily.

I nodded, exhaustion now getting the better of me.

"I tried to say no."

"You're best to go along with it. These days he seems incapable of doing much. When I was young, he'd be at it all night then, I'd have to be up at five while he was still snoring his head off." I lay back in the lumpy bed. "I never realised," I said. "No wonder Mrs Phillips fell for the man at the stables."

Rose sat bolt upright in bed. "Who told you that?" I started to say that she had, and then remembered, it was Isobel she'd told.

"Can't remember," I mumbled.

It seemed like I'd just shut my eyes when Rose was shaking me awake.

"Come on its five o'clock." I couldn't think where I was for a minute which considering all that had happened, was not surprising.

Once in the kitchen I was given a hot cup of sweet tea followed by a bowl of porridge. I was then sent to clean and tidy the downstairs rooms, before waking first Mr Phillips and then Isobel with their morning tea. She was grumpy and rude. Told me to run her a bath and sort her blue dress and undies out for her to wear. She didn't say one word of thanks.

While she was bathing, I went to Mr Phillips' room to clean the bathroom and tidy it up. He was already downstairs eating his breakfast. I then went back to Isobel's room to clean the bath and make her bed. She clearly expected me to pick up the clothes from the previous day that were scattered around the room and sort her hair out.

There was no let up, breakfast was cleared, luncheon set, laundry done. It was my job, it seemed, to iron the frilly aprons for the servants too. James had been right when he'd said to me that a servant's life was from five in the morning until late at night.

On Wednesday afternoon Cook told me it was my turn to have the afternoon off to visit my mother. She gave me half a game pie that had been left over from the previous evening's meal and a large wedge of cheddar cheese.

I took off my cap and apron and set off. Where to, I had no idea. I stood outside the house wondering which way to go when James drew up in the car.

"Get in quickly before anyone sees you," he said.

He drove me to the edge of the village where a few cottages stood at the end of a muddy road.

"It's the middle one," he said. "You will have to find your own way back. Don't be late."

I tapped on the cottage door then pushed it open. It was gloomy inside. There was a woman sitting in a wooden chair with her foot on what I realised was a cradle that contained a baby. She was rocking the cradle with her foot in an ineffectual effort to stop the baby crying. She looked up and smiled at me, her smile widening when she saw I carried a basket of food.

"Hello Lottie, nice to see you," she said, as the baby's wails got louder. "Pick him up will you, his cries are going straight through me."

She struggled up out of the chair, the effort causing her to pant. I picked the baby up, his nappy was sodden and he didn't stop crying, I put him over my shoulder and patted his back. It worked for a short while, but soon his cries turned to screams.

"Is there a dry nappy for him?" I asked. She pointed to the

wooden clothes horse in front of the fire, where there were several items of baby things drying. I handed her the baby and a nappy; I had no intention of changing him myself, I didn't know how. She looked at me and shook her head. "You'll 'ave to do this one day. You can't get away with being squeamish all your life."

She dropped the soiled cloth on the floor, it was clear that she expected me to pick it up. Instead, I went over to the fire where a kettle was simmering and made a pot of tea. I was getting used to loose leaf tea and a teapot. On the sink was a jug of milk and some dirty cups. First, I washed up and poured the tea. I'd sneaked a large slice of fruitcake from the cake stand that afternoon. I cut her a large slab. She looked as if she needed nourishment, and ate it hungrily. As the baby started to fuss again she unbuttoned her top and fed him.

She handed him back to me once he had finished.

"Put 'im down will you and pour me more tea." I put him in his cradle and topped the pot up with hot water.

"No not like that, wind 'im first." She took him back and started to pat his back. The baby responded with a burp that wouldn't have shamed a grown man, she sighed and laid him in the crib. As she straightened, she coughed, a horrible painful hacking cough shook her body. When she stopped, I handed her the tea,

"Have you seen the doctor about your cough?"

"You're 'aving a laugh," she grimaced and said doctors cost money.

"I'll pay from my wages."

"You're a good girl, but 'e charges a shilling."

I was feeling most uncomfortable. She sounded ill, she

looked ill and here she was with a small baby. What was to happen to her and the child?

She asked me what was happening in the Phillips house. She'd heard about Isobel's engagement.

"You wouldn't believe all the fuss and bother. Her dress is being designed by someone in France, they had the engagement party on Saturday."

"The whole village is talking about it. Will it mean extra work? Will you get paid more?"

"I doubt it, I can't work much harder than I do."

"Huh, you 'ave it easier than we used to. The parties they used to 'ave back then."

"Do you know what happened to Isobel's mother?"

She paused for a while, thinking. "Well, I knows what was said. It were a sad thing. The poor lady was ill after Isobel was born. The villagers were told that she lost 'er mind, but there was talk that she was pregnant when she were put away."

"Where? Do you know?" I asked.

"Could 'ave been she were taken to the asylum. They did say she were shouting and screaming when they took 'er away." She started coughing again, really badly this time, she took a gulp of cold tea, but it didn't help much. I thought I shouldn't ask any questions. I had learnt some more.

Cook had told me to be back to help clear up after dinner. So not having any way to tell the time, I decided I needed to start walking back to the house.

I got back in time, just. Again, I felt black looks from cook and Rose wasn't happy with me either.

The week passed, I got used to what was expected of me,

but I lived in dread of being grabbed by Mr Phillips. Thank goodness he was away during the week.

I could not believe how ill-tempered Isobel was, I dreaded going into her room in the morning. She never said a word of thanks, she found fault with everything. Blamed me for clothes screwed up on the floor, for wine stains on her beautiful dresses. She was so spoiled. I started to think that she and Lionel would make a perfect couple. I hoped my time with them would soon be over. However, every morning I woke in that lumpy narrow bed, with a stiff neck and sore head. My skin was sore from the itchy undergarments, I longed for my own clothes, my own time.

It was true that I had learned a great deal from my experiences. I had been unaware of so much. I would never have learned it from books. I continually felt sorry for myself, why had this happened?

This morning, I sat on the edge of my bed reluctant to take off the warm nightdress. It always felt cold up in this tiny room. How could I get away? Last time I thought I saw an opening it was a disaster. I certainly didn't want to go back to that cowshed. I didn't want to stay here as a servant, being ill-treated.

Rose's voice broke into my thoughts.

"Come on Lottie get a move on."

"Leave me alone."

Rose frowned, "It's up to you, it won't be me getting in trouble."

I reluctantly drew the garment over my head and put on my day dress. My apron had fallen on the floor and had several large creases across the front. I put it on hoping that no one would notice. I could sneak into the laundry room later and iron it free of creases.

The sitting room took longer than usual to clean, the fire had been lit the evening before, so the hearth had to be cleaned and polished as well as the whole room dusted. I thought of the winter when the maids would have to light fires in the morning before the house rose. Colder, darker mornings and fires to be lit, things could only get worse.

My name was being called and I rushed to the kitchen.

"You need to change your apron, it's filthy." I was told when cook saw me, so instead of eating porridge I had to iron an apron, sipping my tea as the iron warmed up.

I was in a bad mood when I opened Miss Isobel's curtains. She, however, was in a worse one. Demanding pills for her headache.

"Immediately, don't dawdle, girl I have a splitting head."

I thought, and you deserve it, I looked at her clothes strewn around the room and started to pick them up.

"Pills, I said pills, you stupid girl, are you deaf? Leave the clothes."

I went to the bathroom cupboard, I'd put some aspirin in there to save my legs, she asked for them so often.

She started to shout at me, but I was back with the pills and water, which she grabbed and swallowed quickly.

"Run my bath," she demanded. "I must meet Mrs Miles by ten o'clock. Why didn't you wake me earlier?"

I wanted to say because you didn't tell me, but I didn't. I had to remember Lottie needed this job. While she was bathing, I warned the kitchen that her breakfast was needed as soon as she came down. I was busy tidying up the bedroom, so missed James when he came for her.

When I went back downstairs Rose told me that we had to clean the bedroom that had belonged to Mrs Phillips. It was a beautiful room overlooking the front of the house. I don't think it had been entered since Mrs Phillips left. There were still sheets on the bed; they had yellowed with time. Everything had to be moved, cleaned, washed, polished and the drawers and wardrobes emptied. It was a large task. I asked Rose about Mrs Phillips as we worked.

"She was a lovely lady, but she found it difficult after she'd had Isobel," she said.

"She was lonely, none of her friends had babies and they were all still meeting, going for drinks and coffee. She realised she no longer had anything in common with them. She found their conversation silly and couldn't relate to them. One friend she'd been very close to, had married and moved away. Mrs Phillips felt all alone, Isobel was such a difficult baby."

"Still is difficult," I said.

"What she would have done if she'd been one of us with no help I dread to think. As it was, she tried hard but never really took to the baby. Of course, he wasn't any help, hardly ever home, stayed in London. We all decided he had a fancy woman. When he did come home there were dreadful rows. She would accuse him of no longer loving her and not caring about the baby." It was the longest I'd heard Rose speak.

"Need to get on with this we'd get into trouble if anyone heard us. I did like her though; she was a lovely lady. He was besotted with her until she fell pregnant. She always said thank you and was kind not like her daughter."

"Must be hard if your mother is taken away from you," I said.

"Trouble was Isobel was spoiled. Everyone tried to make it up to her, not him. He never really took any notice of her. We thought he'd wanted a son. Then when she gets older and pretty, he realises he has a daughter. All the young men around here did too and we started to get a bit of life in the place. That's why he employed you, when we had dinner parties and such. Mind you, she thinks you're there to be at her beck and call. Doesn't do with you helping with the housework. She really wants a lady's maid. She seemed a bit better when she first got engaged but she's back to her old ways now."

"You looked after Mrs Phillips, didn't you?"

"Well, she had a French woman when she first came here, but he got fed up with the expense and what he called encouraging her in fancy ways. So, I was made to help. I learned a lot from her before she went. That was when Mrs P was first pregnant, she was sick a lot and he seemed to stop caring about her, got rid of her maid."

"I wonder if that's when she first got melancholic, perhaps the maid meant a lot to her?"

"Could be, she took to her bed for a while. Now look here Lottie, you need to carry on here. I'll take the bedclothes down with me and set the table for luncheon. I think it's only Miss Isobel. But I need to check with cook."

All the time Rose had been talking, we had been working hard. I wondered if she felt guilty for discussing the family history with me. She picked up the clothes and hurried down to the kitchen. Cleaning was such hard work especially when it involved moving the heavy furniture. Rose had taken the bed linen and given me instructions to put all the clothes in a large trunk that had come down from the attic. I decided to fold them up and do that next. The clothes were beautiful, some very delicate. I imagined the joy of a charity shop being given these. Of course, there were no such shops. I wondered what would happen to them.

I filled the trunk and went upstairs to find another, glad to stretch my back. I remembered seeing lavender bags and decided to put these in to deter moths. I tried to think where I'd seen them, they were not in the chest. I looked in the wardrobe, the middle part was sectioned off into sets of shelves and drawers. One hadn't been emptied, it contained lacy hankies and lavender bags. I wondered if Rose had left it on purpose. I took most of the bags and placed them in the trunks. The drawer went further back than I realised, I pulled it right out and found the hankies covered several slim books. I took them out and saw they were diaries. Had they been hidden there by Mrs Phillips? I opened one and it was filled with fine writing. I looked in the back of other drawers and there were more. This was a captivating find. If no one else knew they were there, would it hurt if I took them? I collected them up and held them under my apron. I took them upstairs and hid them in the trunk under my bed. Just one quick look had told me they were a fascinating glimpse into this woman's life. I was sure they would be destroyed if Mr Phillips knew of their existence.

Chapter 12

Isobel was dining out, so once we had cleared the table and tidied the kitchen, I spent a little time in the laundry room. Then, much to our relief after our strenuous morning we had the rest of the day to ourselves.

Rose announced she was going to visit her sister. I thought this would be a good opportunity for me to look at the diaries. Once upstairs I got them out from under my bed, the early ones didn't have much written in, just engagements and dates that she met up with her friends.

I found the one for 1910 when she was pregnant with Isobel. She writes of terrible sickness and her French maid giving her lemon and ginger in the mornings to lessen the effects. Towards the end of her pregnancy, her writing is full of how Arthur is staying in London and doesn't speak to her except at dinner when he is home. She is desperately unhappy, feels fat and unloved.

Entry after entry says she is sure he has a mistress, and how her only comfort is Estelle. She starts to feel sick again and the doctor tells her she must eat, or the baby will not survive. Estelle makes her special broths, the only thing she can eat.

She feels that she looks like a great belly on stick legs. She has lost so much weight.

Arthur comes home and tells her the business isn't doing so well and they must economise. He says Estelle must go, she responds by telling him to get rid of his mistress and his London flat. They have a terrible row, and he tells her she is unstable, and he will have her committed. She threatens to throw herself down the stairs if he gets rid of Estelle.

She wakes up the next morning and the doctor is there. Arthur explains that she is unbalanced and threatening to kill the baby. The doctor gives her an injection and the next thing she knows she is in a nursing home, being guarded day and night.

When she refuses to eat, they force feed her saying it's for the baby's sake. She writes that she was out of it for most of the time.

Every day I was in a daze, made to drink greasy soup that the forbidding nurse fed me. I wasn't allowed out of my bed except to go on the commode.

I complained my back hurt and they gave me an enema, which was dreadful and humiliating. After that the pain got worse and they said I was in labour.

Two days of the most extreme pain anyone ever suffered followed.

When Isobel was born, I was so exhausted I couldn't hold her. They took her away and again a prick in my arm made me senseless.

One day Arthur came to see me, said it was disappointing it was a girl, we would have to try again in a few months. I asked him when I could come home. He said in another week providing I didn't have another episode.

When I asked what he meant he said I had to be less excitable and 'toe the line', as his mother had. Be like that mousey little woman. I started to laugh. He left saying I needed to calm down. Perhaps I needed more than a week?

From the dates, it looks like she was there for another two weeks having very little contact with Isobel because they said she made the baby cry.

What an awful situation. She finally came home. Arthur fetched her in the car and the baby cried all the way home. When they got in, he instructed her to stop the crying. He disappeared immediately to his study. She hardly knew what to do and Rose appeared with a bottle of milk.

She asked where Estelle was. She couldn't work out why she wasn't there to help her. She was told Estelle had gone. She had been sacked the day after Rachel was taken to the nursing home. She left the baby with Rose and went to Arthur's study to confront him. He told her the doctor thought Estelle's foreign ways had contributed to Rachel's breakdown, so he had sent her back to France. Rachel was distraught, she might have been able to cope with Estelle's help but without her, she felt all was lost. Forgetting about the baby, she went up to her room and sobbed.

The next day the doctor was called and prescribed medication. She was to take it every day to help her cope with her new life as a mother.

There were spaces in the entries for the next few months. What writing there was, made little sense and the text was blotched and spindly.

She wrote she was sad and lost, she had no fulfilment from the baby who seemed to cry incessantly.

A few friends called to see her and made cooing noises over the baby, but she had little interest in them. Their lives were still going on as before, her own was totally changed.

By the time Isobel's birthday arrived, Rachel had started to find her interesting.

A large party was planned, all her old friends were invited plus the Miles family. It was a huge success and she felt life was starting to get back to normal.

She started to see her friend Vivienne Miles once a week. Lionel, Vivienne's little boy and Isobel are both entertained by the nursemaid.

There are many hints in Rachel's diary that Vivienne wasn't happy in her marriage, thinking that her own husband was unfaithful too. Arthur returned to Rachel's bed at the weekends. She doesn't appear to enjoy sex but she is pleased he is taking an interest in her. A couple of months later she feels sick and realises she is pregnant again. She tells Rose who brings her the lemon and ginger remedy Estelle used to make for her.

Arthur, once he knew she was pregnant, stopped coming to her bed. When she asked him to join her, he tells her his job is done. She is pregnant and it had better be a boy this time. Her misery is extreme. She'd thought he loved her again. Her diary is full of wondering what she could have done differently. She had tried so hard to be what he wanted but had failed.

There are several weeks where the only entry is '*I feel sick,*' or I' *wish I were dead*'.

This is all so sad and when I hear footsteps on the stairs, I realise it's late and I must hide the books away. I can't take any more misery and injustice, and I need my sleep.

But I hardly slept that night and when I did, I dreamt I was Rachel with a screaming baby in my arms. When I woke from the dream, my arms ached just as they did in the dream. I was frightened to open my eyes in case I was in Rachel's body. When I did, I saw I was still Lottie, but how my arms ached, across my shoulders too. I wondered if I could tiptoe down to the pantry to find some aspirin. I couldn't sleep like this. I got out of bed and in doing so I awoke Rose. I told her about my shoulders, and she said there was some aspirin in the drawer by her bed. She was grumpy at being woken.

"It's all the moving of the heavy furniture we'd done. You're such a lightweight Lottie. I swear you get worse."

I took the tablets gratefully and tossed and turned for the rest of the night.

For once, I was up before Rose. I felt if I lay in that lumpy bed any longer my back would break. She was right I was a lightweight, I'd had such a cosy life compared to her. She had started as a maid before her thirteenth birthday.

Life had been hard then she'd told me, never feeling warm enough in winter. Getting up to light fires and heat water for the people she waited on. No electricity in the house, cooking was by gas and the big coal range. The place was lit by gaslight and oil lamps. She shuddered when she told me how much cleaning there had been. So much dust. Madam had insisted on candles every evening in those days, which made even more work.

Later that morning I asked her if she knew why we

were sorting out the bedroom that hadn't been touched for so long.

"Cook reckons once Miss Isobel moves out, when she's married, Mr Phillips will move his mistress down from London. She would have the room then. It's the best room."

"Wonder how cook knows?"

"Cook could be wrong; don't know how she knows what's going on? He might be planning to marry someone himself," Rose said. "It makes sense to get rid of all this stuff."

"Do you think he might sell the house and get somewhere smaller when Miss Isobel leaves?"

She looked at me, eyebrows raised, "Why would he do that?"

I shrugged. I was looking at it with modern eyes, there would be no need for him to downsize, another instance of how life was so different for the rich.

Well, I thought to myself, the next war will change things. Now women were servants, mistresses or bored wives of men, who thought their own lives so important. Then I thought of all the wives of working men struggling to make ends meet, no control over their lives or bodies, living in abject poverty. Not much better in the 80's. When would women get true equality?

We were cleaning the silver before setting the table. Rose asked me if my arms still hurt. I said not so much but still a little sore. She told me I looked miserable enough to turn the milk and reminded me it was my afternoon off, so I'd better cheer up.

Isobel's friends were coming for lunch, so I had to go

upstairs to help her get ready. My heart was not in it. Why did she need help? She was a grown woman.

She was sitting on her bed in that lovely dressing gown I had worn. I imagined her anger if she knew, and it was the first time I smiled that day.

I took several dresses out from the wardrobe before she decided what to wear. She started to talk about her wedding, which was soon. She was going for a fitting for her dress the next day and she was clearly anxious. It made her snappy and fussy. I did her hair, and it was wrong, so I damped it down and started again. A drip went down her neck and she shouted at me and called me stupid and clumsy. At last, she was satisfied. I thought if she's like this today what will the wedding morning be like?

As if she'd heard me, Isobel said, "thank goodness I have a professional coming to look after me on my wedding morning."

"That's good then Miss." If she intended to hurt my feelings, she did the opposite.

"Yes, Elise from the boutique is coming to help me get ready."

I thought I should say something nice. "You'll look lovely in the dress from Paris, Miss."

"Yes, I will. Not every girl has a Worth creation to wear on her big day."

Smiling, she went down to greet her friends whilst I cleared up the mess she left behind.

That afternoon I took the rest of the diaries I'd found and made my way to the church. One of the things that had kept me awake was wondering how I could keep them safe.

I decided that whatever happened the church would still be there, if I suddenly returned to my own time. I don't know why it was so important to keep them safe I just felt I had to.

I sat quietly at the back of the church reading another diary. Rachel wrote in such detail about her unhappiness, she was dreadfully sick each morning and so alone. She was too ill to even see Vivienne. The only mention of Isobel was of her coming to say goodnight before her nurse took her to bed. Poor little girl, a mostly absent father and a mother too wrapped up in her own misery to care about her. No wonder she was unlikeable now. I turned the page feeling less sorry for this woman, thinking of the child.

Miscarriage was written across the top of the page. She awoke in dreadful pain in the middle of the night and by morning was bleeding. She was losing the baby.

The doctor was sent for, he confirmed that she was no longer pregnant and gave her a sedative. She slept. She was convinced it had been a boy. She had failed again in her eyes and in Arthurs. The doctor told her she must wait for six months before she tried again for another baby. He told her she had produced a healthy child once and, in his opinion, could do so again.

I sat on the hard pew wrapped up in this woman's misery, wondering where she was. I remembered the phone call I'd had just before I went into the void when I was still Isobel. The voice on the other end had called me Imogen; told me to look in the asylum for Rachel, surely, she wasn't there? I didn't know much about the treatment of patients in those places, but I knew it wasn't good. Cold baths and electric shock treatments, with patients enduring hours or days in solitary confinement whilst wearing straitjackets, was what I'd heard. Poor lady surely that hadn't been her fate, she sounded sad not mad.

Vivienne, it seemed, had been a constant visitor; she tried to persuade Rachel to have a dog, thinking it would be good for her to take it for long walks.

Several entries show that she tried hard to get Rachel to lessen the dose of the pills she took.

After much persuading by Vivienne, Rachel agreed to accompany her to the Miles's stables. She had previously been a good horsewoman but hadn't ridden since she was pregnant with Isobel.

On her first trip she took Isobel with her, the little girl loved the pony that Lionel rode.

The stable hand lifted Isobel up on the saddle when Lionel dismounted and gently led her round. Not only did she smile, but she also chuckled with delight. When it was time for her to get down, she kept saying.

"More Mummy more." We were all so delighted she was led round again.

The diary entry says.

For the first time I took pleasure in my little daughter. She was fearless and so happy I forgot to be sad."

She doesn't say if she rode herself but after that once a week, the nanny and Isobel went to the stables.

It seemed finally, life was bearable for her.

I was touched at how kind Vivienne was shown to be. She certainly seemed to be a good friend.

After a few weeks the entry read.

At last, after all this time, I've been out for a ride. It was exhilarating, I'd forgotten how good it is to ride and be free.

The next day she moans about her legs aching but says it was worth it.

At the weekend she tries to tell Arthur about how good it felt but he doesn't want to listen. He tells her it will soon be time for them to try for another baby and once that happens, she must not ride for fear of not conceiving. Her mood sinks again. Her entries start to mention Frank, a friend of Vivienne's brother. They ride out together, she notes several times how he tells her what a good horseman she is. It's so long since anyone has told her she is good at anything, and she is obviously impressed by his comments. She writes he is good company and handsome.

The diary is full of Frank, reading through it, I can see that she is falling in love. My stomach muscles tighten as I read. I feel fear for her. This is not a path she should take. She is too vulnerable. Vivienne is happy to leave them together.

I seem to be spending more and more time with Frank. He is a perfect gentleman, but I can't help noticing that his hand lingers on mine when he helps me dismount. It makes my heartbeat so fast as if it is trying to escape my chest. Yesterday I slipped as I left my horse. Frank steadied me. I had to put my hands on his shoulders for support. I looked up into his eyes for a long time then he bent and kissed me gently on the lips. I stepped back quite shocked, but I must admit I was delighted. He apologised but Vivienne came into the stable yard, so we said no more. She said I looked a little flushed. I blamed the exertions of our ride, but she gave me a look. Did she suspect? I haven't been able to stop thinking about that kiss. Will it happen again? Vivienne came with us today. I so wanted to be alone with Frank. I stole a look at him when we were in the stable yard. He looked at me most tenderly.

I'm torn as Vivienne is a good friend. She has helped me so much, but I must admit it's Frank's company I yearn for.

She is firmly hooked. I wonder, does he really care about her, or is he just interested in the chase?

Chapter 13

It's getting late, the light in the church is dim and her writing is small, I can take a book back with me in the pocket of my dress. The others I need to hide away to keep safe. At the back of the church is an old chest. It smells musty when I lift the lid. There are a few old bibles inside, but it doesn't look as if it's ever opened. Hoping this will be a safe place, I bury the journals under the bibles. There are long wispy cobwebs and a spider scuttles out. I'm sure no one will be looking in here.

I hurried back to the house convinced I'd be late for dinner, but I arrived just in time.

There was no sign of Rose, cook had said she wasn't feeling well. I served Isobel and her father their dinner; they talked of how he would walk her up the aisle of the church.

"Isobel, I have told you and Vivienne I will not go to a wedding practice, you must be content to have me there on the day. I never heard of anything so ridiculous, the woman needs something to occupy her mind."

"But father..."

"That's the end of the matter."

She wasn't happy I could tell, but she didn't argue with him, there was a pause then she asked him.

"Father, why is Mother's old room being cleaned and restored?"

"It's time it was done. You will have your own place to worry about soon, so don't worry your head about it."

I thought, why won't he tell her? Perhaps he thinks she will disapprove?

I cleared the dishes when they were finished eating, she turned to me and said, "I need you to come to see Madame Marianne with me tomorrow, Lottie. There will be plenty of packages to carry."

"Oh yes, Miss," I said. "Will it be the dress, Miss?"

"No, my trousseau, but I will need to try on my dress, now the alterations are complete."

"Alterations? I thought that Worth chap was the business didn't he get it right? The cost was high enough."

"No father, it's nothing, that girl at Madame Marianne's had got my measurements slightly wrong. Stupid girl. It should be perfect now."

I wondered if they had made the dress to my measurements taken before the dieting, it would account for the dress being a poor fit. That poor girl would have taken the blame.

Later, when I'd finished my duties, I went up to the attic room where Rose was asleep. I didn't want to disturb her so sat in the bathroom on the landing to continue reading the diaries.

It was as I first thought, Rachel was deeply in love but what about Frank? It was hard to say, she thought he loved her. Of course she did.

As I turned the pages, she appeared to be deeper and deeper in love. The day she was longing for finally arrived.

The weather was beautiful, and Frank suggested that they rode out to a meadow to have a picnic. No mention of Isobel. I guess that for a while now she hadn't been on their rides.

We rode out in the warm sunshine. Frank had a picnic hamper attached to his horse and we stopped in the far meadow. He spread out the blanket and we sat down, side by side. Soon he was stroking my knee and kissing me. This time he didn't stop though, and I didn't want him to. I took off my jacket, my heart was pounding. I was sure he could see it through my thin blouse. He slowly undid the buttons and kissed the tops of my breasts. Somehow, we were lying down, and his hands were under my skirt. I wanted him to make love to me. I didn't expect much but thought it might bring us closer together.

Instead of thrusting himself into me and coming with a few grunts, as Arthur always had, he started to stroke me. As he bent down and gently kissed me he slipped his tongue around me. I had never felt pleasure like it. I could feel my back arching and my whole being throbbing. I lost all sense of where I was, aware of nothing but the mounting pleasure inside my body, I thought I was going to burst. I was so desperate for him to be inside me. I found myself tearing at the buttons of his trousers, at last he sank into me. I was so wet with desire it was easy, not painful, as I had previously experienced in my marriage bed. As he thrust, I felt myself burst, again and again. I have never known such pleasure. I have no words for how I felt. Afterwards, when we were both breathing normally again, he kissed me tenderly and stroked my arms, saying how good it had been for him. I just smiled. I still had no words. The picnic remained untouched. I didn't think I'd ever be hungry for food again.

We arrived back at the stables as the sun was sinking behind the trees, luckily nobody saw us.

Rose noticed grass stains on my riding habit today. I told her I'd slipped from my mount the other day and slid on the grass. Then I felt guilty because she offered to massage my back in case I'd strained it in the fall.

She would have been so shocked if she had known how those grass stains happened. I'm still a little shocked myself. I never knew a woman could feel such intense pleasure.

Arthur was home at the weekend asking again when we would be able to make another baby. I never want to do that travesty of lovemaking with him again. I made feeble excuses. He wasn't happy, and said we needed an heir. It's not as if we have a grand estate like Vivienne. I thought.

I heard him in the night he had Rose in his bed and I could hear her protesting. Women have no choice. I hope she doesn't fall pregnant. I would miss her and anyway I like the way she does my hair.

I was shocked at her callous attitude to Rose, could she not have done something to help her?

The next week it rained every day and they couldn't go riding.

I am so desperate to see him and feel his lips on mine. I shall be sad all week.

Several weeks follow of her being in heaven with her Frank. She notes that England is at war with the Kaiser and they say it will be all over by Christmas. She seems concerned that the big houses will lose their male servants as most young men are signing up to serve their country. Then disaster strikes:

I haven't bled for over two months. Rose knows; she does my washing.

I must be carrying Frank's child. Fear engulfs me.

I will let Arthur in my bed tonight.

But it doesn't work. He notices her swollen breasts and belly and thinks she is fat and refuses to be intimate with her.

She decides she must tell Frank but when she goes to the stables there is a note for her.

My dearest,

I have decided that I cannot shirk my duty. By the time you read this my brother and I will have signed up. We will ....

I couldn't bear to tell you face to face and witness your tears. My love, we will be home in a few months, after showing the Huns the stuff of which we English men are made.

When I get back, I will come and see Arthur and tell him myself, he must give you up. The world will be changed. We will get married. Be brave.

I love you forever my dearest.

Frank

The note is discoloured with tears and so are the many entries after.

When Arthur finally realises that she is pregnant his fury knows no limits. She says he strikes her then locks her in her room.

To save a scandal he says if she has a girl, he will allow her to keep it, but if it's a boy, he will send it away for adoption.

He has that right as she is married still to him so he is legally the father and can do as he wishes.

She is kept in her room for weeks. Vivienne is told she is ill and not allowed to visit.

Vivienne knows she was distraught over Frank leaving and believes Arthur. There are several little notes from her tucked into the diary, sending her good wishes and saying she will visit as soon as Arthur says she can.

Finally, Rachel goes into labour and delivers a boy, she calls him Frank.

Arthur keeps away for over a week. When he visits, he says the boy will be adopted. He names him Paul, and says she can keep him until he has made arrangements for where he is to go. After two more weeks, a woman comes and takes baby Paul away.

Rachel goes mad with grief, stops eating and becomes sick. Her description of how she feels is frightening. She threatens to kill herself, and burn the house down. She has little thought for Isobel, her little daughter and hates Arthur with all her being. Her writing is a scrawl and difficult to read. She sends letters through Vivienne to Frank but doesn't know if he gets them.

She is told that unless she pulls herself together, she is to be sent to the Asylum. Vivienne finally hears the truth and comes to see her. She is shocked at how Rachel looks and tells her she must get well. She brings letters from Frank saying when he comes home, he will help her find Paul and look after them both.

Rachel gradually starts to eat and Rose looks after her. The servants were all told by Arthur that they must say nothing about recent events . He has the right to do as he wishes with his family.

Rachel starts to look forward to Easter when she is sure she will see Frank.

Vivienne came today. I greeted her with pleasure, expecting her to be delighted with the fact I'd put on weight from eating properly. When I drew close to her, I could see she was pale, her makeup couldn't hide the fact she'd been crying. She held out her arms to me and started to sob, unable to say the words. "Tell me," I cried. "What is it?" She shook her head and after several seconds, she told me. She came with dreadful news. Frank is dead. Dead, dead. My life, my love is dead.

I must have fainted. I was half in the chair, half on the floor. Rose was holding burnt feathers to my face. I didn't want to regain consciousness. I didn't want to live. Frank is dead. How can I live without him? I can't, I won't.

All over the page the word dead had been written in large letters, the writing scrawling, smudged, I guess by large teardrops falling on the pages.

There were no more entries, but my guess is that's when she was sent to the asylum.

I sat there for a time, I don't know how long, I felt sad, I almost wished I'd not read the rest of the entries. Life was so difficult for women and what would happen to poor little Paul. Would the people that had him love him?

I went to bed but was woken by Rose while I was still deep asleep dreaming of Rachel.

"You have to accompany Miss Isobel to the dressmakers later this morning, and there is much to do first," she said.

I decided to tell Rose that I'd found the diary, only the one that I'd been reading that night, not the ones I'd hidden in the church. While we were cleaning, I told her I'd found it when I was sorting out the clothes, which was true in a way. I gave her the diary confessing that I'd read it. I said that I looked at it but couldn't stop reading once I started. She took it, looked at the date and put it quickly in her pocket.

"This was a dreadful time. I thought Madam was going to die. No one was allowed to speak to her. I had to take her meals up on a tray once Mr Phillips found she was pregnant. We were all sworn to secrecy. He said it would harm her if anyone found out, and none of us wanted that." She paused and blew her nose.

"We thought she was going to be allowed to keep the baby at first. It would have been kinder if he had been taken away at birth really. Mr Phillips didn't want to be kind, he wanted to punish her."

"Did anyone believe he would have the baby removed? Why didn't she try to escape? How could she have let him be taken?"

"The day the baby was taken the doctor came to examine them both. While he was with Mrs Phillips, a woman in a nurse's uniform came in and took the baby. She started to panic but the doctor said the nurse was going to check the baby over. By the time Mrs Phillips realised what was happening, he had gone. We never saw him again. Mrs Phillips went mad and started screaming and attacking everyone in the room. She tried to get out, but she was weakened, and the doctor quickly injected her in her arm, and she soon went limp. I had to put her in her bed. I was told to give her tablets when she woke."

"It must have been an awful experience for you too."

"When I came up to her later that day, she had scratched her arms and was bleeding, when I tried to help, she attacked me and screamed I was on his side. She then started to cry and pleaded with me to help her. I've never seen anyone so desperate. I can still hear her screams sometimes they wake me in the night."

Rose's eyes were full of tears, some had escaped and she rubbed them roughly away. She was polishing fast and repeating, "it had been a dreadful time."

"Mrs Miles seemed to be a good friend," I said.

"Yes, she was different back then. Cared for her friend, not hard like now. I think Mrs Phillips went mad when she heard that the captain was dead. Mrs Miles was affected too."

"Do you think she did go mad?"

"Of course she did, who wouldn't. I think she would have recovered, though if he hadn't been so unkind."

"Why did he care so much, he wasn't faithful to her?"

"No, he wasn't but it was keeping up the image. Women aren't allowed to be like men, and he wasn't going to let another man's son inherit, was he?"

"Has she been locked away since then?"

"Yes, I think so. If you'd have seen her when they took her away, she looked so dreadful. Her face and arms were scratched, her hair dirty and uncombed. She'd torn at her clothes and she was screaming she'd kill him."

"Is she still alive?"

"As far as I know. Come on," she sniffed and blew her nose. "You need to tidy yourself up, it will be soon time for you to go with Miss Isobel." She looked at me "don't get any ideas about trying to find Mrs Phillips and no word to Miss Isobel mind." She wagged her finger at me and looked so fierce. "No one wants it all dragged up again. We need our jobs, all of us."

I went to change my dress and wash my hands and face; I

couldn't stop thinking about that poor woman. I knew I had to keep quiet though.

James was waiting in the car for us. He looked surprised when he saw me.

Chapter 14

Isobel looked beautiful in her dress and it now fitted perfectly. Even Mrs Miles should be satisfied. I sat quietly at the back of the shop, while Elise danced attention on Isobel. She was busy fitting the veil on her head when Isobel shrieked.

"You pulled my hair you clumsy idiot." She went quite red in the face with rage. Elise who had been so carefully arranging the dress and veil stepped back as if she had been stung.

"I'm so sorry Miss, I think it was the grip in the veil."

Madame Marianne came forward, forgetting her French accent.

"Elise, take care. Would you like me to continue Miss Isobel?"

"Yes, keep that fat fool away from me."

Elise looked tearful and shocked; Isobel had called her fat. She actually called her fat. I found it hard to believe my ears.

Madame sent Elise out the back, talking to her through clenched teeth.

I followed her out. She looked at me.

"What are you staring at me for?"

"Your nose doesn't go red even though you're crying, how

do you do it? You really are pretty, you know don't let her upset you."

"You're joking, it's not funny. She complained about me getting the measurements wrong, now this. I'll lose my job. Madame doesn't allow mistakes; the customer is always right. After all, they pay a lot of money."

"That shouldn't let them be so rude," I said. I was still shocked.

I heard Isobel calling Lottie and remembered that it was me.

"Yes, Miss?"

"Have you got my packages; I trust the stupid girl has at least got that right."

I forgot myself. "That's hardly fair," I said. "It wasn't her fault I saw you move."

She gasped. "How dare you." She slowly walked over to me and slapped me hard. The room started to spin. Oh no, please not now, why hadn't I been more careful. I should have kept quiet. As if I'd said them aloud, I could hear the words echoing.

"Quiet, keep quiet."

I was in a vortex, spinning, or was the room spinning I didn't know. I thought I saw James's face, then Isobel's looking shocked, before it all went black. I was in a tunnel being pulled along by a force I couldn't see or understand. As I came towards the end I could hear voices, pots clashing. Was I back in the house?

I looked around me. Strange, the walls were tiled, and I could hear the rustle of starched aprons, feet marching along the corridor towards me. I saw two nurses, pushing a trolley containing equipment that for some reason, made me shudder. White enamel jugs and basins, lengths of red rubber tubing. I was in a hospital. I heard cries and shouts coming from further down the corridor. I walked towards the double doors. They were locked. The nurses came up and one took out a large bunch of keys and unlocked the door. I slipped in with them. Realisation dawned. I was in the mental hospital, the asylum. Panic began to set in. Had I morphed into Mrs Phillips? Was I locked in here?

The nurses took no notice of me; they didn't seem to see me. They went up to one woman and told her to get up. She looked terrified and clung onto the chair she was sitting on. They pulled her to her feet. A man in a white tunic came over. He grabbed her arm, and dragged her over to a door, kicking it open. It was a bathroom. A board covered the bath. He pushed her on to it and she started to cry loudly.

One of the nurses told her sharply,

"Be quiet. You should have eaten your food. You know the consequences."

She clearly did and tried to fight them off, but they restrained her by putting her arms in the brackets on the board and tied her down. The nurses proceeded to push the tube down her throat, even though she was gagging. They were so rough with her. Once the tubing was in place, they put a funnel in the other end and started to pour what looked like gruel into her. They emptied the jug, sat her up and held her mouth shut.

There was no compassion shown. My throat hurt. I knew it was only a sympathetic reaction. I could look no longer. I went back into the large room that held many people, most of them sitting in chairs beside cast iron beds. Some were crying, nearly all had a vacant stare, sitting tapping or picking at their clothing. I felt sorry for them but was more interested in how I could get out. I was in a locked ward. How long would it be before I was noticed? Would they think I was a patient? Was I a patient?

One woman was calling out. She was holding a towel in her arms the way you'd hold a baby. I walked over to her. She held the towel out to me.

"My baby's hungry."

Could this be Mrs Phillips? I asked her name.

"Rachel. Rachel Phillips. Please feed my baby." I turned my head away, what could I do? She had clearly lost her mind. She was wearing a drab blue cotton dress. I looked at the food stains on the bodice and thought of the dresses that I'd packed away. Delicate, beautiful, fashionable for their time. I had seen photos of her looking proud, haughty even. How had she sunk to this?

I wanted to tell her that her baby was safe, happy, but I guessed she wouldn't understand. She believed her baby was right there in her arms. Of course, I had no idea of what had really happened to the baby. Rose thought he had been taken to a farm in Wales.

All the women were wearing those plain badly fitting washed out blue dresses. It was difficult to see them as individuals. She started to wail; the noise increased as some of the other women joined in. She was rocking in the chair, her tears mixed with drool and her wailing was so loud I wanted to escape.

I thought how foolish I had been to think she could be

saved. Brought back to normal living. She had been destroyed. How much by her own actions? How much by the cruelty of others? I couldn't tell. She would never leave this place alive that was clear.

I looked around me, I needed to get out of here. The nurses didn't seem to be aware of me. Perhaps I could slip out when one of them opened the door. The two with the trolley were walking back along the room. I followed them and successfully went through the door. What was I going to do now? There were chairs at the end of the corridor. As I walked towards them, I saw the doors leading to the entrance. I sat down thinking, perhaps I could use the same method to get outside. I was shaken by what I had seen. The stale smell of cabbage drifted up the corridor. I had to get out. I stood up and pushed the door, to my surprise, it opened.

Once outside I ran down the steps and sped away from the building. I didn't know where I was going. I needed to leave this dreadful place. The grounds were huge, a tree lined drive led to large iron gates. As I got closer, I could see that they were locked. The walls were too high to climb. They didn't want anyone to escape. Nausea overcame me and bending over against one of the trees, I vomited until my stomach was empty. My head throbbed and I started to cry. How did I get into this mess? I wanted to go home. I was sick of the past.

I wiped my eyes and told myself to get a grip. I'd never expected others to sort out my problems, but I needed help now. There was a small wooden door beside the gates, it was almost hidden by ivy. I walked over and found it hadn't been open for some time. I pulled at the ivy; it came away easily revealing a lock. Of course, the door was locked. Angrily I looked around. The drive was lined with large stones. I wrestled one out of the ground and used it to bash the lock. Anger gave me strength, after a few minutes, the rusty lock gave way. The gate still didn't open. I saw there was a large bolt keeping it closed, it was stubborn, I broke several nails working it free. At last, I was able to open the door. I stepped through into my own room.

Chapter 15

I looked around, was this really my room? I sat down on the bed unsure what to do. I had an acrid taste in my mouth, I remembered being sick. I was no longer wearing a maid's uniform, my jeans felt strange on my legs. I got up and looked in the mirror unsure of who would be looking back at me.

"Hello," I said to myself, my hair was straying out from its bobble in its usual unruly style, my tee shirt pale from the many washes almost reaching the top of my jeans.

I walked over to the wall, I could neither see nor feel a doorway. The doorbell buzzed loudly. 'Pizza for Imogen' came over the intercom when I pressed the button. I let him into the hallway and went down.

I still felt so strange, I didn't take my purse, had no idea where it was, but the delivery boy said it was prepaid. He looked disappointed when I thanked him, and I realised that he had been expecting a tip.

The pizza tasted so good, it felt like months since I'd eaten anything. I started to think about all my experiences, how much time had gone by?

Panic set in, had I missed my deadline? I looked at the pages of work on my table. I knew I'd finished my exams. I couldn't remember what I had left to do. I'd worked so hard, was it all lost now? I was back but to what. I was so tired, I looked at the essay on the table, it was lacking a conclusion, I could soon write that but, was it too late to hand it in. I'll sort everything out tomorrow I thought as my heavy limbs sunk into my bed.

When I awoke the next morning, I didn't know what day it was. I turned on the television and found that I'd only missed the weekend. How could it be, so much had happened. I had time to finish and hand my work in, what a relief. I could walk over to the office, then return my library books. A stern letter from the University Library was open on the table reminding me I would not receive my degree if there were any books unreturned. Walking home I felt pleased but a little lightheaded, I had forgotten to eat. I noticed a large black car driving slowly towards me. That's an old motor, I thought, then saw the driver as it slowed to a stop.

"Get in," he said.

Without thinking I did as James told me.

"Where are we going?" The car was moving fast, everything outside the windows was a blur. Inside there was music playing *Time After Time*.

"No." I cried. "I'm not going back, it's not fair, why are you doing this to me?"

It was too late and I couldn't get out, I thought when it stops at traffic lights I'll get out. It had to stop sometime, but it didn't. I could feel time rolling back. No matter how many questions I asked he didn't answer.

This time there was no vortex, it reminded me of when I first went on the underground with my mum. That strange feeling just before the train arrived at the station. The rush of warm air, before the speed overwhelmed me. Mum told me I had fainted, and she didn't know what to do. Someone had come up and told her to give me a boiled sweet and said it was a lack of sugar. She had done so, and I'd recovered enough to go to see the dinosaurs as she'd planned. I sat on the plush car seat remembering my mum's face, she'd loved the museums. Took me every school holiday, but we'd always travelled across London on the big red buses after that first time. Oh Mum, I thought we were so close then, how did it go so wrong. A picture of him came unwanted into my mind. He was so handsome, so believable, swept Mum off her feet, me too.

We met him at the school gates. I vaguely knew his daughter, Lisa. She was in the class above me, and so we didn't see much of each other. One afternoon Mum and Lisa's dad were talking as we came out. He said they were going for a burger so why didn't we come too. Mum hesitated, even at that age I knew we didn't have money for eating out in the middle of the week. He saw her reluctance and said it would be nice for Lisa to have someone to talk to, so Mum said yes. Lisa and I stared at each other, both of us shy. She asked me if I'd seen the latest Disney film when I said no, she told me all about it. Mum and her dad were talking, I noticed Mum was doing most of the listening and had a soppy look on her face.

Soon after that Lisa and I waited for each other, and Mum took us to the park or back to ours for some tea. Her dad would come and pick her up when he'd finished work. Sometimes on a Friday, we would have a sleepover, always at ours. Lisa never spoke much about her mum, said she stayed mainly at her dad's. Then one day Lisa wasn't at school anymore, they had moved away.

The next Friday though, Lisa's dad, Roger came to our house. Mum was pleased to see him. Fussed around getting him a coffee. He was still there when I went to bed. He became a regular visitor at the weekends, but I didn't see Lisa again. Mum told me that she was living with her mum now in another town. I asked if she could come and stay during the holiday, but she never did. Roger became an almost permanent fixture at our place and Mum seemed very happy. Even if she and I didn't spend so much time together, it was nice that she had a friend of her own.

Mum started to work longer hours and he started to pick me up from school.

Eventually he told me I was big enough to walk home on my own. One day I got in from school, the door was unlocked but there was no one in the kitchen. As I was getting myself a drink of water I heard footsteps on the stairs, it was a dark-haired woman followed by Roger. She went bright red and hurried out of the house. He said she was there because he was planning a surprise for Mum, and I was not to say because that would spoil it.

The next day he met me with a large chocolate bar and again said I must keep quiet. I was only seven and the chocolate tasted nice. Soon after this, a new girl, Cassie, started at school, she was quiet too and my teacher asked me to be kind to her.

We made friends and before long, I was invited to her house. Roger came to pick me up when it was time to go home. When she asked me if Roger was my dad I said no, but he was my mum's friend and he lived with us.

Soon Cassie told me Roger was her mum's friend too. I thought that was strange but didn't say anything. He got a new job in the evenings, so I didn't see much of him. Mum started to be unhappy. She said she was lonely with him working in the evening and soon they started to have rows about money, about him being out so much. It turned out that he wasn't working; he was spending evenings with Cassie's mum. He'd spent my mum's money and never paid her for living with us .

Mum threw him out, but she was bitterly unhappy, I don't know if she drank much before. I was too young to notice. After he left, most evenings she would be slumped in her chair with an empty bottle beside her by the time I went to bed. We didn't go to London to the museums although she did take me to the library. I noticed her books weren't read.

Chapter 16

The car stopped.

"Here we are," he said. I looked up, to find we were in the middle of the countryside. He pointed towards a grey farmhouse, as he got out of the car and came round to open the door for me.

"Out you get," he said. I was unsteady on my feet so I held on to his arm.

"Where is this? I need to get on with my life."

"You wanted to see what happened to him," he said as he got straight back in the car and vanished. I trudged through the smelly mud, full of cowpats towards the farmyard. A woman came out with a bucket and a few hens came clucking up to her as she threw grain to them.

She looked up and noticed me.

"Those shoes will be no good here, you were told to bring wellies. Let's hope you have some in your bag. It came yesterday so we were expecting you." I stared at her, finding her strong Welsh accent difficult to follow.

"Come on in then, you'll be hungry after your journey."

I went inside, a large, blackened kettle was simmering on the range.

"Wash your hands in the scullery, we don't stand on ceremony here," she said as she poured water into a large teapot.

"There's not much of you, don't know how you'll replace Paul when he's gone. Know much about cows? I thought not. Still, you'll have to learn quick. He's off in a few days. Got his papers last week. Thought we'd have to wait weeks to get a girl, but they said we was priority as they need the milk."

One corner of a large, scrubbed table had a white cloth across it. She motioned me to sit and placed a large cup of tea in front of me.

"We're lucky here to have eggs and milk not like in the towns. Heard they're short there, powdered eggs, Gladys says they have."

I wondered if she ever stopped talking. I drank the tea; she took my cup and refilled it and placed a large slab of cake in front of me.

"Apple cake. You'll like it."

I did.

"We'll have supper when the men come in, what's left of them, only the old ones now. All the rest gone for soldiers. That Hitler, he's got a lot to answer for." She sniffed, "I'll miss Paul he's a good worker, allus has been. Cows'll miss him too." She wiped her eyes on the corner of her apron. "He'll be in soon so that he can show you the evening milking."

Paul. Had the baby Paul, survived and grown to be a good cowman?

Seemed that I was here to replace him, was he going off to war? She mentioned soldiers and Hitler.

So much for being in the present I thought. She was still talking and singing his praises.

"Paul, is he your son?"

"He is. Well in a way, we've had him since he was a baby. I couldn't have children and he wasn't wanted. Born out of wedlock he was poor mite. He was a scrap of a thing when he first arrived, needed feeding up, mothering. He kept me awake, worse than lambing he was. Father said I'd have to give him back, but that wasn't going to happen. By the time he was ten he was already good with the cows, he's clever mind. Teacher wanted him to stay at school, but he was needed here. Learn more on the farm than in books, father says. I reckon he's right. Farmers don't need books."

She looked at me. "You a book lover?"

"Yes, I am, I've always read a lot."

"No time for that here you'll find, too much work. Can you cook? Be good to have another woman in the kitchen?"

Luckily, she didn't wait for me to reply. I didn't think microwaving a ready meal would count, especially if this was the late thirties. It looked as if the large range was the only means of cooking here.

"Your cake is good," I said rather lamely.

'I'll show you how to make scones with buttermilk tomorrow, after we've churned the butter," she said.

I asked her how many cows they had. She told me twelve milkers, plus four of them coming into calf soon.

"We must list them all for the ministry of food and how much milk from each one every day. Bookkeeping nonsense. Still, you can do that now, can't you?"

Milking, churning butter, cooking and bookkeeping. What a list my head was spinning. She showed me to my room on the third floor, well the attic. It was spacious, had a single metal bed and a chair and table. A big wardrobe took up most of one wall and a small window looked out onto the yard. In the middle of the room, a large trunk sat on a colourful rug. She saw me looking at the rug.

"We make those in the winter. Pegged it is." I muttered something about finding work for idle hands.

"You get none of that here, our hands are busy," she retorted as she went down the stairs. "Find your boots and something more suitable to wear so you can round up the hens and collect the eggs before it gets dark." I sat on the bed, I could feel the lumps in the mattress, the label on the trunk said, *Sally Harkness c/o Mrs Jones, Valley Farm*. Sally - well at least I knew my name and the farmer's name. Why had I got in the car? I'd had no choice. I felt like a pawn in someone's game. I was out of my depth this time.

"Sally, do you plan to be up there all day? You have work to do." Her voice grated on my senses. I opened the bag, found boots and saw the overall folded on the chair. The overall fitted over my jeans and I carried the boots down to the kitchen. She nodded in the direction of the door.

"That's better now go and get those eggs."

As I went out the door, she thrust a basket into my hands and pointed to a wire enclosure.

"You'll find most of the eggs over there," she said, "but keep your eyes open, we can't afford to miss any."

The boots were uncomfortable, but I was glad of them, there was mud everywhere. By the time the basket was full, my back was aching and my feet sore. This was much worse than being Lottie, at least I'd been warm and clean most of the time. Everywhere looked drab, grey and dirty.

"You must be Sally the land girl. Not used to being on a farm then?"

A young man came across the yard. "You'll soon get used to it. Look, you've only got half the eggs. You need to fill the other basket too. I'll show you where the little blighters hide them, else Ma will be bending your ear." He took the full basket and disappeared for a moment, soon back with an empty one. I would never have found all the eggs on my own. The second basket soon filled up. He chatted in a friendly manner while we were collecting, telling me his name was Paul and that he'd always lived on the farm.

"Been milking the cows since I was a youngster. I shall miss my girls. You'd better look after them."

It took me a minute to realise that he meant the cows. He said once we'd done the eggs, I could come with him and bring them in and he'd show me how to milk.

The water to scald the churns had to be drawn from the pump in the yard, put into the large copper that had a fire under it. We went over to the milking shed; I could hear the water hissing.

"Always keep water in here," he said. My heart sank, that was heavy work. He then ran steaming water into each churn, swirling it round before draining it again. He made it look easy.

"Never take shortcuts, they will reject the whole lot if there's anything wrong. Right fussy they are. Not like the old days, when we sold the milk ourselves. This war let the government control everything. We must give them our quota. Milk's feeding the nation now they say."

I desperately tried to remember what I'd learnt in history lessons. Pitifully little, now I needed to know.

"Ministry of Food, is it?"

"That's right the lorry comes every day, at the moment they're milking well so there's plenty for Ma to make butter as well." He looked at me. "You'll be doing that too. Come on, let's get the girls, then I can see how good you are."

The cows were waiting by the gate, udders full and heavy. He didn't need the switch to encourage them. Once the gate was open, they slowly walked up the lane towards the shed. He called out gently to them, he knew them all by name, it seemed.

"Friesian cows give up to twenty pints each milking and will produce milk for up to three hundred days after calving."

Each stall had a name over it. It didn't matter that I didn't know their names, the cows did. Each going to their own stall to eat the hay in the container hanging on the end. Paul washed his hands in the bowl of hot water, stood back and motioned to me to do the same.

"We wash the cows udders before milking them. Come on we'll start with Betsy, she's placid and won't mind you learning on her."

We went to the far stall, after showing me how to wash her he got up.

"Now sit down, relax, lean against her and pull gently but firmly."

He put the bucket in place. I did as I was told, the milk gushed out.

"There now," he said. "You're born to it." He sounded

impressed. I thought I'd better not tell him I'd tried to milk a cow three or four hundred years ago.

We took it in turns to milk the cows. He told me so many facts about the cows and how to run the herd that my head was spinning. In the end, I just listened to the music of his voice and the splashing of the milk in the bucket. I would have to get him to tell me again when I could write it all down. He was going in a few days.

"Da knows it all but his arthritis is bad, and he only has another old'un to help in the fields, so he has no time."

We had most of the milk in the churns and were scalding out the buckets, when an old man put his head round the door.

He looked straight past me. "Is she any good?" He sounded as if he was expecting a negative answer.

"A natural Da. She'll not take long to learn."

The old man looked me up and down." Need fattening up a bit I dare say, don't want any fainting in here. Won't be no-one to pick you up."

"I'm not in the business of fainting. I can do a day's work." I stared back at him. It was bad enough being here against my will. I rolled my sleeves down.

"He doesn't mean to be rude. It's just his way," Paul explained. "Come on, you've earned your supper."

We walked back to the farmhouse. I thought I'd be too tired to eat, but the smell of the meat pie soon changed my mind.

"I shall miss this food." Paul said as he scraped his plate.

"No home cooking in the army boyo," said his ma, her

hand hovered over his head, as if she wanted to stroke his hair, but instead she bent to clear the plates.

"You'll need to help in the kitchen," she said to me. "Women's work only stops when we go to bed."

"Tonight, Sally needs time to write down the procedures for the milking and recording Ma, to make sure she has it right."

"Don't make a habit of it then."

"She only has two more days before I go, so I need to make sure she's got it all down."

Her voice softened. "Oh, I know, you'd better get on with it then while I do the pots."

Paul went to a drawer.

"The books are all here. Make sure you copy the numbers down every night, no matter how tired you are, so you don't get behind."

He took the scrap of paper from his overalls that had the morning and evening figures and started to fill them in the book."

Without thinking I said how much easier it would be with a computer, he looked at me, shook his head and I apologised saying that I was tired. Not thinking straight. He painstakingly drew a table with a ruler for the next day's figures.

"I need to write down everything you told me this afternoon. I shall never remember otherwise," I said.

He smiled and went back to the drawer. "I thought of that." He pulled out a folder. In it neatly written down were instructions. The cow's names and the expected yields from each of them were on the front page. What a relief.

"All you must do is read this and see if you have any

questions. I think I've thought of everything you need to know," he said as he handed me over a small notebook. "Put this in your pocket tomorrow and note down anything that bothers you or you want to know. I think you need to make your way to bed now. I can see your eyelids drooping and you need to be up by four."

He went over to the large black kettle and poured water into a cup.

"Horlicks, take it up with you," he looked over to Mrs Jones, as if to stop her complaining but her head was nodding, her knitting forgotten.

I fell into bed without cleaning my teeth. The Horlicks tasted creamy, hot and welcome.

I was awoken by a cockerel crowing. It was barely dawn and it took me minutes to realise where I was. I thought I was still dreaming, then wished I was as the memory of the previous day came back and the knowledge that I had to get up.

I staggered out of bed, aches in my legs competing with those in my fingers and arms. The thought of sitting on that stool milking the cows was repellent. I made my way down the stairs to the welcome smell of toast.

Chapter 17

Paul was waiting for me in the kitchen. "Get this down you," he said, thrusting a mug of tea and a plate of toast across the table to me.

"Ma will have a proper breakfast ready for us when we've finished."

Once out in the cowshed we tackled the milking procedure, this time driving the cows out to the field when we had finished. The heavy churns were loaded up onto a trolley, which we pulled out to the front of the farm.

"That's good now we can eat while the water's heating up then we'll scald down the buckets and muck out the stalls. You need to follow a system to make sure everything is done right. Most importantly, don't forget to save Ma some milk for her butter. He pointed to the container in the corner."

I nodded, already feeling like I'd done a day's work. Breakfast of bacon, eggs and fried bread put my energy levels back up, there was no hanging about. Once Paul had scraped his plate, we were up and back in the stalls. He handed me a large rake.

"No time to waste." He laughed at my face.

"The smell seems worse after eating breakfast."

"You'll soon get used to it."

"Guess I'll have to," I said grudgingly.

When everything was clean and sluiced down, we went back to the kitchen and filled out the logbook for the milk quota. Mrs Jones saw me yawning. "We'll leave the butter till tomorrow," she said.

"You're not used to the country air, nor hard work by the look of it. You can make the sandwiches for midday." She pointed to a large loaf of bread and a slab of cheese.

"Don't put too much cheese in."

"The bread smells delicious, is there a local bakery?"

She laughed and pointed to the fireplace. "That's it. The oven, I make enough for three days at a time."

After I'd taken the sandwiches to the fieldworkers, I ate my own, then was set to work peeling potatoes and picking beans for dinner. Soon it was time to collect eggs and start milking again. I knew I only had one more day to learn from Paul, I was relieved when he told me that his Da would help me with the churns once he had gone. I scarcely had time to wonder how long I would be stuck here, the work and rain seemed relentless.

Later that evening I sat on the bed thinking about the day. Paul told me I'd done well.

"You've taken to milking and the girls really well. I was worried about leaving them with a townie but you're not bad, not bad at all. Let's hope we all survive this dratted war."

I was sorry he was going. He was the first person who had been kind to me since I'd started this strange journey. I wondered when it was going to end. Why did it happen? The more I thought about it the more confused I became. I was cold, my hands sore and beginning to be chapped from the harsh soap and hot water. My feet were blistered, and I ached all over. I didn't want the responsibility of the milking when he went, something was sure to go wrong. I didn't know how to get out of this. I was happy being a student and I'd never been much good at practical things. How would I get back home?

The next morning Paul was very subdued, I thought he was quiet but there was a heaviness to his mood. I asked him if he was worried about going away.

"What do you think?" Came his scathing reply, "I've not known anything else but this place."

I stopped feeling so sorry for myself then, he was going off to war, a very uncertain future. I started to say, "I'm sure you'll be fine." But I had a dreadful feeling that he wouldn't. He had been kind to me and in the short time I'd known him I'd got to like him. I wanted to tell him that his mother had loved him, but he would think me mad if I did.

That afternoon true to her word, Mrs Jones cleared the table.

"Butter making," She announced. "Gladys will be here directly; she always helps me with the cheese and butter. You can pass me the churn of milk ready."

I turned to the small churn I'd brought in with me.

"Not that one, it's too fresh. Milk needs to be at least two days old for butter." She tutted, "I forgot you know nothing." She put a wooden barrel that had a handle sticking out of its side onto the table. I guessed that was the churn. I had seen something similar in a visit to a National Trust house when I was at school.

"Won't the milk be sour?" I asked.

"Of course," She said sharply. I fetched the churn that she pointed to and unscrewed the lid. It was sour. "Perfect," she said. She meant the milk, not me.

As a woman walked into the kitchen she looked up and sighed, "Gladys thank goodness, this one knows nothing."

I smiled, held out my hand and spoke. "Hello, I'm Sally." She ignored my hand and looked at me with disdain.

"Oh, I know who you are. Miss Perfect cow woman so Paul says. He never stopped talking about you all evening, saying again and again how wonderful you are. Well, you can forget any designs you have on him. He's mine." She thrust her left hand in front of my face. "We're engaged."

"I don't want him," I said. "I don't even know him. I'm just here to work on the farm."

"Fat lot of good you'll be, coming from town," she said disdainfully.

"Well, she's made a hit with the cows." Paul's voice came from the doorway. I wondered how much he'd heard. Why on earth did Gladys think I was interested in him? I was upset by her behaviour, it seemed that I wasn't a hit with the women around here. I felt like saying to both of them to get on with it, I don't need you and don't want to be here. What would be the point of that though? I was stuck for the time being. Again, I longed to be back home.

"Get on with it, pour the milk in Gladys, we haven't got all week." Mrs Jones was glowering now at both of us. Paul came over to Gladys, kissed her cheek then went over to the teapot and poured himself a cup, saying he'd see me later for evening milking. Once the milk was in the churn Gladys started to turn the handle, after a few minutes she told me to take a turn. It was harder work than I thought it would be and was glad to let her take over again.

"We do this for about an hour. You can feel the resistance as the butter forms."

Mrs Jones seemed to have got over her annoyance with me and explained the procedure as we took turns to churn.

"When we've done churning, the buttermilk that's left is drained off. That's kept for baking bread and scones, any left is mixed with potatoes and fed to the pigs."

I hadn't met the pigs yet. I wondered if that was yet another job I'd have to do. Gladys took the butter out and put it on a wooden board. She mixed a handful of salt into the golden mass then took up a pair of butter paddles and started to pat the butter into shape. I watched her fascinated. Mrs Jones handed me a set of butter pats smooth one side and ridged the other. Gladys laughed at my attempt.

"Think you'd better stick to milking," she said. Her words made me try harder.

"You'll soon get the hang of it," Mrs Jones said. "For now, you can make us a fresh pot, this is thirsty work. Gladys will collect the eggs; you can go and get the cows after you've had a cuppa."

I couldn't believe how the time had flown. Mrs Jones had been right when she'd told me there were no idle hands on the farm.

I went back to the farmhouse after milking, leaving Paul to say goodbye to his girls. I was surprised to see Gladys still there.

"I'm staying for dinner," she told me. "Paul wanted me

to be here for his last night." I felt a shiver as she said, "last night." I wondered if he would ever come back.

I shook myself. I had no reason to doubt that he would. Gladys mistook my expression. "Yes. He wants me to be here, not you."

"I'm getting washed," I said, deciding to ignore her. I went up to my room. I didn't want to join the family party, I wasn't part of it.

I sat on the bed, feeling sorry for myself again. There was no one to relate to here. The only person that treated me like a human being was Paul and he was about to disappear. I wasn't used to feeling so alone. I didn't know how to cope with it. Gladys's open hostility had shocked me. She and I were of a similar age and we could have been friends. No chance of that now I could hear them downstairs. I had never felt such an outsider. The clock ticked. Time was mocking me. Tick, tick, tick. The swallows were swooping. I could see them outside the tiny window. Even the birds had a community. I got up and watched for a while. There were benefits of being in the country. I'd never seen them before. Paul had pointed out their nests in the barn; he said they gathered on the roof in September before they flew off to Africa - such small creatures to fly all that way. Paul knew so much about nature. He was a nicer man than he would have been in the artificial setting of his mother's family.

I wondered what it was about him that made me feel as if I knew him. I felt a connection to him that I couldn't explain. I felt as if I was losing a good friend, not a man I'd only met a few days ago.

There was a tap on my door, followed by a hand on my shoulder. It was Mr Jones.

"Come on lass dinner's ready and it's Paul's last evening with us."

I shook my head. "No, you go ahead, I'm not hungry."

"You're upset. They can be harsh those two and they can't deal with losing him. You need your food, can't have you wasting away."

I turned around to look at him despite his brusque manner. He was kind too, perhaps that's where Paul had learnt it. He handed me a grubby handkerchief.

"Come on now. I'll tell them you were tired, but you'll be down in a minute."

I went down the stairs and Mrs Jones got up.

"Come on, sit yourself down," she said. "You've had a busy day."

Even Gladys gave me a weak smile. She was sitting next to Paul putting food on his plate as if he were a child. Mrs Jones didn't look impressed. When the meal was over, she got up saying, "You two love birds can go for a walk. Sally and I will tidy up and Da you can clear." He looked shocked at being told to do women's work but immediately picked up the plates and lifted the heavy black kettle over to the sink. She stood at the sink grating hard green soap into the hot water, whisking it until it melted and formed bubbles. I picked up a tea towel.

"Can't be doing with all that canoodling stuff and sad eyes. We've had him since he was a baby. She goes on as if she owns him." I was shocked to hear that she didn't approve of Gladys, it made me feel better.

"Well, she will when they wed and you will have to put up with it," Mr Jones told her. He gave her arm a squeeze, which she shrugged off.

"That's not likely to happen yet, nor for a long time and who knows what's in store for us all."

No, I thought of those old war films I'd seen.

"He's not off 'till eleven, so he can help you with the milking. Then we'll have breakfast together as a family and you'll have to fill the gap, missy."

He was including me as part of the family. I gave him a big smile.

"I'll do my best. I know it will be hard for you."

"It will that," they said together.

Next morning I was in the cowshed before Paul. His girls were making a heck of a noise, then quietened down when he came in. I hoped they would be okay with me when he'd gone. Once milking was done, he went to each one in turn calling them by their names telling them he would be back and to behave for me. He had tears in his eyes and came over to the end of the barn wiping his nose on his sleeve.

"We'll scald the pans and clean up before breakfast," he said. "I don't want to leave it to you this morning. Da is coming to lead the girls out to the field, once he's taken the milk to the gate."

I was ready for my breakfast by the time we'd finished. Ma had made a special effort. Her boy wouldn't go off hungry. She gave him a fruitcake in a tin to take with him. Actions - not words - of love.

Da was at the gate in the evening when I went to get the cows.

"This is not going to be regular, but it'll ease you in."

I was pleased to see that I milked faster than he did. He nodded to me saying, "Not bad."

We walked into the house together. It was a subdued meal. I thought about how hard it was for them. No phone in the house. They would have to wait for a letter to find out how he was.

Chapter 18

The next two weeks passed uneventfully, to my surprise the milking went smoothly. I had learnt to put the buckets out of reach of the cow's hooves. It was hard work. I could feel my muscles getting stronger. I could wash and scald the buckets and churns without being exhausted now and I was used to getting up so early. I found a strange contentment from doing the work well.

Mrs Jones had shown me how to make cheese. She placed a large flat bowl on the table and added fresh, warm creamy milk. From her store, she fetched what looked like a large, dried piece of skin. She cut a piece off and dropped it into a small jug of warm water. After a few minutes, she added the liquid to the milk. She told me the skin was a dried calves stomach. It contained the rennet that would turn the milk into cheese. I turned my nose up, but she laughed and told me to stir. As I stirred the milk started to curdle. We left it for a while, soon it looked solid, she cut it up into squares with a wooden knife and liquid ran out.

"That's the whey, the pigs get that," she said. "We want just the curd."

I had to carry on breaking the curd up until it looked like

cottage cheese. Then we set the bowl on the solid plate beside the fire.

"It needs to slowly heat to nearly boiling point," she told me. Once it cooled, she put both hands into the bowl and removed all the solids into a fresh one that she had lined with a muslin cloth. All the whey dripped through. After a while, she told me to pick up all the corners of the cloth containing the curd and squeeze as hard as I could. Once I'd done this, Mrs Jones added a large handful of salt and mixed it into the solids. As instructed, I then put the mixture into a round container, pressing it down well before putting it into the cheese press. She then showed me other rounds of cheese that were maturing in her pantry.

"The longer you leave them the harder and stronger they get." I was very impressed.

I was thinking about the cheeses as I hosed down the cowshed. My thoughts were interrupted by old Jimmy, who helped Mr Jones.

"You'd better come quick, he's bleeding bad."

Mr Jones had tripped while he was scything and cut his arm. I ran trying to remember what I'd learnt in first aid. By the time I reached him, there was more blood that I'd ever seen and his pallor was grey. I took some twine and tied it around his arm using a bit of stick to get it tight. I sent Jimmy off to fetch the doctor. I knew the tourniquet had to be released every few minutes to stop the hand going dead. It was frightening to see how much blood gushed out when I did that. Mrs Jones came running up not looking like her usual calm self. She started to grumble at him for being careless, saying how much it would cost for the doctor to come out.

I was cross and said it would be much more costly if he died and told her to hold his arm up above his heart. It seemed like forever that we waited, at last we heard a cheery voice.

"What have we here then?" I was glad to hand him over to someone who knew what he was doing.

Mr Jones couldn't walk so we managed to put him on the milk churn trolley and get him up to the house.

The table was cleared and the patient, who was barely conscious, heaved on and laid out flat. Dr Borrows took antiseptic from his bag and told me to swab the arm. Mrs Jones was sent for towels and hot water plus brandy for Mr Jones.

"You've made a good job here. I doubt he'd still be with us if you hadn't acted so quickly," he said to me as he worked.

He was efficient, I had read about general doctors working in cottage hospitals before the war. Now I was seeing one managing on a farmhouse kitchen table, where the day before we had made cheese. He asked me where I'd learnt to apply a tourniquet. I was vague - said I'd gone to first aid classes.

"Do you want to be a nurse?"

I laughed, "no thanks I'll decline that honour." The drama of the morning had been enough for me.

"Right, well your first aid is good. Can you put Mr Jones' arm in a sling for me?"

I nodded and started to fold the bandage he handed me.

"Now Mr Jones you must drink plenty and have liver, and lots of gravy for dinner."

"That'll be no hardship doctor."

"Lots of blood to replace," he said as he packed his bag. Mrs Jones asked him to sit down and have a cup of tea, which he did while demolishing a large piece of fruitcake too.

We helped Mr Jones into the comfy chair by the fire. He had started to shiver, and his wife wrapped a blanket around him.

"It's only shock. Give him some sweet tea now that he's back with it. I must be off. There's a difficult birthing I need to attend. I will pop in later to check on him. Keep that arm still but keep wiggling your fingers." He gave Mrs Jones a strip of aspirin.

"He's had morphine which will stop him feeling pain for now but give him some of these later. If his temperature rises you call me straight away." He picked up his bag and rushed off. I noticed his jacket had slipped on to the floor by the table. I picked it up and ran after him. Luckily, his car was slow to start. I handed him his coat and he gave a big smile.

"Thanks, and well done again. You should think about nursing, you know. You're a natural." He drove off, his car making more noise than speed.

I went back to the cowshed to finish up. I was glad my muscles were stronger now it looked like I'd be putting the churns out on my own for a few days.

Jim put his head around the barn door. "Good job you was there. I didn't know what to do."

"You got help Jim, that was the most important thing to do." He smiled and tugged at his cap.

"Paul said you was a good un. He were right. Let me know if you want any heavy lifting done."

That evening when I went in for food, Mrs Jones looked stressed.

"It's alright for the doctor to say keep him still, I reckon I need chains."

Mr Jones had tried to remove the sling. "How can I work with this on?"

"Da you're not meant to work, the doctor said you're lucky to have your arm after that cut. You need to stay still for a few days."

"How is that going to happen? Farm won't run itself."

"No, it won't, Jim and I will do what's necessary." I'd called him Da without thinking. Just like Paul did. He did look flushed, I didn't know if it contrasted with his earlier paleness. I reached over and touched his forehead. He was hot. Too hot. His arm looked swollen, around the stitches it was an angry red colour. He seemed to be getting hotter by the minute.

"We need ice," I said to Mrs Jones.

"No chance of that but the well water will be very cold," she said.

I found Jim and asked him to get me buckets of cold water. Then Mrs Jones and I dragged in the tin bathtub and filled it with cold water. I told her to strip him down to his underclothes then put him in the bath. She looked shocked.

"His arm is infected and he's heating up. We need to reduce his temperature." The sweat was standing out on his forehead now.

"Are you sure we can't just put a cold poultice on his arm?"

I said we could try but I didn't like the look of him, he needed antibiotics.

Young Jimmy had been sent for the doctor. He came back looking worried saying the doctor was busy and would come as soon as he could. After an hour of cold poultices, Mr Jones was worse, and his wife took off his clothes and we got him into the cold water. An hour later, the doctor arrived. He looked harassed and tired. When he took the patient's temperature, it was 104.5 degrees centigrade.

"Well done," he said.

"It was Sally insisting, I'd have thought he'd catch his death in there."

He looked at her seriously. "You know how quickly a temperature can rise with an infected cut. That's what will cause a death."

"Will he be alright?" she asked, knowing he couldn't give her an answer.

He sat with us most of the night. They sent me to bed at one o'clock knowing I had to be up for the milking.

In the morning, Mrs Jones was asleep in her chair beside the bath.

I made a pot of tea and Dr Burrows told me his temperature was high but stable. The next few hours would be critical.

It was difficult to concentrate on the milking and I wished, not for the first time that Paul was there. I could hear his singsong voice calling out the girl's names as I walked them to the pasture.

Alwen, Aeelwin, Betsy, Bertha, Blodwyn, Cari, Cerys, Dilys, Gwen, Olwen, Seren. Wynne. He would half whisper to them as they slowly walked. I cleaned up the barn, fearful of what I would find when I returned to the kitchen.

Chapter 19

Mr Jones was sitting in his chair wrapped in a blanket. He looked deathly pale now. Mrs Jones was by his side, smiling.

"The fever's broken. You should've seen the pus that's come out his arm."

Mr Jones turned to look at me and gave me a weak smile.

"I reckon he'd ave been a goner if it weren't for you."

"I'm glad you're feeling a bit better," I said.

"Bloody cold though."

"That's enough of that language. You were much too hot before." She sounded fierce but looked at him fondly.

"You've just missed the doctor, he said he'll be back later."

I wondered what it was about the doctor he seemed familiar, but he couldn't be. In fact, he reminded me a little of Paul, but I knew he was no relation to him. Whatever it was I liked him, I found myself thinking of him while I was working. I wondered if he was married. I don't know why? This was forty years before my time. I couldn't get him out of my head though. He'd visited and left again before I managed to get back to the farmhouse.

The next time Gladys came, she told me about the village

barn dance, saying everyone would be there and people were anxious to meet me. I wasn't sure who the people were.

"I can't go, the cows need milking every day."

"I'll come and help you on Saturday, then you can go," Gladys said to my surprise.

Mrs Jones saw my hesitation, "Yes, you go, you deserve some fun, girl."

I wasn't sure it would be fun but gave in and said I'd go.

Of course, there were more women than men, but that didn't matter. Much to my surprise I enjoyed myself and Gladys introduced me to several people. Towards the end of the evening, I saw Dr Burrows. He came over to me and said he would give me a lift back to the farm. He'd been to check on Mr Jones and they'd told him where I was. I was grateful and indeed ready to leave. It had been a long day, and I was tired. They had been right; it had been good fun. I found Gladys and said goodbye.

"That will set tongues wagging," she said. I laughed and thought nothing of it.

Once in the car, he asked me how I was and said how pleased he was with Mr Jones' recovery.

"You are a very interesting young woman," he said. "I wanted to get a chance to speak to you." I was glad he was driving and didn't see me blushing.

"Tell me about yourself. Where do you come from?"

I told him about the village where I had lived with my mum. I thought if I told him I came from a time in the future when the war was a distant memory, he'd throw me out of the car. I was beginning to feel very firmly fixed here. Sitting next to him felt a good place to be. I asked him about himself. He told me that his name was Robert.

"My dad was a doctor, I never thought about doing anything else. My parents were elderly when they had me, my mum a typical village doctor's wife. I worked with my father once I was qualified and now my father's retired. A nice life but uneventful."

"Have you ever thought about living anywhere else, or working in a hospital?"

"Good heavens, never in a hospital. I had enough of that when I was training. I love it here, and my dad needed a partner. Now of course the practice is mine."

"Will you look for a partner? You seem to be busy."

"Possibly, when this war is over, my wife and I have no children. There won't be anyone to pass on the practice to when I'm old."

I was sad when I heard that he was married, I don't know why, he wouldn't have been interested in me. We soon drew up at the farm. I thanked him and he got out of the car and opened the door for me. He held out his hand to help me out. Was it my imagination that he held mine longer than necessary?

That night I had difficulty getting to sleep. When I closed my eyes I could see his face, while a voice in my head was saying, *'he is married.'*

Mr Jones was better, so he said. He was still having difficulty with his injured arm. It didn't stop him giving Jim plenty of instructions. Dr Burrows called in most days to see him.

"Reckon, it's you he comes to see." He grinned when I turned red.

"That's wicked of you," said Mrs Jones. "You know he's wed."

"Much good she is with her fancy town ways, ain't given him no babies as she?"

Mrs Jones shushed him, but I saw from her expression, she'd noticed my red face.

It was true, Robert did come and talk to me when he came to the farm, and I looked forward to seeing him.

"He's trying to persuade me to sign up to be a nurse," I told them. I enjoyed his company, even though I knew it might cause gossip.

I'd nearly finished hosing down the barn at the end of the following week. I didn't hear the Doctor come in. He made me jump when he spoke, and I nearly tripped over the coil of pipe. dropping his bag and stepped forward to steady me. He held on to me.

"Can't have you falling and being hurt," he said. He was still holding me. "Do you work in here every day?"

"I do, there's no one else." I was very aware of his hands on my arms and how closely he was holding me. I stepped back but he held on.

"Are you steady now?"

I nodded, but my knees felt weak. I wanted to stay in his arms forever.

"You just made me jump. I'm fine."

"You look pale. They're working you too hard. You shouldn't be working every day. Even I get time off. I'm going to talk to the Jones's. I'm sure they are entitled to another land girl." He let go of my arm, and my heart slowed down a little.

"Your pulse seems very fast, that's not good."

"It's because you made me jump. I'm used to being alone."

"You're too pretty to be alone." I blushed again. "I'm sorry that was personal, I shouldn't have said it." I was glad he had. He found me pretty. I found him incredibly attractive.

"It was nice of you."

"Nice - it was unprofessional. I don't know why but I feel I know you very well, when of course I don't. I wish I was free to tell you how I feel."

Without thinking, I came close to him and kissed him. He put his arms around me and kissed me back.

"Well, I think you know now, and it feels mutual."

"It is."

After a while, he said that he was going back to the house to talk to the Jones about sending some forms off to the ministry to ask for more help. I watched him go feeling happy, even though I knew we couldn't have any future together.

In my room that evening, I relived that kiss. How could I be in love with a man from the past, a married man too? I told myself it was ridiculous. It couldn't be, it wasn't real, how was I even here? I had no idea of how I could get back to my own time. I had seen nothing of James since he'd dropped me off at the farm. Sheer tiredness overtook me. I fell asleep, dreaming of Robert in a time where we could love each other.

After milking, the next morning Mr Jones told me that they'd applied for another girl to help me. He said they were both sorry that they'd overworked me. I knew they had expected no more from me than from themselves. The loss of young men's labour had hit them hard, and they were still expected to fulfil their quota for the ministry.

Chapter 20

Mr Jones was able to do a full day's work again, he took the growing piglets to sell in the market, along with Mrs Jones's butter and cheese. After his successful day, he handed Mrs Jones money for the eggs, butter and cheeses. She counted it out then handed me a shilling and half a crown.

"What's this?" I asked, not being familiar with the money.

"Three and six, your share of the butter and cheese money," she said. When I started to protest, she quickly silenced me.

"You deserve it, you worked hard. It's only fair."

It was another two weeks before they heard from the ministry. A girl was being sent from London to help. They were scathing, asking what would a Londoner know about farm work?

"She'll have the wrong clothes and expect to be waited on. Have her head full of flighty ideas," was Mrs Jones' verdict. I reminded her that she hadn't seen her yet. She sniffed and said she didn't need to. It was funny, she now counted me as her ally against the invasion of Londoners. I thought another pair of hands would be welcome. I loved the cows but longed for a break from the hard work.

The following week Alison arrived; she had been working in a bridal shop.

"Don't know nothing about the country. Cor its mucky and smelly here."

I remembered thinking that when I arrived. I was used to it now. I wondered if she would settle. Mrs Jones exchanged 'told you so looks' with me.

Upstairs in the bedroom Alison prattled on about London and how it was difficult to get food and that it was rumoured that clothing was about to be rationed.

"Even buttons and elastic. They said my job was not essential. My mum's not best pleased." She looked round the room which now contained another single bed.

"Roomy in here anyway. There's three of us in a tiny room at home. Tell me what we have to do." She barely paused for breath.

"We'll have a cuppa first, then I'll show you the cows."

"Cows. No one said nothing about cows. I thought I was here to get the hay in."

This is going to be fun I thought. Mrs Jones is probably right.

Alison enjoyed her tea and fruitcake. Mrs Jones busied herself by the sink, not wanting to be drawn into conversation. I told Alison about the cows and milking times. I swear she went pale when I told her she'd have to be up and dressed by four o'clock in the morning.

"You'll get used to it," I said. "I did." I gave her a clean pair of overalls and found some wellies and thick socks for her to wear. "You'll need to tie your hair up," I told her.

"Don't forget the eggs," was the only comment from Mrs

Jones. Alison thought the chickens were cute but was a little afraid when I took her to the pigsty.

"Don't worry, we don't have to clean them out," I said, as she held her nose.

If she'd been afraid of the pigs, she was terrified when she saw the cows.

"Great big lumbering creatures. I don't like the look of them. You'll not get me close."

"You'll do more than get close, we will be milking them in a minute," I told her crossly. It was a good job Paul wasn't there. She stood right back, as I herded them into the barn.

"Watch," I said. "They all know where to go and they are placid and won't hurt you. They want to be milked. Their udders are so heavy. We'll start with Betsy." I sat down and showed her how to milk as Paul had done with me.

"Here. Now you have a go, it's easy, and she is a lovely beast." I thought to myself, it would be dark before we'd finished if she didn't buck up. She was being a hindrance. I wanted to get on with the other cows but stayed with her to encourage her. As the milk started to spurt out of Betsy's teats, it hit the bucket and splashed Alison's arm. She shrieked so loudly she made me jump and scared the cow, which kicked out and hit my head with her hoof. Everything went black for a moment; the stupid girl was screaming. I straightened up and held on to the post. This was not the time to black out.

"You told me she was safe." Alison was shouting at me. The bucket was on its side, milk flowing over the floor and poor Betsy was making such a noise.

"She is but you scared her. Now sit down quietly and try again." But she ran off.

"There is no way I'm staying here."

"Good riddance," I thought. I was now so behind, and we'd lost a whole bucket of milk. It didn't take me long to soothe Betsy and the other cows quietened down once she was okay. After a while, Mr Jones came into the barn. He looked at me, shook his head then calmly started to milk.

While we were cleaning up, he said, "that girl come into the kitchen sobbing and crying, saying one of the cows had tried to kill her. She says she's leaving in the morning." He sniffed and rubbed his nose on his sleeve. "Ma gave her some food and told her to pen the chickens up then get off to bed. Ma thinks it will be okay in the morning, but I wondered what you think?"

"If you really want to know, I think she's a pain in the neck and the girls don't deserve her. Paul wouldn't like it."

"No, he wouldn't that's the truth. He took to you though, even though you're English."

"She is just stupid, nothing to do with being English. Anyway, Paul was English by birth." He stopped what he was doing and looked at me.

"How do you know that?"

Sally wouldn't know. I quickly thought of an answer.

"Ma told me he was adopted; she must have mentioned it."

"He came from border country. We was told on our side. He is Welsh."

"Oh, sorry I must have got it wrong. Don't know why." I hadn't realised it mattered so much. He was still looking at me in a puzzled way.

"Not like Ma to tell anyone he was adopted." I had tripped up there, and wished I'd kept quiet.

"The bump on your head. It looks nasty, it's got bigger. Reckon we should call Dr Burrows if it gets any worse."

I told him how it had happened, "I feel all right now." When I touched my head, I was surprised how large the bump felt. "Ouch, I wish I hadn't been bending to help Alison when Betsy kicked out."

"Ma can put some witch hazel on it for you," he said, kindly.

We finished up and walked back to the house. I tripped as we got to the back door. The jolt made my head pound, it really did hurt now, and I felt queasy when the smell of cooking came from the kitchen.

Ma took one look at me. "Send for the doctor," she said to Mr Jones. "That looks bad and she's far too pale."

I muttered. "It's too expensive, I'll be okay." The heat of the room made me dizzy, and I was glad to sit down. Ma put a cool damp piece of linen on my head, the smell reminded me of something from childhood.

"Witch hazel will help, but I want Dr Burrows to check you out. We'll dock the money from that girl's wages, she caused it." She sounded cross.

The smell made me feel safe. It reminded me of my grandma's, when I went to stay with her when I was little. I must have been about three. I slept in a big girl's bed, which had a pink silky cover that I'd loved. She had a big tabby cat, which used to curl up on her knee. When I was on her knee she used to move the cat and it would sit beside us, head on her lap and purr. Granny was good at reading stories. She said after family, books were the most important things in the world. I thought her cakes were second most important.

When I fell in her garden and hurt my knee, she mended it with witch's brew and kisses. It got better quickly, and I thought she was magic.

I wished my Granny were still alive, she would know what to do. She might not understand what was happening to me because I didn't. I felt sad and realised that I was crying. I didn't know if it was for the loss of my grandmother, or if I was crying because of the impossibility of my situation. I had fallen in love with a man I could never be with, he was out of my time. I'd never felt like this before, and didn't know how to cope. The tears started to fall faster. It won't be me I thought that gets to make love to him, it will be Sally, and she will have his child. I saw a woman tenderly holding a baby in her arms. She looked like me, but I knew it wasn't me. It could never be me.

"Sally, Sally." It was his voice, sounding worried.

"Oh, hello I was thinking of you. Are you real?"

"Of course I'm real, but I think you may be concussed."

"I might not be here much longer, but I want you to know I love you."

"Of course you'll be here, it's only a bump but you need to rest."

He turned to Mr and Mrs Jones. "I would like to take her to the cottage hospital for observation tonight. I think she will be fine, but I want to be sure."

"The cows?" I asked.

"Don't you fret. I will look after them and make Madam Alison help," said Mr Jones.

I looked around the kitchen. I had been happy here once I settled in. Perhaps she would be too. I felt it might be the last time I saw it. I had that strange, not quite real feeling as if I was only half there. I must have said it aloud because they all started to reassure me that I would be back soon.

Robert helped me to his car. He started the engine. It throbbed in time with my head. I didn't want to go. I wanted to stay with him but I couldn't find the seat belt. He asked me what I was looking for.

"Shh don't worry," he said when I told him. I realised they hadn't been invented yet. When he pulled up at the little hospital, he bent over to me and gently kissed me.

"I will sort something out. We will be together. I love you too. First though we need to sort your head out. Stay there, I'll help you out." I could hear strains of music.

"I'm going," I said. "I can feel it." The music was louder, he helped me out of the car. When I held on to him my hands went straight through his tweed jacket, I could no longer hear his voice. He grew fainter and fainter, until he was a paper cut out waving in the wind.

"I love you," I called. My words were hollow in my ears. And he was gone.

Chapter 21

I was lying in a bed. Not my own, I immediately realised. The sheets were coarse and there were blankets, not my duvet. My head ached, when I felt there was no lump. I must have left that behind with Sally. A bell rang loudly. The clock beside the bed said five thirty. Quite late, by farm standards. There was a persistent knocking on the door.

"Hurry up Betty, you can't be late again. Sister will have your guts for garters."

I swung my legs out of bed. Betty? Sister? There was a washstand in one corner and a nurse's uniform on the chair. I washed my face - I was used to cold water on the farm. I looked at the tin of well-used, pink paste lying next to the worn-out toothbrush. I was getting used to this, but I shuddered at the thought of cleaning my teeth with someone else's brush. I dressed in the uniform, there was nothing else and put on a very sensible pair of black shoes. When I opened the door, there was a young woman in a nurse's uniform waiting. Her name badge said Nurse Margaret Barnes.

"Oh hello," I said, wondering what was going to happen next.

"Come on, there's such a queue for the lavies, we'll be

late." She grabbed my hand, and I followed her along the corridor and down the stairs where we joined a queue of women all dressed like us.

I followed Margaret into the hospital, the building was large and imposing. I hoped we would be working on the same ward. I hadn't a clue where I was going. I guessed I was a nurse from the uniform. How much was I supposed to know? I didn't even know what year it was. It was late spring or early summer. I could tell from the temperature.

We walked down a long corridor, Margaret turned left, and we went through double doors past small rooms, one of them a bathroom, another looked like a small kitchen. Margaret stopped beside a line of pegs, took off her cloak and hung it up. I hurriedly did the same and followed her past a large cupboard full of sheets and towels. Next was a closed door, Ward Sister was written on it for all to see. Finally, we were in the main ward. As far as I could see there were beds full of men, most of them lying quietly under tightly tucked in counterpanes. In the middle of the room, there was a desk where two women were sitting talking quietly. Both were in dark blue uniforms. I looked around and I saw two nurses dressed like me, in striped dresses and white aprons. They were moving quickly between the beds.

"Ah, at last, the day staff. I've reported to Sister Simmons so now I'm off for a well-earned rest." She smiled at the other woman in the dark blue dress. "I shall be glad to get my feet up. It's been a long night. Some of these boys have the most dreadful nightmares." Off she went and the two nurses followed her giving us a weak smile as they walked out. I could guess who had been doing most of the work during the night.

"Nurse Barnes, Nurse Johnson. Sit down, sit down, we have a great deal to get through before the doctors start their rounds and we are short staffed." Sister Simmons gave us a summary of what was wrong with the men, which ones needed special attention and the ones that made a fuss. The night staff had already bed bathed some of the sicker men. A few were allowed to get up and use the bathroom.

"Most of them need assistance." She looked at me, frowning. I know you're new Johnson but I'm expecting you to pull your weight today. And don't be too soft with them. They are soldiers, I'm hoping the ambulant ones will be discharged later to free up beds." She looked up and down the ward. "We have more men expected later today. God only knows where we will put them." She sighed and took her glasses off.

"Hurry up will you, there's a war on. We need to get these men well so they can go back and fight. That horrible little German man has pushed us right out of France, but as Churchill says we're not beaten yet."

Margaret had been making notes as sister had been giving out her orders. I decided I must look for a notebook in my room. I could never remember all that had been said, even if I'd understood it.

As we walked over to the beds, I whispered, "I forgot my notebook."

"I noticed. I thought you were getting cocky. Never mind we work together. We need to start down the far end as most of them can get out of bed."

They all looked pretty sick to me. There was a smell of sickness and sweat as we got close to the beds. Most of the men were heavily bandaged. Some had broken arms, some had legs in the air in a pulley-contraption.

"I presume they can't get out of bed," I said.

"Of course not they are in traction, broken legs, have to be careful of embolisms with fractures like that. If they complain of chest pains take it seriously. What did they teach you in Maidstone?"

"Nothing like this. I shall need your help. I didn't know the men would be so injured."

"Goodness Betty you're such a child. They've been chased out of France, blown up and shot at on the beaches. What did you think, they'd have a few scratches? They are arriving every day from Dunkirk in small boats. Lucky to survive, but badly injured or they wouldn't be sent here."

We started by getting bowls of hot water as she spoke and taking them to the men who could wash and shave themselves. I got out their wash stuff from the lockers and gave it to them with a small towel.

"I've not worked on a men's ward before." It was the truth. I'd only ever visited patients in hospital.

"That explains a lot. Well, you'll soon pick it up, it's not that different."

A man in dark trousers and a white top was walking towards us.

"Oh good, an orderly. He will shave the ones that can't manage." She smiled at him. "Good morning. We'll leave the shaving to you."

Many of the men were friendly, grateful for our attention. The ones closest to the desk were the sickest.

"Need to make sure they are turned regularly and have

surgical spirit rubs so that they don't get bed sores. That also goes for the traction patients. Not the turning of course but checking for bed sores." Margaret was a good teacher. I was so grateful I was with her.

At last, we had all the men washed and the beds made. Several had hobbled to the bathroom and were now sitting on chairs by their beds. I hadn't accounted for the fact that the bedbound would need bedpans and bottles and wasn't ready for the ensuing stench. I told myself it was no worse than the cows but that didn't help.

I nearly made a bad mistake when one of the men asked me for a bottle. I went to the linen cupboard to look for one. Margaret, who was on her way to empty a commode asked me what I was doing in there.

"Bottles are in the sluice," she said, giving me a withering look. I thought that was a strange place for a hot water bottle, then was glad I hadn't voiced my thoughts as she picked up a urine bottle for the man to pee in.

"Cor blimey Nurse, I was getting a bit desperate," he said as I came back.

We had just finished when there was a clanking sound in the corridor, and a smell of food. The breakfast trolley had arrived. We handed out food going back to help those who couldn't feed themselves. The porridge looked stodgy and thick with obvious lumps. Mrs Jones wouldn't have been impressed, no cream here. Toast with margarine wasn't much better. I was helping a man with two broken arms who pulled a long face.

"Hardly The Ritz."

"No," said Margaret, who was carefully spooning porridge

into his neighbour's mouth. She'd added more milk to improve the consistency.

"But with this rationing it soon won't be much better there."

"I wouldn't take bets on it. The toffs always manage." I was unaware of Sister moving up the ward.

"Nurse, you are meant to be feeding, not conversing with the patients. There is still plenty to be done."

The soldier whispered, "sorry nurse didn't mean to get you into trouble."

Sister was giving out medication, pushing the trolley with dignity up the ward. She asked each man how he was and what sort of night he'd had. I didn't hear anyone complain.

With breakfast over it was nearly time for the doctor's round.

The ward door opened and an important looking military man walked in. Sister was all smiles, as she smoothed her skirt and prepared to follow him around the room.

"Come on." Margaret took my arm. "Time for toast." We went to the kitchen where the orderly had sliced bread in the toaster and tea in the large stained pot. Nothing had tasted so good for a long time.

We helped the patients the doctor had discharged to gather their things together. A few had bedraggled photos. Most had nothing personal, except shaving tackle and wash things, given to them when they arrived. They were all given knitted socks and clean uniforms, which the orderly had sorted out for them to wear. I was shocked at how coarse the khaki felt. I wouldn't fancy wearing that next to my skin.

I noticed that one man was sitting on his chair silently

weeping. When I asked him what was wrong. He said that they were going to send him back.

"It was awful there. You have no idea, so many of us were killed. Sitting targets we were. They just gunned us down." He started to sob, "I can't go back, I can't."

He looked so young, I felt sorry for him. I remembered seeing a film about Dunkirk. It was awful. I couldn't sit through it. This young man had lived the experience and was going to be sent back, Heavens knew where?

I took his hand not knowing what to say. I could hear someone muttering.

"Bloody coward. Get on with it. We need to beat 'em."

He shouted. "It's alright for you. You're not being sent back."

Sister had come over to see what all the fuss was about. She saw me holding his hand.

"Corporal. Pull yourself together man. Nurse in my office now."

"Now you're for it," the man in the far bed muttered.

I went to her office and waited.

"That man could get arrested for cowardice and you were encouraging him. We are here to get men well to return to fight. Never forget that. Do not let me see you holding a soldier's hand again or you will find yourself back in the provincial hospital from whence you came. We pride ourselves on serving our country here. Now go and clean the sluice."

When I came out he had gone, but I couldn't get him out of my mind.

After lunch, I was sent to make up the empty beds for the new arrivals. I was pleased that my mum had been trained as a nurse. Our beds at home were always made with hospital corners. I went backwards and forwards to the linen cupboard feeling confident about what I was doing for the first time that day.

When I came onto the ward the next day, six more soldiers had arrived from France. Two had serious back injuries. Two had broken arms. One was suffering from exposure, the first little boat that rescued him had capsized. The last one had been shot in the leg, and had a bullet wound to the head. Sister said his head injuries were mainly superficial, but his leg was badly injured. The man suffering from exposure was calling out asking for help. Sister told me to go over to see if I could help him. He clung on to me and begged me to help his mates who were drowning in the water. The man was hot and feverish.

When I reported what had been said to Sister, she told me the boat had been strafed by German planes and all the others had perished. When he'd been picked up, he was holding up another man who was dead. He'd had to let go of him, let him sink in the water. There wasn't enough room on the rescuing boat for all the living, let alone the dead.

"These men have had a terrible ordeal," she said, and sent me to fetch ice to reduce his temperature.

We had an even bigger rush to get everybody ready for the doctor's round. The night staff, despite being so busy all night, had again done several bed baths for us. I was told to get on and do the 'obs once all the washing was complete. I was so glad I'd watched all the nursing soaps with my mum when I was younger. I did the temperature, pulse, and respirations and Margaret came along after me doing blood pressures for those that needed it. She soon caught up with me.

"Why are you so slow," she whispered. She watched me then told me not to take the pulse for a full minute. "Fifteen seconds and multiply by four, or you'll be here all day and Sister will be furious." She told me to do the same for respirations, then read the thermometer. I had no trouble filling out the charts, but I did have difficulty watching the men's chests rise and fall. To be truthful I made half of it up. It didn't seem to do any harm and I guessed if I couldn't see them breathing, they must be normal. The ones that were ill, had laboured breathing, which was clear to see.

When I got to the man with the head injury, I saw what could be seen of his face was swollen and discoloured. Even though the bandages hid most of his face, I knew straight away that it was Paul. I was shocked and stood staring at him. He had a metal cage over his lower legs to stop the sheets from pressing on his injured leg. He opened his good eye and asked for a drink. I held a glass of water with a straw up to his mouth and he took a few sips.

I said, "Paul it's me." He looked at me blankly as if he didn't know me, and I realised he didn't recognise me. Of course, I was no longer Sally. Margaret came up and asked me what the problem was. It was difficult not to say I knew him.

"He needed water," I said.

"We need to dress his wounds, but first he must have some painkillers."

He looked at her so gratefully when she told him she was getting him something for the pain. Luckily, his head injuries were indeed mostly superficial. A bullet had made a glancing blow. His leg however looked a mess. We cleaned it up.

"He's to be taken for an x-ray later, so that it can be set." Margaret popped a thermometer in his mouth. "I thought so, his temperature's raised. If you get a basin of clean water, I'll sponge him down, while you tidy away the dirty bandages."

No men were discharged that day, nor for the rest of the week. One day blurred into another. We couldn't save the man who had been in the water. We had to put him in a side room, he disturbed the other patients so. It was the first time I'd seen a death. I changed my mind about Sister being cold and callous. She was gentle with him even when he raged. She told me not all deaths were as bad as this. I will never forget the look of terror in his eyes, or the stench of his legs that had started to rot. In the end, as Sister said, death was a merciful release.

Paul's leg was set in a plaster cast but after a while, he started to complain of it being hot and painful. His head was healing well, but when the doctors examined his leg, they found an infection. They looked serious and Margaret said they were thinking of amputation.

"They can't do that," I cried. "He's a cowman. How would he look after his cows if they took off his leg? The farm wouldn't manage without him." Margaret gave a hard look.

"How do you know that?" she asked. I muttered something about him saying about what he did in peacetime. She looked at me again.

"Sometimes there is something not quite right about you Betty. It's as if you know things you shouldn't, but don't know the simplest things you should. Anyway, I hope you

Chapter 22

Margaret was sent to the surgical ward; her skills were needed there. There was a new staff nurse in charge of me and two other junior nurses. She had been on the boats that brought the men back from Dunkirk. The boats had made many journeys picking up men under fire from land and sky. The conditions had been horrendous, Sister told us.

Staff Nurse Talbot took an instant dislike to me.

"Sister might be pleased with your progress Johnson," she said. "But quite frankly your corners leave a lot to be desired. Go and make those beds again." She pointed to the empty ones, the men sitting next to them. Uncomfortable in their chairs, longing I knew, to be back resting. Easing their aching bodies on top of the counterpanes.

"But Staff Nurse." I knew that it would take up valuable time and I didn't think it was necessary. "The men need to get back on their beds."

"I will decide when that happens. They can stay in their chairs until after lunch. These are soldiers Johnson. They can take a little discomfort and it will do them good. They are getting too soft in here. Barnes ran a shoddy ward. I intend to get it shipshape again and before you put your pennyworth in, Sister agrees with me."

I tried to compose my face, she had pulled out the sheets from the offending beds so there was nothing to do but set to and make them up again. I was fuming.

Anne Marshall was more senior than me, but still not fully qualified. She came over to help me but was soon called away to help with a dressing. I could hear the rattle of the lunch trolley and still had six more beds to finish. Two of the men decided they needed to empty their bladders at the same time, so I rushed to the sluice to get bottles for them.

"Nurse." It was Sister. "A good nurse doesn't run or look rushed. Always look calm nurse. Always look calm."

"Yes Sister," I breathed. Trying to walk quickly but sedately back to the waiting men. I knew I needed to get the used bottles back to the sluice before food was served.

"Nurse." It was Sister again. She sounded angry. "What is the meaning of this?" She pointed to the unmade beds.

"I'm trying to finish them, Sister."

"Trying is clearly not good enough. Nurse Marshall come and help Nurse Johnson." She didn't say because she is incapable, but it was implied by the look she gave me. Sister and Staff Nurse stood by the food trolley looking at the watches pinned to their uniform until we finished. I did notice Nurse Marshall's corners were not as neat as mine. It gave me a small feeling of satisfaction.

Once the meal was finished, we had taken round tea. It was bedpan time again, followed by washes. The men who'd been drooping in their chairs, were allowed back in bed for an afternoon rest. Finally, we were allowed to go for our break.

The ward was clean and tidy, the men as comfortable as we could make them.

The food in the canteen looked unappetizing, meals started at noon. It was now after one thirty. I ate my mince, lumpy mash and grey vegetables without pleasure. The apple pie that followed was better but very short on apple. Well, I thought there was a war on. I knew though, I'd been kept past my break time to teach me a lesson. Anne, who never cared what she ate, was unbothered, she said she knew I'd worked hard.

"It's just bad luck that she picked on you, that's what it's like. I always think the important thing is to remember not to do the same when you're qualified."

I wished I had the same temperament as her. I longed to be me again. Would I miss my degree ceremony, I didn't even know if I had got the 2:1 that I needed to carry on doing research. Thank goodness I'd managed to hand in my dissertation. Anne was talking to me.

"You look miles away, don't let this get you down. We're doing important work helping the men back to health."

"She hates me. I don't know why."

"She has a reputation for picking on juniors. If it's any consolation, usually the good nurses get the worst of it. How about coming out tomorrow? I've got a friend with a car. We can go into Southampton and see a film and have something to eat. That will take your mind off things. It doesn't do to be cooped up here all the time."

We both had a day off. I was wondering how I was going to spend it. I usually walked along the river breathing in the fresh air when I was off duty. It could be lonely though and now Margaret was on a different ward I didn't even see her. Cinema sounded too good to miss.

At the end of our shift, Anne put her head round the door of the sluice. Staff Nurse had sent me back to finish up in there saying, "don't think about going off duty yet, the sluice needs to be done. It must be perfect before you leave."

Anne said that she would see me the next day at noon, by the entrance of the nurse's home. It made the polishing of the bedpans less onerous. I wondered what film we would see. It would be black and white of course. I thought of Harry from Uni. He was obsessed with old black and white films.

I used my notebook to write down all the things that I had learnt during the day together with little diagrams of the trays that I'd been shown how to prepare. These were laid out in a very specific way for the different procedures. Dressings, removal of stitches, catheterisation, injections, and drips all required their own tray of equipment. I was pleased with my little book, and I'd started to write my thoughts down too, almost like a journal. I found when the day had been particularly hard it helped to put down how I felt. This night it was particularly helpful to rid of myself of feelings of hurt and grievance. I started to think how helpful it would be to more like Anne and Margaret, so I wrote:

I want to be someone who is quiet, contemplative. I want to be calm and reassuring. Not this busy feather brained person dashing from bed to sink, over cooking the toast, annoying, trying, failing. Never getting things quite right.

I want to be someone who doesn't go red when scolded who doesn't look guilty. I want to be someone who is calm, not one who has anger spilling up over my throat into my mouth threatening to choke me when the angry words, and feelings have to be suppressed and not come out.

The next morning when I re-read what I had written it made me feel angry again.

They had no right to make me feel like this. I had begun to doubt myself why was it necessary? Is this what had happened to all junior nurses I wondered. I thought it was a helping caring profession. Then I remembered how kind and helpful Margaret was and how Anne had helped me yesterday and started to feel a bit better. I took my undies down to the washroom and washed them out and put my uniform in the laundry bag. My clean dresses and aprons were on the shelf waiting for me to take them back up to my room. At least that part of the system worked well. At a few minutes to twelve, I went down to the entrance in a much better mood and waited for Anne and her friend.

Chapter 23

A bright red sports car drew up. Anne was squeezed in the back and two young men were in the front.

"Hop in," one called out. "I'm Johnny and he's Tony." Ann and I sat down, our knees up to our chins.

"It's a two-seater plus," She said laughing at my discomfort. "It's not far and it's fun." It was very noisy, and we felt every bump in the road. We came to a bridge and were stopped by soldiers. They wanted to know who we were and where we were going. When they heard that we were medical students and nurses they waved us past. Which was a good job, as I didn't have any papers. I told Anne, she said, "they only need to see your identity card."

"Identity card?"

"Yes, you must carry it everywhere. You've been stuck in the hospital too long. It will be in your bag I expect." It was. A small buff coloured card with my name, the hospital's address, and a number. It was like my NHS medical card but didn't have the national health number on it. I must have said this out loud because Anne asked.

"Do you mean EMS?" I repeated EMS, not understanding.

"Emergency Medical Services. I didn't know you had a

card for that. I expect it's because you were seconded from your cottage hospital through it."

I was uncomfortable, desperately trying to remember when the NHS was formed. I vaguely remember my mum saying it was after the war so that was why Anne was questioning me. Luckily, we had arrived at our destination. The Gaumont Cinema. Johnny stopped the car, Tony helped us it was harder to get out then getting in, laughing at our unsuccessful efforts to be ladylike. I asked Johnny where he was going to park the car.

"Here of course there is no point in walking further than we need to."

No traffic wardens, I thought not many cars around either. Johnny put his arm around Anne.

"Come on then let's get settled before the film." I had wondered which of them was Ann's friend. I looked at Tony. Was he a sort of date for me?

"Think this is a bit of a girl's film, apparently, it's a good story. The suspense in Hitchcock's last film was amazing. If you get scared, you can cling on to me."

"Oh," I said reading the lettering above the cinema. "Rebecca. It will be good. Do you know who is playing the lead?"

"I read the guff about it. Joan Fontaine is Rebecca and Laurence Olivier plays her husband."

"No, Rebecca is dead in the story, the heroine is his new wife, that's who Joan Fontaine will play."

"Well, you know all about it then. Have you already seen it?" asked Tony.

"I've read the book, it's good, very good."

"You don't mind then that you know the plot? We could try somewhere else."

"No, it's an excellent choice," I said. We went inside, and Johnny bought the tickets. I tried to pay him, but he refused my money.

"Only two and six. You girls work hard for little pay, it's our treat."

We went into the dark following an usherette with a torch. I stumbled, unable to see. Tony held my arm and didn't let go until we were settled into our seats. There was a film playing, not Rebecca, a cowboy film with waggons in a circle being attacked by Indians. Soon there was triumphant music and the cavalry arrived. The invaders fled and it all ended happily. The credits rolled by, followed by a few adverts.

At last our film started. I was enthralled, some of it seemed over acted but I loved it. When she came down the grand staircase in the dress that was a replica of the one Rebecca had worn, I could feel her despair and hated Mrs Danvers. Tony put his arm around me, and I snuggled into the comfort of his warmth.

I had forgotten how it ended and again wondered if he was a murderer, or had Rebecca taken her own life. The credits rolled. The national anthem played. *God Save the King.* We hurriedly stood up and the lights went on.

"We enjoyed that," said Tony to Johnny and Anne. "Did you?"

"Oh yes. Hitchcock's a master of suspense," said Johnny.

"I loved it. Isn't Olivier great, slightly menacing, but he's so dishy," said Anne.

"Hey you. I'll be getting jealous," said Johnny.

"Well, you're lucky he's only on the screen. But since we don't want to walk back, I will allow you are dishy too."

"We usually go to a little place round the corner for something to eat. Is that alright with you?" Anne asked me. I said it would be great, anything rather than hospital food sounded wonderful.

Fish and chips, bread and butter with huge cups of tea. There was plenty of vinegar and H.P. sauce and no one to frown at the amount of salt I put on the hot fat chips. Blissful.

"You look as if you really enjoyed that," said Johnny.

"Oh, I did. Such a change from lukewarm, hospital food. Thank you so much for bringing me here."

"It's a pleasure. You must come with us again."

"Yes," said Tony. "It's good to be with someone who enjoys cinema and has an understanding of the story." We sat over more tea discussing the film.

"You know a lot about psychology and Hitchcock," Anne said.

"It's a subject I've always been interested in." I thought I'd better not say any more about Hitchcock. The film, *The Birds* wouldn't have been made yet, and people would know nothing about his cruel treatment of Tippi Hendren.

Tony picked up the Hitchcock theme and talked about some of his early silent films, and *Blackmail,* which was his first sound film. He knew his subject well and the focus was luckily taken away from me.

"Come on, pubs will be open. You two film buffs can carry on there." Johnny called for the bill. We all paid our share, Tony put in a shilling for the tip.

We walked to the pub where the men had pints of beer.

I wasn't sure what to have. I thought a pint of beer might not be what women drank. I hesitated and when Anne asked for a snowball, I had the same. It was a mixture of eggnog and lemonade, very sweet and not unpleasant. Anne got very giggly and snuggled up to Johnny.

"Remember we have to be back by ten or we will be locked out," she said.

"We have plenty of time for another round. My turn." Tony got up and went to the bar.

"You seem to be getting along well. Are you glad you came?" Anne asked me.

"He's nice and interesting. I can't remember when I last had a normal conversation."

"Talking about me?"

"Not likely," said Johnny. "The word normal was mentioned."

"I was saying what a good time I'm having."

"I'm enjoying your company. It's not often I talk to a girl with a brain."

"That's because they have more sense than to talk to you," bantered Johnny.

"Take no notice of him. We've known each other since school," Tony told me.

We drove back to the nurse's home, just beating the deadline. Anne and Johnny stood in a clinch by the car. Tony pulled me to one side and said he hoped we could see each other again. He bent and kissed my cheek. When I didn't move away he kissed me gently on the lips, saying until next time. I felt happy and a little giddy as I went inside.

Chapter 24

I was still feeling happy the next morning as I walked into the ward. My mood was strengthened by the absence of Staff Nurse. Some of the men called out to me that I had a spring in my step, followed by rude comments about Staff. I pretended I hadn't heard, but it was nice to feel that they were on my side. Everything went smoothly. No remaking of beds, no hurtful comments. One of the men called out to me.

"Nurse, my arm don't 'alf hurt." He held up his bandaged arm and I could see the wound seeping through the dressing and re-took his temperature. It was raised. I told Anne, who told me to get the dressings tray. We cleaned up his wound with antiseptic, which made the poor man gasp.

"We need to get rid of this infection," she told him. We were busy and didn't notice what was going on at the far end of the ward until Sister came by, walking faster than usual.

"Nurse Marshall. With me now."

Anne quickly followed her leaving me to finish the dressing. The curtains were drawn around a bed at the far end. One of the men who was ready to be discharged must be ill. Two doctors came hurrying through the ward. I carried on with my duties wondering what was happening. The men were noticing that something wasn't right.

"What's up Nurse? Is it 'Arry? 'E were complaining of a bad 'eadache yesterday." Sid, whose arm I had been dressing, always seemed to know what was going on.

"Did he tell the nurse that he was in pain?" I asked.

"No, 'e were keen to get home to see his wife and new babe, didn't want to be kept 'ere any longer. 'E'd been in 'ere long enough with that broken leg 'e reckoned."

One of the ambulant men walked down to the end of the ward only to be sharply told to go back to his bedside.

"I reckon he's a goner," he said to the ward in general. I told him not to say such things. Harry was well enough to go home and see his family.

Anne returned. "We have to do the lunches," she told me. "Sister is too busy with the doctors." It was unheard of Sister not to preside over the lunch trolley.

"What's happening?"

"Come to the sluice," Anne said.

Once in there she told me that Harry was dead. "Apparently he'd had a dreadful pain in his head but not told any of the staff," she said. "He collapsed and was gone. We couldn't do anything, when I got there it was too late."

"But how? Why? He was going home."

"The doctor thinks it was an embolism."

"A what?"

"An embolism. Sometimes a clot comes away from a broken leg and gets into the bloodstream. It can then travel into the lungs or brain. That's why it's so important to notify chest pain or headache when we do the obs. Trouble is he was so keen to get home he didn't complain until it was too late. They will take him to the morgue to do an autopsy."

I was so shocked; I knew the problems of infection but had never heard of this. I made a mental note to take special notice of anyone with a broken bone.

"What do we say to the men?"

"Nothing yet, Sister will decide what we tell them. You can just say he is poorly, but you don't know any more if they ask."

It was a sad afternoon. Harry had been well liked and apparently very brave when he was in France. When they got to the beaches, he helped others to get on the boats. He didn't bother about himself, until as the men put it, *'The Hun got him and did his leg in.'*

The Padre came on the ward and spoke about his bravery before he did the Sunday Evening Service. "He will probably be given a medal which his widow will receive," he told them.

"Much good that will do." One war weary man commentated. "She won't be able to feed her kids on that."

He was silenced by the Padre commencing the prayers. I found myself praying fervently for all the men. Even though I didn't believe in the God they were praying to.

Even Staff Nurse was quieter when she came on duty on Monday. I thought she might make sarcastic comments about slack nursing when she wasn't there. I told Margaret about it later that evening, she said she thought perhaps Staff realised she hadn't noticed it the evening before, when the other men said he had been in pain.

"There would have been nothing that could have been

done. I've seen it before," she said sadly. "Tell me about your day out, we need to cheer up."

I told her what a lovely day I'd had, and she told me that she had been to visit Paul in his convalescent home.

"As soon as he is released, he is going to take me to Wales to meet his family."

I said how pleased they would be to see him and the woman that had nursed him back to health.

"Oh, as his fiancée," she said shyly, showing me a ring. "Of course I can't wear it at work." I looked at her and she was glowing with pleasure.

"You will be perfect for him. You are both such lovely people."

"You sound as if you know him."

"Well, you get to know people quickly in here and you got to know him didn't you?"

"I did, he is so lovable."

I agreed with her, but I wasn't sure that his parents would be pleased with him bringing a woman from England home with him. I just hoped she wouldn't run into Gladys.

"You've gone very quiet, are you okay?"

I was thinking that he will be able to show you his cows, he never stopped talking about them," I said.

"I'm not so sure about that," she said.

"I get the impression it's love me, love my cows," I said.

"Hope not. Anyway, tell me more about Tony." She was keen to change the subject, but I noticed she kept looking at her ring and smiling. A lady in love, I thought.

"How did he manage to buy the ring?"

"He went on a trip to Southampton with a couple of the

others. They do that to make sure they're fit enough to discharge. He is just waiting for his final check from the doctors now." She sounded so happy.

I asked her how she was finding her new ward.

"I really like it. The cases are all post op and need careful nursing, much more demanding. We have a new doctor who comes from Wales. Paul recognised his name thinks he might be from his village."

"Oh, that's nice," I said, trying to sound as if I wasn't particularly interested. "What's his name?"

"Doctor Burrows, why? You can't know him."

"No, I wondered if he might have come on our ward."

"Apparently his interest is surgical, but he went back to his village to join his father's practice as his father was getting old. He wanted a change from General Practice though, so when he heard there was a shortage of doctors on the front line he came here. He seems very switched on for a country doctor."

It was strange to hear her talk about him. My heart was beating fast at the thought of seeing Robert again. What would he think about me being here? I didn't sleep very well that night. Every time I woke, I thought about being in Robert's arms.

The next morning dragged by. There were no little cheeky comments or jokes from the men. After lunch, Staff Nurse called me over. I wondered wearily what I had done.

"Nurse, go with the orderly to the surgical ward. There is a patient to be transferred here." I smiled at her; something was in my favour. I might bump into Robert. I could hear my pulse beating in my head. I held my shaking hands under my apron. The orderly stood by my side. I looked up at him. It was James, from where had he appeared?

"You look a bit flushed. Are you okay?" James was looking at me. "Let's walk the long way round. Sister won't know and it will cool you down." I nodded.

As soon as we were outside, I turned to him.

"Where have you been? I haven't seen you since you dropped me off at the farm."

"I have been watching you. You didn't need my help; you've managed very well."

"Why are you here now if you can't help me get back? What is the point of you?" My words were harsh. I knew as soon as they'd left my mouth, he looked down, biting his lip before he spoke.

"I believe you need support at this moment, so I'm here."

"I need to be back in my own time, my degree."

"You needn't worry about your degree, and you will get back I promise you."

As we approached the ward, I saw him. I'd have known him anywhere. I could feel my chest fluttering.

"Robert." He turned and looked around, wondering who was calling him, looked straight at me then turned back.

"Robert. Hello." He stopped and looked at me again. He seemed to be looking straight through me. "Robert."

"Sorry, do I know you."

"Of course you do. It's me." He looked puzzled.

"I'm sorry nurse, you must be confused."

"But." James pulled my arm. "Come on, we have work to do."

"But I do know him from Wales, I know him very well.

How can he not recognise me." I was in tears. I didn't understand what was happening. Surely, he wasn't just saying that because I was only a nurse, and he was one of the god-like doctors. He wasn't like that. I knew he wasn't. Robert had turned and quickly walked away. James was whispering in my ear.

"Come on, he doesn't know you. Don't make a fool of yourself. Doctors don't speak to nurses. You know that."

"But I do know him."

"Sure, you do, but he doesn't recognise you."

I was bereft. What was happening? Was it because I was in uniform?

Then realisation struck and punched me in the stomach. I folded over as if winded. Of course, he didn't know me. I wasn't Sally, I looked different. It wasn't the uniform. I was no longer the girl he loved. He loved Sally, she would have his baby, share his life not me. I couldn't stand upright. This was all so unfair. I had been managing well until I saw him now, I couldn't go on. What was the point? James was holding me up. My legs had no strength.

"Come on, you can do this." He was stroking my back. I leaned into him, and his hands held me. He felt warm and for a moment, I felt secure. He wiped my tears away. It felt good to have him there and I regretted my earlier harsh words.

"I don't understand, what is this all for?" He stepped back, releasing his hold on me.

"I promise, eventually you will understand." He squeezed my hands in his and disappeared. I was there on my own. So alone. I wanted to go home. I'd had enough. What was it all for? Where was James? It was true, I hadn't needed him at the farm. I did now.

"Betty what's wrong?" It was Margaret's voice.

"He didn't know me." She didn't understand what I was talking about. James had gone but John, the orderly was by her side.

"Tell Staff, Nurse Johnson is ill," she said. She sent him back to the ward with the patient and a nurse from surgical.

"Come on," she said, taking my arm. "It's my lunch break. We're going to the canteen. I don't know what's wrong, but you need some nourishment."

"Staff Nurse," I said weakly.

"Never mind her. I think the events of the last two days have been too much for you." We walked over to the canteen, which gave me time to get my breath.

"I'm sorry that was silly," I said.

"It didn't look silly. It looked painful. Will you be alright to go back on duty?"

"Yes, but I'm worried what Staff will say."

"She'll survive, she shouldn't work you so hard. Just apologise."

When I went back Staff gave me a hard look and asked if I was fit to work. I said I was so she sent me to the sluice where I scrubbed as hard as I could. I felt rather embarrassed now. Later during our tea break, Anne asked me if I was okay.

"John said you had a breakdown. We didn't expect you back today."

"I thought I saw someone I used to know, then felt terribly homesick."

"Glad you're okay now. Johnny said that Tony was asking when you're off duty again. Sister is putting the list up later."

"Oh, I think I'll give it a miss next time."

"Nonsense. Go out and enjoy yourself. Tony is nice."

I said I'd think about it, and we went back to do the patient's supper.

The next day Robert came to our ward to examine the patient who'd been transferred from surgical. I was glad I was too lowly to attend the bedside. There were several men, well enough to be transferred to a convalescent hospital. I was busy sorting out their belongings and remaking beds. Things were getting a little easier.

Then the bombing started not on us, but in nearby Southampton. The cinema we'd been to only a short time before had been left in smoking ruins. The Luftwaffe was going for the docks, we were told. Many people were injured, including soldiers guarding the docks. These were sent to us and so the empty beds were filled again. Weeks went by and men slowly got better and their beds were refilled. There was talk of a British Expeditionary Force being sent to Africa and the desert to fight. It was all hush hush but we heard about it. That's what we were repairing the men for I thought, to send back to fight again. Paul recovered, but Margaret said his leg still gave him painful moments. They'd had some precious time together before he'd had to re-join his regiment. Although Margaret had a near miss the night the cinema was destroyed by a direct hit. She had been asked to work because they were short staffed and had cancelled her cinema date with Paul.

"It must have been fate," she said. "Southampton was being destroyed by the bombing." Later, Paul heard Swansea and surrounding towns and villages had been bombed. He had been desperate to see his parents, but the army cancelled his travel permit. They didn't want to lose any soldiers. Margaret said it gave them a little more time together, but soon he was gone. Training again for the desert mission. Margaret told me that he had asked for leave, so that they could get married.

They gave him one night. Margaret got a special licence. One of Paul's army friends and myself were witnesses. I was so pleased for them. Paul said after the war, they would have a service in church, where their parents could attend. He wanted to marry Margaret before he was sent away. He was in his uniform with two stripes on his arm now. She wore a pale blue dress. Some of us had given her our ration points so that she could get a dress and a pretty nighty for the one night they were allowed.

Several nurses who weren't on duty came to see them and wish them good luck. The Sister from her ward had managed to get the canteen to make a cake. They had a small reception at one of the hotels still standing in the shell of Southampton. The next day he went off and she donned her uniform again.

Chapter 25

I awoke with a start. I had been dreaming that I was getting married to Robert in a church and as he bent to kiss me, I saw that he was Tony. "No." I cried out, "You're the wrong one." The vicar sternly told me that I was married now and would have to make the best of it. It felt so real and in the light of what had been happening to me, it took a while for me to realise that it was only a dream. I remembered I had another day off, so unusual to have two days so close together. I decided to look around the grounds of the hospital. I'd been told that there were graves from Crimea and the Great War at the far end. I'd never ventured very far along the riverbank either. I could spend the day exploring. Get away from the smell of sickness and disinfectant.

As I walked across the grass towards the graves, I couldn't help thinking about Harry who'd died from an embolism. Somewhere at the back of my mind, I knew I'd heard that word before.

The grass was quite long, and I could see swings in the far corner. "That's strange," I thought. I could hear boys, young boys calling out and I was back watching my brother and his friends playing cricket in the park.

"But Tommy, why not? I want to play."

"You're too small, you'd be no good. Go away." Another boy, not Tommy, answered me unkindly.

I started to cry. "I'm a big girl. I'm nearly four. Please Tommy."

"Tom," the other boy said. "Send her away, she's a nuisance, we can't play with babies around."

"I'm not a baby. Tell him Tom."

"Go over to the swings and I'll play with you later," my brother answered.

"I'm going home to tell my mummy. It's not fair. You were supposed to be looking after me."

Tears run down my cheeks, and I try to wipe them away with my sleeve, but they won't stop. I can feel the unfairness so strongly and one of the boys says, "girls can't play cricket anyway."

I turn around to say. "Yes, they can," just as the ball hit Tommy on the head. He falls over, as I get to him, I can see his eyes are closed, the boys push me out of the way, and I start to howl. One of them tells me he's okay and I can see he's sitting up now blinking.

"Blimey I saw stars." He was trying to laugh but I knew he was scared.

"You've got a big bump on your head," I said.

"It's a real egg, getting bigger," said one of the boys. "I reckon you should sit down for a while."

"What's going on here?" It was Daddy. "Goodness Tom, you're out of my sight for ten minutes and you get hurt. I came to get your sister, but I think we'd better get you checked over." Tom protested that he was all right but when he got up, even I could see he was dizzy. The boy who'd thrown the ball kept saying that he was sorry. One of the others said Tom walked into the ball, because he was watching me. That made me cry again.

"Oh, dear what a pair." Dad picked me up and put his arm around Tom. "You all right old fellow?"

"I'm fine now Dad."

"I think we'll make a trip to the hospital. We could do with Granny here; she'd have some of her special stuff to put on it."

The hospital was close to home and Tommy didn't have to wait long to be seen.

The doctor came out and said to Daddy that they would x-ray to be sure, but they thought he was fine. We went along corridors to another place. The walls had big yellow stickers with big black crosses on them. We sat in the comfortable chairs and Daddy read comics to me. It seemed a long time before Tommy came back to us. He had a big sticker on his jumper.

"Is that because you have a broken head?" I asked him.

The nurse who was with him said, "no it's because he has been very brave."

"I've been brave too," I said. The nurse laughed and found me a sticker, not as big as Tommy's but it was pink, my favourite colour.

"We can go home now. The doctor's say that Tommy is okay." Dad sounded pleased.

When we got home, Mummy was already home from work. When she heard what had happened she shouted at Daddy. She told me and Tommy to go up to our rooms and play. I was getting hungry but didn't dare say. I knew when

Mummy was cross, we kept quiet. Tommy let me play in his room with his Lego. He decided to lie down on the bed. He said he felt tired. I made a big castle. This was good. Usually, Tommy didn't let me play for long with his Lego, he made spaceships and said what I did was silly. I found a Lego man in a space helmet and pretended he was a knight coming to rescue the princess who was trapped inside by an evil giant.

Tommy sat up in bed.

"I feel sick." He said knocking over my castle as he got out of bed. He threw up, he kept being sick. Sicker than when I'd had a sick bug at play school. He was sick all over the Lego. Then he fell back on the bed. I called Mummy. She came upstairs, Daddy followed her. Tommy was white and very still. He didn't answer Mummy when she spoke to him.

Daddy said, "I'll get the car."

"No, carry him downstairs, he's limp, not responding." Mummy was cleaning him up. I started to cry. I was frightened. I could see they were too.

We all went in the car to the hospital. Daddy took me for an orange juice and to my surprise let me ride in the Postman Pat car. Then we went back to where we had left Mummy and Tommy. A nurse told Daddy where they had gone, and we hurried off to find them. Daddy carried me most of the way. Telling me, the doctors would make Tommy better.

"What if they can't?"

"Don't be silly of course they will."

We went to a place where there were lots of rooms with beds and scary looking machines with flashing lights.

"That's so they can find out what's wrong with Tommy," said Daddy.

After a long time, they let us see Tommy. Mummy was sitting beside him holding his hand and a tube was going into his other hand. He was still not awake. I was more frightened now. Mummy and Daddy talked quietly, then Mummy gave me a big hug.

"Daddy's going to take you home now."

"What are you going to do?"

"I'm going to stay with Tommy."

"Why can't he come home? I want him to come home."

"Now stop crying Imogen, you must be a brave girl and go with Daddy. Tommy must stay here so the doctors can make him better." Mummy handed me a tissue. "Now blow your nose and wipe those tears away. Tears won't help." Mummy had her *'don't argue with me voice.'* I blew my nose, but the tears wouldn't stop. I looked at Daddy, his face was red, and he was frowning.

"Call me, if there is any change," he said, bending to kiss Mummy. She turned her head away and didn't answer. We had fish fingers and chips for tea, but I wasn't hungry, nor was Daddy. All I could think of was Tommy, with all the wires and tubes, next to that machine thing with the lights.

Chapter 26

I was sitting on the grass looking at the white gravestones. Corporal Thomas Hadley, the wording said. Died from injuries. I could read no more. My eyes were so full of tears. Of course, it wasn't my Tommy. He had died that summer day after being hit by a cricket ball. He was only eight years old. Playing cricket one day, dead the next.

Mum blamed Dad, for not insisting that the hospital kept him in on the first visit. Dad got angry and wanted to sue the hospital. The boy that had thrown the ball thought it was his fault, even though all his friends had said that Tom had walked into it not looking where he was going. The school talked about banning cricket balls in the park. I kept quiet. I knew it was my fault. If I hadn't made a fuss Tommy would have been looking at the ball. He wouldn't have been hit.

Everyone said it was no one's fault, but I always knew it was mine. It was my fault everything was broken. Not just Tommy's head. Dad got a job away from home and came home less and less. Once I started school Mum worked every day but always fetched me from the school gate. Mum and Dad must have got divorced. The only difference for me was Dad stopped coming home and the rows ceased too. I saw

Dad at weekends for a while, then just in the holidays. I think he found it hard to see me. I reminded him of Tommy. Then he met Megan.

I became aware of someone behind me. I sniffed and looked for a hanky.

"Here, have this one." The voice was familiar. It was Robert. I knew he didn't know me. He offered me a large clean handkerchief. I started to apologise and mopped my face.

"No, please don't be sorry. I can see you are very distressed. Keep the hanky."

I looked up at him breathing, "thanks." His dear, kind face so close to me.

"I know you, I think. You're a nurse here. I'm Doctor Burrows. You were feeling ill the other day. Is it recent news?"

"No, that's my brother's name, although it isn't him, it reminded me of when he died."

"Grief has no time limits or boundaries. It attacks us without warning, even when we think everything's sorted. I'm sorry you lost your brother."

I felt a little more in control now his words were kind.

"If you are ready to get up my dear, hold on to my arm it will steady you."

The sun was getting low. I didn't know how long I'd spent there. I needed to get back if I was to get anything to eat. He helped me up and we walked towards the hospital. I asked him how he came to be working there. He wasn't military. He told me country doctors were being called up to help because of the shortage of medics.

"I worry about my patients at home. There was no one locally to replace me."

"In Wales?"

"Is my accent so strong?"

"No faint, but I can hear it. Thank you for your help." We had arrived back by the nurse's home. "I'll wash your handkerchief and let you have it back."

When I got to my room, there was a note pushed under the door from Tony. He must have asked one of the nurses to deliver it for him. There was no way the Home Sister would have let a man in the building. I smiled to myself. They still behaved as if we were all nuns.

Come out for a spin and a bite to eat. I heard that you are off duty. I'll be around about five o'clock. Do come. I could do with some company. Tony xx.

Anne must have told him, my first thought was to ignore the note, then I decided I needed some company too, so at 5 o'clock I was waiting by the door. He looked so pleased to see me I was glad I'd changed my mind.

"When Johnny knew you had time off, he said I could have the old banger to see if I could tempt you out." Waving the car keys at me. "He knows I'm a bit keen on you."

"A bit keen?"

"Well, a lot actually, he says I've not stopped talking about you."

"You must have run out of other things to say."

"Perhaps that's why he let me borrow the car, so I came up with something new. Where do you fancy driving to?"

"New Forest would be nice. I don't fancy Southampton, do you?"

"Good idea, don't want any close shaves with the bombs."

We climbed in the car; it was the first time I'd been in

the front. It was more comfortable, but I was a bit apprehensive. However, Tony drove at a slightly more sedate pace than Johnny did. After a while, I settled in my seat enjoying the scenery.

It was impossible to hold a conversation because the car was too noisy. It didn't stop Tony talking though. At least he didn't turn and look at me while he spoke.

He stopped the car when we got to a bridge where ponies were gathering.

"This is my favourite spot, come and look at the water." He helped me out of the car, and we walked along the stream for about a mile where it broadened out into a large shallow pond.

"Look, you can see the fish." I couldn't see them at first. When my eyes adjusted, I saw so many of them darting about, in and out of the flat stones. It was peaceful and lovely.

"You've turned my day around," I told him. We sat chatting for a while watching fish and birds.

"I used to come here with my Mum and Dad," he told me.

"My brother and I would make dams in the stream and play all day." I asked him where his brother was now. He said he was in the army waiting to be sent somewhere in Africa.

"He was one of the lucky ones that got home from Belgium safely. Mother's worried sick that he's used up all his luck now. Can't wait until I'm fully trained, so that I can go and help."

"Used up all his luck?"

"Yes, he and his mates were travelling to Dunkirk and the German tanks were behind them all the way. They were trapped. In the confusion, my brother and his sergeant managed to hide, but the other officer and some of the men were captured. He said he felt bad, but they all were running, and he didn't realise the others weren't with them until it was too late. A Belgian farmer helped them. Then the sergeant was hit on the beach. They both managed to get home, Harry without a scratch. Mother thinks it's tempting fate to go back in the firing line."

"But they have no choice, do they?"

"No, but if he had, he would still go. It's about fighting for your country. Doing the right thing."

"Is that why you'll go?"

"Of course." He looked at me," I say, you're not a pacifist are you?"

"Well, I'm finding it hard to help men get well just to send them back. It must be awful to know what you are going into."

"Mm, I suppose that's why women nurse and men fight. It's in our blood."

A heron landed on the opposite bank. It stood on one leg looking in the water. We both sat very still watching it. It's head darted into the water, and it came up with a fish wiggling in its beak. Looked across at us then flew off. It was a breath-taking moment, I no longer wanted to think about men being killed or injured.

"Shall we go and look for something to eat?" he asked. "Can't promise fish but there is a chip shop in Brockenhurst." We walked back to the car.

Luckily, the chip shop was still open. "Just about to close," the man said. "Plenty of chips, no fish left, but lots of bits of batter."

We sat on a bench and had a feast. "I can hardly move, I hope I can fit into my uniform tomorrow."

"Let's walk across the green to the pub. That'll burn a bit off, then we can swill it down with a couple of pints." I looked at him.

"I will on one condition." He dropped his arm from my shoulders.

"Sorry, am I getting too fresh? Difficult not to put my arm around you when you're so close."

"It's not that. Can I have a pint? I can't stand that yellow stuff. It's so girly." He looked relieved.

"Wow I knew you were special, of course you can, and I won't breathe a word to Margaret."

We walked across the green giving way to cows as they made their leisurely way past us. Tony grabbed my hand.

"They won't hurt you." He held on to my hand even though I assured him I wasn't afraid of cows. I thought of the farm and wondered how the herd were doing. Would Paul ever be reunited with his girls? A great wave of sadness went through me. What would happen to Paul and all those other men?

"Penny for them?"

"Sorry. I was thinking of the men who have recovered and wondering what would happen to them. Paul, who Margaret married, is a farmer. He has a herd of cows."

"I can't imagine Margaret milking cows."

"Stranger things have happened," I said. We'd reached the pub. We went inside and found a seat. Tony went to the bar to order. He came back with two pints.

"I got you the same, they didn't have much choice." I took a sip then a gulp.

"It's nectar. It's so long since I've had a proper drink." We sat in a comfortable silence downing our pints.

"I know something about you that no-one else does now."

"What's that?"

"You know about films, read books and drink pints. You're not afraid of cows. I wonder what other secrets I can find out?"

"There's not a lot to know," they weren't really secrets. "We'd better get back to the car I mustn't be late in." I needed to change the subject. There were, of course, so many secrets that I couldn't tell him.

He drove slowly back to the hospital, neither of us wanted this day to end.

Chapter 27

More bombing in Southampton, more casualties, I was so sick of blood and broken bodies and more blood, but I did as I was instructed. I knew I was helping in a small way. Often a smile and smoothing of the bed sheets made things a little more bearable. Gentleness and kind words as we changed dressings kept spirits up. I longed for modern medicine. These men had so much confidence in us, and we had so little to help them. I was in the sluice cleaning bedpans, the spray of water hit the side of the pan. Sister must have heard my yelp of surprise. She found me covered in an evil smelling brown slurry. I expected a dressing down, told to concentrate, and to be more professional. Instead, she helped me to take off my dripping apron, and handed me a towel.

"Sometimes life seems unbearable and then it gets worse, dry yourself off and clear up here, then go back to the nurse's home for a bath. You can't sit with the others for an end of day report smelling like this." She looked at my now tear stained face. "Shit happens."

We both burst out laughing. "Don't tell anyone I said that. They wouldn't believe you anyway." I hurried out of the building, head down, hoping not to see anyone.

Luckily, the bathroom was empty and the water was hot. I stood in the bath, rinsed myself off, before filling the bath with very hot water. A shower would have been good but of course only deep old cast iron baths were available. It was the first time for a while that I'd thought about my other life. My real life. I had become used to the hospital; the poor pay and difficult conditions. How long was I to stay here I wondered? What would become of Tony was he really going to join up? As I sat there soaking in the cooling water, I knew I wouldn't find out. What about Margaret? Newly married, she'd told me in a whisper she thought she was pregnant. Would Paul survive the war? Would Margaret survive a life on a lonely Welsh farm?

The water was cool now, too cool to lie in any longer. I stood up reaching for the towel as I did so the room began to blur. I could hear James's voice saying come on if you stay there any longer you will be stuck. As I wrapped the towel around me, I could hear music. It was faint and as I strained to listen, I stepped out of the bath onto – nothing, no bath mat. I fell. It felt as if I was falling through space.

I was back in my room. A copy of my completed essay was on the table, a half-eaten sandwich and a glass of wine beside it. I picked up an envelope, which had been pushed through the door. I held my breath; the letter was from the university. It stated *we are pleased to inform you that you have been awarded a first-class honours degree.*

I barely had time to take it in before the room was swirling around again. All I could hear was first class, first class, echoing round and round in my head, but I was no longer there.

"James, James," I cried. "I've had enough. I need to get on with my life."

I could hear his voice faintly. "You've not finished yet. There is one more thing for you to do."

"No." I could hear my voice as if it belonged to someone else, sounding as if it was coming from a long hollow tube. "Noooo," going on and on, echoing and distorting.

Nausea overwhelmed me, I was going to be sick. Take slow breaths, I told myself just as I'd told the patients. It must have worked because the room was no longer reeling and the sounds were returning to normal. Normal? Who was I kidding, normal? I could hear a baby crying. I moved over to the window. I think that was when I realised I wasn't in my own room. Looking round I saw it was the same size as mine but instead of my table, cluttered with books, it was neat and tidy. Oh, but it smelt bad. In the centre was a baby's cot. The awful stench was a nappy that needed changing.

Margaret came into the room making soothing sounds as she bent and picked up the baby. She grabbed a clean nappy from a clothes airer, which was standing in front of the fire. Sighing she sat down, the lines on her face sharply etched. She started to change the baby and he stopped crying. I didn't know what to say. How could I explain my presence? She seemed unaware of me. Now she was feeding him some gruel-like mixture from a small dish. He seemed to spit more out than he swallowed. I looked around the room. On the side there was a picture of Paul, he had three stripes on the arm of his uniform. That made him a sergeant I thought.

I looked across to the other side of the room. A curtain half hid a sink and two gas burners. It all looked rather bare, there was a large white tin with blue writing on it, *National Dried Milk*. Next to it were a couple of glass bottles and rubber teats. There was a loaf of bread, a knife, and a bread bin next to a jar of jam and a piece of cheese. No high living here I thought. Under the sink, my nose found a white bucket, although it had a lid, there was no doubt about what was soaking there.

She still hadn't seen me. I went over to her and asked if I could do anything to help, but she looked straight through me. She couldn't see me. I looked at my hand. I was visible, perhaps only to myself. Was that possible? I ruefully laughed at myself. Anything was possible, wasn't it? How had I got here? I needed to ask James and he wasn't here.

I had a strange feeling I'd been in this situation before. I remembered the recurring dream I used to have when I was young.

After my brother died, I had the same dream night after night. He and I would be at a party. Not a children's party with jelly and ice cream. It was a gathering of women. Our mother was there, glass in hand. There was much chattering and laughter, everyone was happy. We were sitting to one side drinking lemonade and sharing a bowl of crisps. I would look across at the bookshelf, wondering if I could pick up a book to read without anyone noticing. One of the women would start to laugh louder than the others and point across at us, as if she'd not seen us before. Her laughter then turned to cackling, her nose growing large, into a point. Standing up I could see her clothes were black, a black cape around her shoulders. I couldn't tell what she was saying but she continued to point at us. As my brother stepped away towards the wall in fear,

I would see him slowly become wallpaper. Tom's head and face, slowly changing into a large flower, his body becoming the stems and leaves. Mouthing "Help me."

Every time I realised too late, I'd been here before and I couldn't do anything to stop it happening. No matter how I cried, the witch would have no mercy.

I would wake sobbing and frightened. Had I caused his death again?

If I could stop myself from looking at the books and hold his hand instead, could I have saved him? I never told anyone of the dream. It was too real. Too frightening.

In truth, perhaps I was going mad. I'd heard that people went mad with grief. Hamlet did. My brother's death had changed my world. I was no longer a sister or a daughter to my father. He didn't function as part of a family now. His grief and guilt seemed to devour him. He and my mother were barely on speaking terms. Indeed, only angry words were exchanged between them. I kept very quiet, wondering how long it would be before they realised that it had all been my fault. I'd sit in the room, quietly reading my Enid Blyton book, thinking I'd disappeared, or at least become invisible.

I looked across at the photo of Paul and it struck me that he too was wallpaper. He wouldn't come back; did she know yet? Did Margaret know?

She placed the baby carefully in the cot, stroking his little face until he settled.

There was something about the way she did it. I remembered someone stroking my face when I was put to bed. A story until I was sleepy, then my face gently stroked. It wasn't my mother. Memories of a hand with freckles on the back came rushing to me. Those gentle hands and the voice laughing.

"No darling, those are called age spots, not freckles."

"But you're not old Granny. I think they are freckles," I'd say.

There was a knock on the door, Margaret straightened up from the cot. One hand in the small of her back and went to answer the door.

"Oh Mum, thanks. He's just gone off to sleep."

A grey-haired woman came into the room, kissed Margaret on the cheek.

"Any news yet?"

"No, I haven't heard anything for weeks. It's a long way for letters to come. He might not have much time to write if they are in the middle of a battle."

"At least he should be safe in that tank. I've heard they are huge."

Margaret was putting on her coat. "Fingers crossed; you know what they say, no news is good news."

"I've brought three eggs; the hens have started laying again. I thought little William could have one for his tea."

"Thanks, that will be good. I was wondering what he could have, it's getting difficult to find something that he doesn't spit out. He likes rusks and that's about it. He likes mashed carrot and potato with a little Oxo cube and of course his milk."

"He needs more solids now, he's a growing boy."

Margaret's voice went up a little. "I know he does, but at least the milk has goodness in it, and he doesn't spit it out. They say it's perfect food."

The other woman looked at her.

"Not for growing boys."

"I know, I know. Thank you for the eggs and for being here for us." She walked over to the cot again. "I must go, I'll be late." Giving the woman a quick peck on the cheek she rushed off. Well, I thought what happens now, will this one see me?

She placed the eggs in a small cupboard on the wall, took off her coat and hung it up before sitting down to read a magazine. I looked over her shoulder. 'Woman's Weekly.' It seemed full of ideas of how to make food go further and leftovers tasty. There was a whole page of 'Ways with dried egg.'

Not my idea of a good read, but I did see when she turned over the page there were stories too.

It seemed I was still invisible. It was a strange feeling. Was I the one to turn into wallpaper now? I had a sudden frightening thought. Was I dead? I knew instinctively that Paul was or soon would be. How did I know that? I thought about what I'd learnt about purgatory. I'd always thought it church mumbo-jumbo, but what if it were true, when people died, they stayed suspended in the ether? Just like I seemed to be, hovering, unseen. Watching what was happening, unable to communicate. I stood there not knowing what was happening to me. From the date on the front of the magazine, it was nearly the end of the war. What would happen to all the soldiers when they returned? So many had gone to fight from ordinary, peacetime jobs, like Paul. Those who returned, survived, would have experienced situations they couldn't have previously imagined. Many had become killing machines. How would they adjust to peacetime? To family life? I don't think much thought had been given to service men's adjustment. I believe they were just expected to get on with it. Women who'd had some independence during wartime had to go back to being housewives and mothers. I'd never thought about the impact on men before.

My dad would never have been suited for war; he was so gentle. He didn't even stand up to my mum when she used to shout at him. I used to think he was weak, walking away from us and Mum encouraged me to think so. I wondered if it were true. He'd only loved Tommy, never been interested in me, Mum had told me so many times. As I stood watching little William with the woman I assumed was his grandma, the things Dad used to do with me came tumbling back. Brushing my hair, making my sandwiches for lunch, taking me to school, and reading me stories.

Dad did love me, but why had he disappeared from my life. I needed to find out. For the moment, though, I was trapped here.

While I'd been thinking about my past, time had moved here. The cot had gone, and little William was sitting on the rug playing with wooden bricks. Margaret was sitting in the chair picking at the worn fabric with her fingernails. On the floor, the paper had huge headlines. 'V.E. Day. The War Is Over. Celebration Time.' With tears running down her cheeks. She spoke to the little boy.

"Not much to celebrate here is there, with your daddy never coming home and granddad dead? Cows are gone and your grannie is ill in hospital. He dreamed of teaching you how to be a cowman." The little boy looked up at her and when she bent towards him, he reached up and tried to wipe away her tears. She picked him up. "Ah well my baby boy at least we have each other." Giving him a loving hug, as he said.

"Not baby, big boy."

I wondered what had happened on the farm. I knew money was scarce, perhaps there hadn't been enough help to keep the cows. Mr Jones wouldn't have managed by himself if he didn't regain his strength after his arm injury. I stood in the room as an onlooker, unseen but seeing the difficulties that these people had to face. A far cry from the family who'd rejected Paul. At least he had been loved by his adoptive parents. He had found love and happiness with Margaret, even though it had been short lived. He had been lucky to find her, she was a warm generous person. She reminded me of someone. Who was it? I found I too had tears on my cheeks. This room was so depressing. There was such a lack of comfort. I only had to look at mother and baby and see the love, but everything seemed so sparse. I needed to get out of here. This really wasn't my time. I wanted to find my father, find out what had happened to him. I went over to the door, not expecting it to open.

I found myself in a corridor, I started walking not knowing where I was going, stumbling as I went. I needed to find the light switch. I'd never been good in the dark. My hand searched the wall and found a doorknob. Again, that feeling of being in a vortex enveloped me, as I reached out for something, anything to hang on to. I was being sucked down a tube of time.

Chapter 28

I was back in that strange room where this had all started. James was sitting behind the desk.

"Oh, it's you. Are you still trying to get back to you own time?" He sounded bored.

"Look here," I said. "I've had enough of this."

"No need to shout." He unsuccessfully tried to stifle a yawn. "Just think of all you've learnt. You should be thanking me."

"Thank you. You impossible man, you've sent me all over the place in an attempt to send me back to my own time. You, well you're incompetent." I was breathing fast and struggling to find the right words. Why wasn't he apologising to me? As my voice got louder, he started to fade. I walked towards him.

"Please don't go. I didn't mean to be rude. I really have had enough of not knowing where or who I am. I need to go back to my own time permanently, not just drifting in and out, as I have been. I've achieved my degree and got a first I believe. I can register for a masters or a doctorate, but I need to be there to do so. Please help me, James."

He looked down his long nose at me. "My name is not

James; it was just one of the personas I inhabited on your journey. However, you may call me that if you wish."

"I wish to go home."

"Yes, you have made me aware of that fact. Many times, though, I wonder if you are aware of what you need to do to complete matters." He made it sound as if there had been a reason for what had happened to me. As always, I was puzzled.

"Go through the door, if you can find it, then look for..."

I could no longer hear what he was saying. Cyndi Lauper's song drowned out his quiet voice. What was I to look for? If I went through the door, would I be back or forward in time, like the first time I'd been in this room? I could see a door materialising in the dark wall panels. I could hardly stay here back in the eighteen hundreds. I had to try.

I opened the door and walked straight back into my own room. I could have cried with relief. The phone was ringing. When I answered it, I heard my mother's voice.

"At last, I've been trying for days. I wanted to know when you were coming."

"Coming?"

"Yes, coming home to see me. Now that term is finished, I thought you would be here by now."

"I rather hoped that you'd come for graduation day."

"Really do you mean it? Of course I will, then we can travel home together."

"Mum I won't be coming back home for good I want to carry on. I am going to do a master's degree."

"But you will come, I've stopped drinking. Really stopped

this time, I've joined A.A. I want you to stay with me for the summer." I could hear her voice wobble.

"Yes, I'll come, but not for the whole summer. That's such good news Mum I'm proud of you." I hoped it was true. She had stopped drinking so many times, but to my knowledge, she hadn't joined A.A. before. I was taking a chance inviting her to the graduation, but I felt that was a necessary risk. Hopefully, she won't let me down.

I put the phone down, remembering as I did the prize giving evening at my sixth form. When my name had been called out, she had clapped enthusiastically, which was okay. As I crossed the stage to get my prize, she stood up, called, and whistled. Loud piercing whistles. I was so humiliated. I grabbed my prize and hurried off the stage.

Later I tried to get her to go home.

"What miss the drinks and nibbles? Why would we do that Imogen?" Despite my pleas, she wouldn't go. She started to complain loudly that the drinks were only tea, coffee or soft drinks. She went up to my head of year and harassed him loudly, saying that everyone expected wine. I could hear mutters from other parents saying she'd had enough already. To my everlasting shame, she was gently led outside.

I was told to take her home. I still can hear her shouts and feel my embarrassment. My friends all thought it was funny and said they agreed with her. They wouldn't have found it so funny if it had been one of their mothers though.

After leaving for university, I'd worried about her. In fact, it seemed as if all my life I'd looked after her. Several times in my first year, I'd gone home to find her in a stupor, empty bottles around her, and stale food in the fridge. I'd clean her up get rid of bottles, shop for healthy food, listening once again to promises that I knew she wouldn't keep.

Finally, I stopped going home. Sessions with the university counsellor helped me to see it wasn't helping her but damaging to me. Now I thought, I can give her another chance and I wanted to see her. If she was really going to AA meetings perhaps, she would get better at last.

To my relief and amazement, Mum turned up well-dressed and sober and stayed that way. Once back home, I noticed that everywhere, although not perfect, was at least tidy and there was no sign of any empties lying around. Of course, I knew she could have tidied up, we'd been there before. I'd think everything was normal, like other people's houses, then after a few days, a bottle would roll out from under the sofa. This time though, on Tuesday evening she got ready to go to her meeting. I walked with her to the church hall, arranging to meet her outside when it was finished. Once back home, I started to look through an old photograph album. There were black and white photos of several people I didn't recognise. I decided to ask Mum about them when she came back.

I met her as promised at the door of the hall, and a tall man came out with her. He introduced himself as her sponsor.

"William keeps me on the straight and narrow," Mum said.

"No, you do that yourself," he said. "I'm there to listen and support. Your mum can call me at any time when she needs me." He looked friendly and said goodbye to us both.

"A new love interest?"

"Definitely not. The relationship is to keep me dry. He is so supportive in a very responsible way. He is firm but kind. He has been there himself." I must have looked surprised.

Mum then told me that all at AA were alcoholics. William had been dry for five years. I didn't ask about the photos that evening, she wanted to talk about her AA meeting and how varied the people were. I think it made her feel normal again and allowed her to have faith in herself. It was good to see her keen and interested. I thought of all the life she had missed because of alcohol. Grieving in such an unhealthy way, for my brother. I tried to talk about him, but she neatly changed the subject. It was still too painful for her it seemed.

"I can't go there without a drink, an' since I'm not drinking, I can't go there. I hope you understand."

I did understand but just for once, I would have liked her to consider my feelings.

I realised I was being selfish, what she was doing was hard. I didn't need to make it harder. She was doing well. The loneliness was quite overpowering, sometimes I think I'm less real now than I was in all those time travelling situations.

I've been home for weeks now. It's been uneventful, boring even. Still, I've kept in my own body and Mum hasn't had a drop of alcohol. Working locally has made me even more determined to do a higher degree.

I've been looking at those old photos again. Mum's not been much help.

"They belonged to your dad. I've no idea how they have survived. I should have thrown them away. Can't think why I didn't."

I think it's because I saved them, knowing they were my dad's. I wanted anything belonging to him, then, I forgot I had them. Mum wouldn't have thrown them away because firstly, she didn't know they were there and second, she never sorted anything out. She'd only been interested in where the next drink was coming from.

That sounds harsh, I know but it was my reality.

"Mum, do you know where Dad is now?"

"As far as I know he is in Wales, He doesn't send me money anymore of course."

"Send you money?"

"Well, he did until you went to university," she bristled. "It was my right he owed me. I had to bring you up."

"He sent money for my keep. I never knew."

"Why should you? It was between him and me."

"But it means he cared about me."

"Suppose so,"

"You always said he didn't care. I grew up thinking he didn't care."

"Doesn't mean he did. He had money, I didn't."

"Huh. I thought you had a children's allowance for me, but it was all spent on wine."

"Not all of it, don't be so harsh. I wasn't well."

"Drinking didn't make you better." I could feel the old bitterness creeping back. I was laughed at for my charity shop clothes; free school dinners and second-hand school uniforms. He cared about me, sent money for me. Why had she said he didn't? The walls seemed too close. I decided to go out, a long walk was what I needed.

I decided while I was walking that I would ask her for my dad's address. I'd always avoided it before. Any mention of him sent her to the bottle and tirades about how he'd left her in her hour of need. When I walked into the kitchen, she was sitting drinking a cup of coffee. From the direction of the oven came a hint of jacket potatoes. Always my favourite, a plate of grated cheese on the table confirmed what my nose told me.

This indeed was a new woman. As we tucked in, I broached the subject. She shrugged and said again, she thought he was in Wales.

"Yes, but where?"

"I think his address is in one of those old photos," she said. "He was always sending photos with the address on the back, so you could visit him." This was news to me.

"Why didn't I ever see them?"

"I didn't want him to break your heart too. You used to cry yourself to sleep after he left. It was best you forgot him. I did it for the best." I stared at her.

"Don't look at me like that. It was tough bringing you up on my own. I had to do what I thought was right. I had no one to turn to and I was ill."

"What about Grannie, I remember her? I remember going to her place in the country."

"Yes, you did but we fell out. She was too interfering, and took your dad's side too. I didn't want her influencing you."

My stomach was churning and my mouth dry. Thoughts were tumbling around my head. She cut me off from people who loved me and then neglected me. Why do I still care about her? Why haven't I the courage now, to say what I feel? I can use the excuse that I'm worried that wine will replace the coffee again. I can't risk being ignored, cold-shouldered. She's all I've got, and she was ill, not thinking properly.

"Did you never think about me, that I might need my dad?" I blurted out.

"You were all I thought about," her voice rose, and she blew her nose loudly.

The words, all you thought about was where you were getting your next drink from, burnt my lips as I clamped them shut. I got up to look at the photos again, the taste of what I'd eaten sour in my mouth.

Chapter 29

I found several addresses, two in London and one in Wales. I'd not looked at these photos properly because they were of places, not of my dad. There was a photo of Grannie standing outside an old cottage. It looked familiar, but that could have been my memory playing tricks. When I looked closely, I could see chickens by her feet. On the back, my dad's spidery writing said, '*Mum feeding the hens.*'

I looked at the Welsh address and wrote a quick note to my dad, hoping he was still there. Then I wondered if I could find a phone number. I could find nothing from directory enquiries, so posted the note, hoping he would phone me back on the number I'd enclosed.

The next few days dragged by. I'd foolishly told Mum I'd written to Dad. Every day she asked if I'd heard anything, nodding and smiling when I said no. She didn't say I told you so, didn't need to. The days seemed long. All my old friends had moved on. They weren't really friends, just people I'd known at school. Once in sixth form, I had made a couple of friends, girls who'd seen me for who I was, rather than my weird clothes. I decided to call at Sam's house to see if her mother was there. She had always been kind to me, often sending me home with cakes and other goodies.

Mum and her almost zealous abstinence was becoming overwhelming. I can't say I longed for the old version back, but I started to understand the saying you can have too much of a good thing. Even labels on take away meals were read and re-read to make sure there was no alcohol included. To be honest I longed for a pint of beer.

Sam's mum welcomed me.

"Come in, so good to see you. I've made a cottage pie so hope you can stay for supper."

"Oh bliss," I said, remembering her cooking. Sam wasn't home. Her course in modern languages was a four year one.

"She's in France practising her French. She has a teaching post for the summer," her mum said.

"English as a foreign language," her dad chipped in. "She seems to be an expert on French wines too." Sam's mum shushed him saying that he was being tactless. I told her it was okay; Mum had stopped drinking.

She raised her eyebrows. "Really," I said and made them laugh when I told them how boring it was to be with a teetotaller.

"In that case," she said. "Time to get out one of those bottles that Sam brought home with her last time." I had a lovely evening and went home with Sam's address and new phone number.

"She'll love to hear from you," her dad told me.

When I got in there was a message on the phone. Missed call, from a number I didn't recognise. It was too late to call, so I decided I'd find out who it was in the morning. I tried not to get excited; it could be someone trying to sell insurance.

My crumpled sheets the next morning gave away the night I'd had. What if the caller had been Dad? What would I say? I was still thinking about what to say when the phone rang. It was Dad.

"Imogen, is that really you?" I knew his voice. Of course, I knew it. I heard my own start to wobble.

"Dad."

"Are you alright? Do you need help?" This didn't sound like the selfish man my mum had described.

"Yes, I'm fine. Actually, I wanted to see you, is that possible?"

"Possible, I should say it is. When can you come? Sorry I'm assuming you'll want to come here. Will that be okay, or do you want to meet somewhere neutral?"

"I'd love to come to you. I can come as soon as possible. How do I get there?"

"I'll send you money for the train. I can meet you at Cardiff station. I'm busy this week, but by the weekend I can be all yours."

We talked for ages, I told him about my degree, and he told me that he ran a campsite he'd established in Gran's old place.

"You do remember your grannie, don't you?"

"I do, I remember how kind she was."

He had to go; he had some guests checking out and loads of things to do. He said he would put a cheque in the post for my train fare. When I told Mum, she said it was typical, trying to buy me back with money. I wasn't in the mood to listen.

I sat for much of the day looking at the photos, dreaming of Dad and Wales. What would it be like?

I found myself work in a local restaurant when I arrived home. The next day I was back on duty, I told them that I needed a week off for a family visit, they said they could cover me for a week, but any longer and they would have to find a replacement. I wanted to save as much as possible before starting back at college. I'd have to support myself, even though there would be the chance to do some paid work for the department. Mum found so many reasons why I shouldn't go to Wales, but I was determined not to listen. Perhaps my dad might turn out to be a disappointment, I had to find out for myself.

Friday came, and I was on the train, excited, fearful, and mixed up. I had plenty of time to think about how I felt. Each time I thought about meeting Dad my hands became clammy and I could feel my heart racing. I tried to read but kept losing my place. What would he look like? I had no idea if he had a new partner, and what if I took an instant dislike to her? An awful thought crossed my mind. What if he had other children, another daughter? Would he have told me?

At last, the train drew into Cardiff. I was last to get off. I stood on the platform. Would he be there?

"Imogen." I turned and saw him, much older than I remembered, but it was my dad. Dropping my case, I stood staring not knowing what to say.

Chapter 30

What if he comes over and tries to hug me? He didn't. He picked up my case.

"Come on, let's get out of this draughty old station," he said, smiling at me. Then case in one hand he steered me with the other, out to his car. It was a big old Range Rover. He opened the door, and I climbed in. There was a big black dog in the back. I could hear her tail thrashing the seat.

"That's Molly, she's old and very friendly."

We both started to talk at once, me out of nervousness.

"How was your journey?"

"Fine. How far away is the farm?"

"About an hour's drive. I do hope you'll like it." There was an uncomfortable silence. I stared out of the window, wondering how to hold a conversation with a man I hadn't seen for years, hoping this hadn't been a mistake. He asked me questions. I answered in monosyllables, knowing I should make an effort. I relaxed a little when he started to talk about the farm.

"It had been neglected after the war. Mother, your grannie had come here to get away from the bomb damage in the south of England. She was quite horrified at the primitive conditions she found." As he spoke, I realised I knew nothing about his childhood.

"What about you, were you with her?"

"Yes, I was a toddler, my grandpa had a stroke and died. Mum felt sorry for my gran, all on her own and liked the idea of me growing up here. Mum eventually got a job as a district nurse, and I became a country boy."

"What brought you back south?"

"I went to grammar school then to university. I wanted to get away from all this. Now I love it and I hope you will too."

We had turned off the main road and were driving down a narrow lane, with fields on either side, green as far as I could see.

"Nearly there now, the house is still a bit old fashioned. I hope you'll be comfortable. At least there is an indoor loo and bathroom. When I was a boy, it was still a tin tub in front of the fire and a dash to the lavvy when you needed to go." He pulled up and asked me to open the large five bar gate, which I did and closed it after he drove through. I still couldn't see the farmhouse. There were several tents, large ones. Further on, I saw a barn and another building, which I guessed was a toilet block. There were several 'Slow Down' signs along the lane and we bumped over a cattle grid.

"Do you have any animals?"

"Only a few hens and a couple of goats. I sell eggs and we make cheese and yoghurt from the goat's milk. The cattle grid goes back to when the farm had a dairy herd before the war." He surprised me. I hadn't thought of him as a cheese maker. As I was thinking this, I remembered my own lessons on making cheese.

"I wonder if you can make butter from goats' milk?"

"I'm sure you can. We can look it up and you can have a go if you like."

He sounded keen, I hadn't realised I'd spoken out loud.

"Butter making is a hard work, I did it years ago." Again, I spoke without thinking. We drew up outside the house. It was like the one I was remembering. I told myself all Welsh farmhouses of that period would look the same. This one though, wasn't tired, and the front was clean and paved. There were large flower pots full of plants. The door was painted a deep blue and a rose rambled around the wooden porch. I could see curtains in the windows. He opened the door, and I walked in. The flagstone floor was old and uneven. Wooden chairs with brightly covered cushions sat around a large, scrubbed table. There was a deep sink by the window, next to a solid fuel cooker. A huge old fireplace was at the far end. Several pegged rugs were on the floor. A Welsh dresser took up almost the whole of one wall.

"I've been here before," I said, reaching for a chair. I was scared, I felt faint, I didn't want to disappear into another time zone. "Not now, oh please not now."

Dad's voice was coming in waves, echoing as I slipped away.

"Good flour is the important part. Get the right flour and the bread follows. It's not magic, it's nature." I could hear her voice, I found it difficult to see her clearly. I knew she was standing opposite me, her hands sticky with dough. I closed my eyes. I didn't want to be back here. Although it was warm, the fire was burning brightly. I could see one batch proving in the hearth.

"What's the matter girl, got a bad head? You need to get

to bed early, too much staying up reading. Does your eyes no good." I could feel myself swaying. I tried to keep my balance. It was important that I didn't give in to this. The room was so hot the smell of the dough was overpowering. I heard the scrape of a chair then felt it under me.

A voice said, "Sit down. You look faint." She faded and I was back with Dad. He had a cup of tea in his hand.

"Here, drink this. You must be exhausted from travelling." I nodded while taking the cup. It felt solid and the tea was hot.

"You had me worried there for a moment. You looked so faint. You're not ill, are you? You would tell me?"

"No Dad I'm not ill but I did feel strange. I've been here before; I know I have."

"Yes, you have, but I thought you were too young to remember. The place was different. The improvements hadn't been done and your mum wouldn't stay. Said it was archaic, not fit for a baby. Tommy loved it. There was plenty for him to explore, but of course, he got muddy. Your mum didn't like that either. She always said my mum disapproved of her and made her feel uncomfortable." His voice trailed off, "I don't want to start slagging your mum off."

"No, will you show me the rest of the house?"

"Of course. Finish your tea. You can see your bedroom first. I hope you like it. There used to be four bedrooms, but one is now a bathroom. You'll not believe this. They used to have a bath in front of the fire on a Friday night. It was like that when I was little. My mum used to get the old tin bath from the outhouse and fill it up for me. I loved it. I had a little wooden boat."

He sat looking towards the fireplace, lost in memories. I

remembered having a strip wash in the cold room upstairs, trying to get rid of the smell of dung. He stood up.

"You know I can remember my gran making bread at this table. The thought came into my head when you were feeling faint. I could almost smell it. She would knead and bash it into shape then --"

"Put it by the fire to prove," I finished. He looked at me in a strange way.

"It's as if you were there too, watching her. You used to have little turns when you were small. You'd go almost into a trance, then say things that had happened before you were born. You used to spook your mum. I said that you'd heard us talking and repeated it." He shook his head. "Now it seems you're doing it again."

I put my cup down. "Coincidence, come on show me upstairs."

It was the same bedroom with a bigger window. The old wardrobe had gone and there were fitted cupboards along the wall. A large, mirrored door made the room look much bigger and the bed had a comfy looking duvet and matching pillows. A dressing table was by the window and an upholstered chair at the foot of the bed. Best of all, my feet sank into a pale carpet.

"It's lovely."

"Hope you'll be comfortable in here, change things round if you want to."

He put my case down beside the bed. "There are hangers in the cupboard." He opened the door to show me rails and drawers. On a shelf, there were pale pink fluffy towels. It felt as if he had made an effort for me. I turned around and hugged him.

"Thank you so much, it's all lovely."

He went downstairs while I unpacked. The room felt warm with the late afternoon sun, more than that, the room was welcoming. I was glad I had come here.

When had I first realised it was the farmhouse I'd experienced as a land girl? I'm not sure. I think when I smelt the bread and saw Mrs Jones. I wonder what she would think of her kitchen now. She would be pleased her table was still in use. A question suddenly exploded in my mind. My dad had been talking about his gran living here, was that Mrs Jones or had someone else lived in the farmhouse after the war?

Chapter 31

"Let me show you the extension, it's the bit I'm most proud of." I was downstairs, questions were rattling around my brain.

I'd found the bathroom upstairs. It looked great. There was a deep bath and a separate walk-in shower. The toilet was out of view in an alcove. It looked like no expense had been spared.

"The bathroom looks great Dad. I like the separate shower."

There is a shower and toilet down here, you get to it from the opening to the old pantry." He opened the door. The old shelves had been varnished and were full of towels, shower gel and cleaning stuff. On one side was another door, which led to a shower and toilet.

"No more dashing outside in the rain then," I said.

He gave me a questioning look. "No, but how do you know about that?"

"You mentioned having to dash when you needed to go, so I guessed the old one must have been outside." This seemed to satisfy him.

He took me to the other side of the kitchen and down

the hall. I vaguely remembered a small dark sitting room. I'd never been allowed in there.

"Only for funerals or weddings, or such like," Mrs Jones had told me. The curtains were always drawn so that the furniture didn't spoil with the sun. I wondered if Mr Jones had been brought back here when he died before his journey to the chapel. I didn't wonder for long. Dad opened the door and the light flooded in. The old, dark room was gone. A beautiful glass and wooden extension covered the whole area. It took my breath away.

"It's amazing." It was big but not grossly so. The armchairs were modern and looked comfortable, but I remembered the table and dining chairs and the old, fancy sideboard. The ancient dresser was full of blue plates and other oddments of pottery.

"I must admit I'm proud of this. The old furniture was my gran's and some of it older. When my mum, your grannie died, I found she had insurance and savings. I had this done with some of the money. She would have loved it."

"Anyone would. I'm so sorry Grannie died, I wish I had seen her again."

He looked unhappy for a minute. "She was always sad she couldn't see you. Still, you have the memories of when you were young and know she loved you. She would have been so proud of you." He cleared his throat and gave a half smile.

"Come on, you must be hungry. I have a beef casserole in the oven."

I slept well that night, but my dreams were of my time in the forties. Of the cows and Paul, cheese making and strip washes. I was so glad to wake in the bright bedroom, knowing there was a bathroom close by. After breakfast, Dad was keen to show me the camping area.

He was proud of all he had done. The old cowshed had been converted into holiday accommodation. I hardly recognised it. The barn was an area for wet weather. A boon for people in small tents where they could shelter and leave their wet things to dry. "A necessity in Wales," Dad said.

What the Jones' would have made of it I couldn't imagine. At one end, there were two large washing machines and dryers next to a deep sink. I recognised the sink I had washed out the milk churns in it. Now campers used it.

"Where are all these campers then Dad?"

"Over in the field. We can go there next." As we walked down the gravelled drive, he pointed out the building I'd noticed from the car.

"That's the shower and toilet block. Look over there." There were tents of all shapes and sizes spaced out in a circle around a children's playground. In the next field, there were more coloured canvas shapes.

"This one's for families and the further one is for people who like it quieter." He seemed to have a good system and plenty of campers.

"People come back year after year. Once the seasons are over I'm getting hard standing, and electricity put on in that area." He pointed to the other side. "People with caravans seem to prefer that and will pay for it too."

I felt proud of my dad. He had built up a business here that seemed to be flourishing.

On our way back to the house, we passed the old pig pens and I heard a snuffling.

"That doesn't sound like goats to me."

"Take a look." So I did. There was a large, very large sow with about eight piglets. "People like the piglets and I have a market for them when they are grown. The goats are over by the small barn."

We walked on and I saw several goats munching grass. "I keep them tethered when campers are around, I don't want any children being hurt."

"Hurt?"

"They have a nasty habit of appearing friendly then butting. This way, the children can see them and the piglets but not get too close. Then everyone is happy."

"Who milks them?"

"I do. I could do with some help though. Not many people are able or want to milk these days."

"I'll have a go. I'd like to." He smiled at me. I could tell he wasn't sure. I hoped I'd be able to surprise him. I was pleased that the farm still had some animals. It felt right.

He opened the door to the small barn. The far end was glazed, very different to the ramshackle building I remembered. We walked along the flagstone floor to where a woman was working. The area was spotless.

"This is Sheila, she makes the yogurt and cheese and pasteurises the milk."

The set up was impressive. Sheila was in a white coat with white boots on her feet.

"Hi. Your dad has been so excited about your visit. He wanted everything to be perfect for you. He sent me to get new towels and bath stuff last week. Hope you like pink."

"Thanks, I do."

"I'll leave you with Sheila, she can show you how everything is done here. I have some accounts to do. I'll see you at lunchtime." He went out saying, "it will give you time to get to know each other."

"Do you work for Dad full-time?" I asked her.

"No three days a week. I love this work."

"What do you do the rest of the time?"

"I have two boys who take up most of my time." I wanted to ask so many questions. How close to my dad was she?

"I can see you've questions to ask, but shall I show you what I do here, before we start on any personal stuff." I nodded, so there was personal stuff then.

For the next hour or so she explained to me about the yogurt and cheese making. I was impressed with all the stainless equipment and the level of hygiene.

"It must be right as we get inspected, so the products can be sold. Frozen yogurt goes down well with the campers too; your dad wants to expand."

She put some of the yogurt in a sample dish for me to try. It tasted good.

"Mustn't spoil your lunch, Will is a stickler for time, we'd better go up to the house." She walked to the other end of the room and took off her white coat and boots. So, she was coming for lunch too. I tried not to make anything of it. It made sense to eat here rather than go to the village.

When we got back to the house Sheila went to the fridge and got out salad stuff, which she put in a large bowl and mixed with a dressing that was already in a jug. I could smell something good cooking in the Aga.

"The plates are over there," she pointed to the dresser, as she fetched cutlery from the drawer in the table. Dad reappeared and took two pizzas from the oven. I put the plates and glasses on the table and filled a jug with water. Sheila took the jug from me, saying the water was already in the fridge cooling.

We sat down. Dad cut the pizza into portions. I felt uncomfortable. Sheila was very much at home here. I was the stranger.

"Well, did you tell her?"

"About the products? Yes."

"About us?" So, there was an us.

"No, I thought that's for you to do."

I looked from Dad to Sheila. What did they need to tell me?

"Who is going to tell me then?"

Dad cleared his throat. "There's not a lot to tell really." I saw Sheila's eyebrows rise. She frowned.

"Looks like Sheila thinks there is Dad."

"Sheila and I are partners, she has her own house in the village, because she has two boys. We have no intention of getting married but we're together." Dad looked embarrassed.

"Your dad and I, we get on really well together, but my husband was a soldier and if we make the arrangement formal, I lose his pension and I need it for my boys."

"Was your husband the boys' father?" As I said it, I thought that sounds crass, but I was wondering. I couldn't help it.

"Yes, they're not your dad's if that's what you're thinking?"

"I'm sorry. I shouldn't have said that." I was pushing salad around my plate, my appetite disappearing by the moment.

"It's our fault we told you in a clumsy way. I work for

your dad and we've been good friends for years. We gradually became closer. I need to be careful because of the boys, but we didn't want to keep it from you. It shouldn't have been difficult to say, but somehow it was." Dad reached over and put his hand over hers.

Despite myself, I smiled at them. They were entitled to their life, and I'd be a miserable bitch if I'd wanted him to stay single all his life. Mum certainly hadn't.

"I'm happy for you. It's just a lot to take in."

"That's alright then. I should have said something last night."

"Dad, it's okay." I was glad I didn't have to meet two little half-brothers. Now that would have been hard. We finished the pizza and had frozen strawberry yoghurt for pudding. Dad announced I was going to help with the milking.

"That's good," said Sheila. "That's one thing I hate doing."

Later I could understand why she didn't like it. The goats were very different to placid cows, but Dad showed me how to tie them up and I persevered and to his surprise, I milked them. Sheila was impressed. She took the milk from me saying she would put it in the pasteuriser, so that it would be ready to work with in the morning. I was surprised she pasteurised the milk. I asked her why, knowing the prebiotic bacteria would be killed off, as well as the ones that spoil the milk. She explained that it was safer to pasteurise when the milk wasn't used straight away. Sometimes campers came for the morning milk, which was fresh and unpasteurised. Many people prefer it that way.

She asked me how I knew how to milk, and I said that I'd spent some time on a farm years ago. Some people from the camping field came along wanting to buy yogurt so she didn't ask me any more questions. I went back to have a shower and to rid myself of the smell of goats.

Once in the shower I started to think about how different my life could have been if I'd lived with Dad. I thought of all those times going to school in badly fitting clothes, being hungry, going to the shop to get alcohol for Mum. If it hadn't been for my form tutor who had encouraged me, lent me the books we were supposed to buy. Told me often I was clever enough, I don't know where I would be now. I suppose she had taken the place of my grannie.

Grannie had been important to me, told me stories, she'd believed in me. I thought my heart was going to break when Mum told me she had died. For years in the summer, Grannie had taken me on holiday to the seaside. Then she became too ill to travel. I'd wanted to go to see her, but Mum said it was too far. I'd written to Dad asking him to fetch me to see her but got no reply.

"Your dad will be too busy," Mum had always said.

I thought of the photos I'd brought with me. I needed to ask Dad about them.

Why had he always been too busy for me? It was really bugging me. He'd made a success of his life. Had he ever thought about me? I mean really thought. Not a glancing *'I wonder how Imogen is?'* When I was struggling to look after my mum, barely coping, did he think of me?

I felt as if I needed to get away, much as I loved it. Oh, I did love it here. I'd been so happy here in that other life. Contented, Paul had shown me how to care for the animals. Mrs Jones had taught me so much. That had all gone, I wasn't sure if it had been real. It had felt real, but how could it have happened? I was here now in the present, with my dad. Why hadn't he sent for me?

I couldn't confront him. I hardly knew him. I couldn't lose him now. I decided to just be grateful for being here, finding him at last. I pushed those niggling thoughts away. I decided to go downstairs, have a cup of tea and calm down. I was good at keeping calm, I'd learnt from an early age.

I walked into the kitchen; Molly was dozing in her basket. She opened her eyes, decided I didn't have any treats and settled down again. Dad was by the sink chopping vegetables.

"Let me help."

"Thanks. Are you okay? I thought you were a little upset earlier."

"I'm fine."

"Sure?"

"Yes, pass me those carrots."

"I'll do the meat then." He moved across to the other draining board and took another knife from the block. Carrots sliced, I reached for the swede.

"You need to peel that first."

"Really. I know I'm a townie, but I have chopped veg before."

"Sorry, just needed to say. The skin is too tough."

"Yes, you need to have tough skin in this family."

"What?"

"Nothing, just thinking out loud."

"Look Imo." He called me by my baby name.

"I'm not Imo. I'm Imogen, and not a baby now. I thought you would have noticed."

"Look. Of course, I know that. It's just that I always think of you as Imo."

"Do you Dad? Do you think of me?"

"Of course I do. How can you say that?"

"How can I say that? How can you ask? I should think I have every right to say. Why didn't you contact me once I was grown up? Why did it have to be me contacting you? Why do I have to be the adult with both my parents?" I hadn't realised how angry I was. I sniffed away the tears. I didn't want to be weak. Crying like Mum, I didn't want to be like her.

"Look... "

"Will you stop saying look. I'm tired of looking, seeing everything from someone else's point of view. Keeping my mouth shut, not upsetting anyone."

"It's not been easy for me, you know."

I looked around me, taking in all the alterations, the expensive kitchen equipment.

"Obviously not."

"I've always sent money for you."

"The local off licence has enjoyed that. I'm sure they will thank you." I wiped my nose on my sleeve.

"Please put that knife down, it feels as if it's my head you're chopping up."

I slammed the knife down, scattering carrots and onion. I watched the blood slowly dripping onto the chopping board from my finger. I'd cut it, not badly though, it was difficult to see clearly through tears.

Molly sensing something was wrong came over. Dad washed his hands and patted her head. He gave her some of the fatty bits he'd cut from the meat and washed his hands again.

"We need to talk properly. I'm not surprised that you're unhappy."

I didn't want him to patronise me. "It's too late. I'm grown now, but I wish you had been there for me when I was little. I'm sorry. I didn't mean to get upset."

"Let's put this in the oven and sit down and talk. There has been so much time lost."

Chapter 32

Once we were seated, Dad said I sounded hurt and angry.

"Will you talk to me about how you feel?"

"I don't know how I feel. I feel mixed up. It still seems as if there is a great big hole where Tommy should be and it seems wrong, it was all so long ago."

"How can it be wrong; you lost your brother? You hero-worshipped him. You followed him around. We used to say you were his little shadow."

"Yes, and if I hadn't followed him, he would still be here."

"Why do you say that?" Dad sounded shocked.

"Because he was looking at me, not at the ball. It was my fault Tommy died and then you were lost too."

"Oh no. Have you always thought that?" I nodded, not able to speak.

"Come here." He put his arm around me. "It was never your fault. Never. I should have been looking after you better. Oh, my poor Imo. It wasn't your fault."

"But you went away, you couldn't bear to be with us. I thought, I've always thought every time you looked at me you thought of Tommy, and it was too painful."

"I felt guilty. I thought you would be better off without your mum and me rowing all the time."

"Why didn't you take me with you?"

"I did try but the courts decided a little girl was better with her mum."

"Mum said you had someone called Megan and you wanted a new life. That I'd get in the way."

"I did have a girlfriend called Megan for a while, but it didn't last long I was in too much of a mess. I'd lost you and Tommy."

"I remember being with you and Grannie, then that stopped too." We sat quietly for a few minutes, his arm tightly around me.

"Yes, your mum said you got so upset and didn't want you to come back like that anymore. She said you cried and couldn't sleep when you got back home with her. We tried to do what was best, but it seems now, we made a mess of it."

"Why didn't you send me birthday cards if you cared about me?"

He looked shocked, "I did, I did, every year. Oh, I should have checked."

He put his head in his hand. "I can't tell you how sorry I am. I am so glad to have you here now. I know I can't make it up to you. What an idiot I've been."

We sat until it was dark, talking. I was glad I'd found him, and it was true it hadn't been easy for him. He could have been more forceful, but Mum had convinced him that it was best for me to be with her. I'm not sure why. I'd often felt I was a hindrance to her.

It seems that adults play games with children's lives. As

Dad pointed out, Mum was a victim of what had happened too. She never was the same after Tommy's death.

"Dad, I found some photos of you and Grannie, that's how I found your address."

"Yes, I used to send photos when I wrote to you, so you did get some letters then?"

"No, I didn't but I found these photos when I was looking through Mum's stuff. Can I show them to you?" I went upstairs and fetched them. When I came down, he had a pile of photos on the table. I handed mine to him.

"Look, these are the ones I found. I thought some of them had been taken here."

"Yes, you're right. Look, that's your gran and me, and there's my gran, she looks stern. She never smiled in a photo." He looked through the photos.

"These are when I was in my London flat. Your grannie came to visit me and looked after you while I was working. Look, this one, you're sitting on her knee. It was soon after that she persuaded me to come back here. I wasn't happy I'd finished with Megan. Or rather, she'd had enough of me, and I hated my job."

"What did you do down here?"

"Well, there were the pigs and a couple of cows, the hay needed cutting. Everything had been neglected. It took me the summer to get things straight. Grannie knew people through being the district nurse and there were several who were glad of someone that could do their books for them. Help them with their tax returns. The farm work helped. Healed me."

"Did you have the idea for campers?"

"Yes, I had help converting the old buildings, Grannie was

really encouraging. It was her idea to get the goats too. She insisted on helping me financially. I couldn't have done it without her."

I reached out and held his hand. "You still miss her."

"Yes, I do. Everyone loved her. She would have been so proud of you. You remind me of her. There is something about the way you bend your head when you listen. You have a look of her too. I'm not explaining it very well."

"I'm pleased you think I'm like her. Do you ever wonder about your dad, what he was like?" Dad got up and went over to his pile of pictures.

"My mum talked about my dad; she never was interested in anyone else. She said he was gentle and kind." He handed me a creased black and white photo.

"This is their wedding day; it was in the middle of the war. He got sent away to Africa after that and didn't make it back."

Paul and Margaret looked at me from the old print. I knew. I did know, but to see the photo of them smiling, as if they had their whole lives to live. I seemed to have forgotten how to breathe. I could hear Paul's voice, his gentle Welsh voice.

"Come on, you can do it," but I couldn't. The room swam. In my ears, their voices were coming and going. Paul was my grandfather, and Margaret, dear, kind Margaret was my grandmother. It seemed my jumping through time had allowed me to see them as real people. I opened my eyes and saw Dad's worried face.

"Paul and Margaret," I whispered.

"Yes, I wish I'd known him."

'You look like him."

"Do you think so? I'm glad. Mum used to say that I was like him. You look faint again. Sit down there and I will dish up the dinner. I think we should get the doctor to examine you. It concerns me."

I assured him that I was well and didn't need a doctor. I couldn't tell him why it was such a shock to see the photo. He would have been concerned if I had. The casserole was delicious.

"The Aga works magic," he said.

It took me a long time to get to sleep that night. Once I allowed myself to work it out, it all made sense. Margaret had come here because the farm belonged to Paul's family and once here, she wanted her son to have his inheritance. From what Dad remembered, she'd liked it and wanted to be where Paul had lived. It seemed she fitted in and the village needed a nurse. The thing I didn't understand, if Paul were my grandfather, surely our name would be Jones too., Something didn't add up. I was wide awake at five o'clock, the question still going round my brain.

I went down to make myself a cup of tea and take some paracetamol for my headache. Dad was up. I bombarded him with questions.

"Hang on, let's sit down with our tea and see if I can answer you." We sat together on the comfy sofa, with the dog at our feet.

"I asked the question myself when I was old enough to realise. Apparently, when my dad signed up, he found the adoption papers had not changed his name to Jones. He was registered as Hadley-Phillips so when they married that was his official name." He turned to me.

"Did I tell you that he was adopted by the Jones' when he was a baby?"

I nodded, he hadn't, but of course I knew. I knew the whole, sorry story.

"He tried to find out about his birth family, but it was war time and his mother had died. No one wanted to know about him so he and my mum decided, after the war they would change the name officially. He owed the Phillips nothing and didn't want their name." He got up and refilled his cup.

"Of course he didn't live to do that. Mum said she and Dad had talked about children and Dad had said that if they had a boy, he wanted him to be called William after Grandfather Jones. That's what she did and dropped the Phillips part of the surname. So that's how I am William Hadley, Will to my friends of course."

"Why didn't she change it to Jones?"

"Well from what I gather the Jones weren't too friendly to her for a start. They thought my dad was going to marry a local girl and Mum had tricked him."

Gladys, I thought. She was the one who'd wanted marriage.

"After Dad was lost in action, Mum wrote to them saying she wanted them to see me."

"And that did the trick?" I said. "Gladys wouldn't have had a chance."

"Gladys?"

Whoops I shouldn't have said that. "Aren't all Welsh girls called Gladys?"

"That's a coincidence, she was called Gladys, but apparently Grandfather liked Mum as soon as he saw her and of course, she had called me after him. He was ill by then and

Mum helped around the farm while Granny Jones looked after me. So, it all worked out well. They left the farm to Mum and me. The rest I think you know."

"I think I do." More than I can let you know I thought.

The next few days went by quickly. There were so many jobs to do around the farm, including a field full of ripening strawberries. It was back breaking work to pick them but rewarding to see the full punnets of fruit. Dad's farm shop was very popular with both the campers and local people. It was good to see how enterprising he was.

On the way to the station, he asked me to consider coming back to work with him.

"We'd make a good team," he said. I pointed out he had Sheila, and another person could make things run less smoothly.

"I think we could all work well. Please give it some serious thought."

I thought he was trying to make up for the time we had lost, but he said I was a natural on the farm and we could make a good life.

I was very tempted, despite the stress of the first few days I had relaxed and enjoyed my stay. I enjoyed being with him and liked Sheila. I was glowing with the feeling of being wanted. I told him, I still wanted to do my master's, but would like to come and work with him in the vacations.

I found it hard to say goodbye when my train arrived.

Chapter 33

The journey gave me time to sort out some of my jumbled thoughts. It was strange to think that Paul and Margaret were my grandparents. Strange but nice, it gave me a warm feeling. I'd not known my mother's parents, they had both died young, he in the war and she when my mother was in her teens. Mum had never answered my questions about them. Consequently, I'd always felt I had no history. Now I knew, at least on Dad's side where I came from. I wondered if Margaret had pandered to Dad. He was an only child, with only her to answer to. That would explain him not standing up to Mum and taking the easy way out. It didn't seem to me he'd tried very hard to keep in touch. I started to feel unhappy again but told myself he intended to make up for his absence now. I found it hard not to feel resentful. I kept thinking of all those years when he could have made my life easier. He said he intended to keep me close now I'd found him again. I needed to believe him.

Mum was out when I arrived home, but she had left a salad and quiche in the fridge for me. She probably didn't want to hear about my newfound relationship with Dad. I could understand that. I spent a couple of days with her.

We skirted around each other, being polite. For the next few weeks, I worked as many hours as possible, so we saw little of each other. It was a relief to get back to university. My friend Sarah had said that I could stay on her sofa until I had sorted out a new place.

I had an appointment to see Dr Sutton, my old tutor to discuss my options. I was glad. I was no longer so sure what I wanted to do. I found myself wondering if I was still the same person who had decided to carry on in education earlier in the year. I'd said several times, "I'm going to do a master's," but felt as if I'd lived several lifetimes since then.

Sarah was pleased to see me. We chatted for hours. She and George were doing four-year degrees and would soon start their final year. She told me that Harry was going to do a PhD and so was Lizzie. It made me realise that I'd not been in touch with anyone since graduation. Because I'd been with Mum, I'd not joined my friends in the usual partying. In fact, I'd hardly spoken to anyone since that night I'd come home from the pub.

Over a glass or two of wine Sarah told me, at the end of term, they'd all been concerned about me. They knew I'd had work to finish, so they'd put my disappearance down to my determination to get a good grade.

"Which you did. Well done you, egghead. So glad you're back. You have some serious partying to catch up on." I grinned at her. I was glad of some light-hearted banter. I was a bit tired of soul searching and I'd certainly had my fill of physical work recently.

I had a sore head the next day and was glad my appointment was in the afternoon. Dr Sutton welcomed me into her office. We sat on easy chairs, chatting about my results and my options. She said there was an opportunity to do a master's in medical physics.

"I know you expressed an interest in psychology earlier in the year but given your results I think this would suit you. You could do your practical work at the hospital, with payment for the hours you spend there. Of course, it could also lead to a permanent position. The hospital's keen to work closer with the university."

I wasn't sure I wanted to do medical physics. I knew it was an interesting field with many opportunities and I could further my studies while being paid for working in the hospital. Dr Sutton handed me some papers.

"Read through these and come back and see me at the end of the week, you don't have to decide now."

I read the papers the next day. The research proposal looked interesting; I liked the idea of doing something which could improve people's lives. I kept thinking of Wales and being closer to Dad. I talked it through with Sarah the following day, I told her about the position in the hospital.

"It sounds great, and you'd be paid. What's stopping you from jumping at it?"

"Well in the vac I went to Wales and found my Dad."

"And?"

"He runs this holiday farm and has goats, and makes yogurt. It seems like a good way to live. It was so good to find him. I could live there. Help him build the business."

"Imogen, what are you thinking? You're clever. You'd be bored stiff after a few months. How does making yogurt compare with medical research?"

"It's not the yogurt, it's being with my dad. I'd like to get to know him."

"You can visit, can't you?"

"Yes of course." I thought of him in the farmhouse and felt my eyes brimming with tears. I sniffed. "I'm sorry, Sarah, I can't stop thinking of all those years when I didn't know him. He'd sent me letters and cards; Mum had kept them back. She said it was to stop me getting upset."

"Oh Imogen, I'm so sorry." Sarah put her arms around me and gave me the biggest hug. "I know you've always struggled with your mum, but you say she's dry now."

I blew my nose again, "She is, it's funny, she's quite boring. Sometimes she could be amazing when she was drinking."

"Yes, I remember our first year, when she turned up and took us all out to the pub. She got so drunk; she made a pass at George."

"Yea, didn't realise he was gay, let alone half her age. I can laugh now. I could have died at the time. I thought none of you would ever speak to me again."

"In a weird way it made us closer though. It feels like we're more family than our blood relations." We hugged again. "You don't have to live with your dad to keep in touch. You've found him now."

"You're right. He has a partner too. He has his own life."

"You can be part of it too."

By Friday I had made up my mind, I would do the medical research. I knocked on Dr Sutton's door feeling a little nervous. She told me she'd arranged for me to visit the hospital.

"I was hoping for a positive answer from you. I thought you could look around the department where you'll be doing the practical work." She gave me a number to ring to organise the details.

"One of the medics will show you round. I thought after our chat, it would be good for you to spend some time there, so you can be sure it's what you want. You can think about how you will plan your first term. Obviously, you'll need to be back here in the library too."

"Thank you."

"Are you excited?"

"I am, but a bit nervous now."

"Hopefully they will put you at ease. Just concentrate on finding your way around. We are not expecting solutions in the first year. You will be an asset to the team."

I left; my doubts forgotten. Sarah was right, making yogurt didn't compare to this. I would find myself somewhere to live then call the number Dr Sutton had given me. I felt more confident than I had for weeks.

Sarah and I trawled around the letting agents. We were shown some awful places. In desperation, I called the people that had rented me my previous flat. It was still empty; the rent had increased but so had the rent on all the properties. Sarah couldn't understand my reluctance to go back there.

"It's a nice room in a secure building, close to the hospital and university. Why are you not biting their hand off considering the others that we've seen?"

I couldn't tell her. I muttered something about a weird neighbour.

"How weird?"

I wondered briefly what she would have said if I'd told her one from another century, who'd had me walking through walls. I realised that I was being too sensitive and eventually agreed to renew the lease. As it was empty, they said I could move in without waiting. They had my details on record and Dad had kept his word. There was money to cover the deposit in my bank.

I moved my stuff from Sarah's the following week. I told myself I was silly to feel apprehensive. I'd had no funny turns; I'd stayed in my own time zone since the summer. I was back living my own life. I was due to go to the hospital the next day. I was to ask for Daniel Markham, a houseman in the cardiac unit. He was going to show me around.

I sat reading through some of the papers that Dr Sutton had recommended. They were quite hard going, so it was a relief to see Grannie's old sweetie tin on the table. I didn't remember unpacking it. In fact, I thought it was lost. A sweet was just what I needed. I reached over to the barrel shaped tin. It was cold. Opening with a click, it released the aroma of old-fashioned sweets. My mouth watered with expectation. It had always been a box of hidden delights. I looked in, remembering the sweet bitterness of lemon drops on my tongue. It was empty. I was sure I'd filled it. I had. Those lemon drops had kept me going last term when I was writing and revising. I always refilled the tin before it was half empty. George had teased me saying that I was as addicted to my sweets as he was to tobacco. I'd left boxes of my stuff with Sarah. Perhaps she'd emptied it. Why was I bothering about a few sweets? She was a good friend. I felt uncomfortable, if she'd left things with me would I have looked through them and taken her sweets? I got up and made myself a coffee, my milk was low. I would need more for the morning. I could get some lemon drops and chocolate biscuits too. I hadn't bothered to cook anything. I was too tired after sorting the flat and making up my bed. The fresh air had revived me and the man in the shop asked me how I was? He said it was good to see me as he reached over and got the lemon drops off the shelf without me asking.

Back in the flat, I opened the tin again ready to pour in the sweets. I noticed torn bits of paper in the bottom. When I looked, I saw it was part of a note. Puzzled, I read it.

'So confused. Sorry it doesn't seem right. Can't do this.' I looked at it for a while, wondering what it meant. My stomach grumbled, reminding me that I hadn't eaten. It wasn't for me, it could be anyone, perhaps I'd left the tin in the flat and someone else had used it. Yes, that must be why I didn't remember unpacking it. Why did I feel so uncomfortable? It was how I'd felt when I had my school reports. Mum had stuffed them into the empty tin without talking to me about them. Then later when she was asleep in the chair, I'd get them out to see what had been written. They usually said things like.

'Imogen is a quiet child, and seems sad at times. She needs to join in class activities.' At senior school, I was good at maths and science, often called swot and nerd. Once here at university I found others like me and made real friends for the first time. I had brought Grannie's tin with me and used it for its original purpose. I needed to stop thinking about the past and those stupid bits of paper. Tomorrow I would be in the hospital starting my next step. I made another coffee and ate chocolate biscuits, then curled up under my duvet.

My alarm was shrill. Time to get up. I couldn't believe I'd slept so well.

Chapter 34

I spent the morning with a pleasant woman in the hospital. I filled in forms while she sorted out my identity card. The picture she took of me was not flattering, but better than my student ID. I had a chest x-ray. 'Routine,' I was told. Finally, she called Dr Markham. He suggested that we had some lunch before he took me to Cardiology. I was gasping for a coffee. We walked to the staff canteen.

"Very basic but okay," he said. We chatted over jacket potatoes and coffee. He told me he was pleased to do this with me.

"Gives me time to breathe, we are the lowest in the medical chain. At everybody's beck and call, night and day. Normally my beeper goes off as soon as I sit down." Just to prove it, a beep started. He switched it off.

"I don't have to answer it until five p.m. That gives us plenty of time to show you round." He gulped his coffee down. I tried to keep up with him. He was experienced at this.

"Helps to have a tin oesophagus," he said.

I picked mine up, "I can finish it as we walk."

"Not allowed. Health and Safety, drink it now. I can tell you a bit about the work we are doing while you drink." It sounded fascinating, but I was having difficulty taking it all in. I drained my mug as soon as the coffee was cool enough.

He had so much energy. I'd been fine with walking down the stairs, but he climbed up with the same speed that he'd downed his drink.

"You'll soon get fit working in this old building. Being in Cardiology encourages us to do the stairs, we don't want to end up like some of our patients."

Once in the ward we passed several people walking slowly, hooked up to drip stands. Dr Markham introduced me to the nurse in charge of the ward, telling me that she was the most important person, and I was to keep on her good side.

She looked at me. "You'd better believe it." Although she smiled, I knew it was true.

Finally, we went down the long corridor, past the day room. I glanced through doors to the sluice and rooms containing equipment.

"This is the one." He knocked, then opened the door. A man in a white coat was sitting in front of a screen. The lighting in the room was very dim. I saw a narrow bed and several other screens. Wires and electrodes were attached to a control board.

"This is Gareth. He understands all the technical stuff and will explain things to you while I just go and check on my patients."

Gareth held out his hand to me. "So pleased to have you on board. Has Dan explained what we would like you to be involved with?" I said he'd made a start. He'd explained why the equipment was important and what the medical team wanted.

"We believe that we have the equipment that can predict someone's tendency for heart failure. We don't have enough data and the machine needs fine-tuning. With the budget, we can't afford to send everyone for further tests. Basically, we can't afford false positives."

"Would that matter? It sounds like it could save lives."

"Only the seriously ill can be treated."

"So it's about money then?"

"Unfortunately, it always is, but if we can fine tune so people who are at minor risk can be identified, they can change their lifestyle to prevent heart attacks."

"At minimum cost."

"You've got it."

A knock on the door. Dan returned with a patient. I watched as she was wired up to the machine. Dan reassured her as she laid back on the bed and the lights on the screen started to flash. After a while, she was allowed to sit up and the printer chugged into life. I watched the trace. Nice smooth curves then a spike. The curve pattern was repeated, but the spike wasn't consistent. Dan wheeled the woman out.

"That's what we are looking for. That spike is telling us all is not well," said Gareth.

Chapter 35

I came away with so many ideas. I loved the thought that I could do some research that would help people. Gareth had so much raw data that needed sorting out. I would have to spend more time with him to understand what was required. Already, I was thinking of ways the algorithm could be improved to be more precise.

I spent time with Dan during the next two weeks following him round, listening to his patients. The consultant, Mr Fredricks, introduced himself to me, he seemed very pleasant, but posh. Dan said he was scary to work for, but the patients adored him. I decided to give him as wide a berth as possible.

Dan and I got on well. We laughed at the same things, and I found him very attractive.

He asked me if I'd like to go to the pub at the end of the second week, warning me, although he was off duty he could never guarantee he wouldn't be called back.

It was a casual invitation, but I felt accepted. I was increasingly glad that I wasn't doing a medical degree. Dan worked such long hours. I could see why Gareth chose the technical side.

On Friday night I put on my best jeans and a sexier tee and

walked to the pub. Dan was waiting by the door. "Come and meet the others," he said.

They were sitting around a table in a corner looking as if they were arguing. I hung back feeling out of it, but they looked up as we approached. Dan introduced me and they told me their names. I had seen one of the girls on the ward.

"Hi," she said. "You're a physicist, aren't you? Just the person. We're discussing Schrodinger's cat. Do you believe that you can be in two places at the same time?"

Wow, that was an introduction. Dan told them to let me have a drink first.

He went to the bar and the subject moved rapidly to out of body experiences. I kept quiet, listened. Two of the girls were arguing that it was possible to go back in time. You just had to find the portal and take the risk.

"Most people can't see, or if they do they ignore it and say they've had a funny five minutes." The girl with short blonde hair was getting really excited now. Dan came back with two pints of beer.

"Don't take any notice of Jules, she's completely bonkers," he said.

"Oh Dan, you're too one dimensional," she replied. "Open your mind."

She looked across at me, "He's lovely but so straight. He won't allow, things happen that we can't explain." The other girl joined in, "What do you think?"

I couldn't deny it. It had happened to me, but I didn't want Dan to think I was mad. "My prof believed that time wasn't a straight line, he has written papers on it, from a mathematical angle of course."

Jules looked across at Dan. "There you are. It's not just us. Imogen you are so welcome you must come to our group; we meet on the last Wednesday of the month here."

Dan looked uncomfortable, but I was interested and thanked her saying I would come along when they next met.

He looked so sexy in his jeans and sweatshirt; I didn't want to do anything to put him off me. When he said, after our second pint he needed to go I was disappointed. He asked me if I wanted him to walk me back to my place, although I was reluctant to leave the friendly group I left with him. He took my hand when we got outside.

"Hope you don't mind," he said. It was so busy in there and I wanted to spend more time with you."

"So, you don't have to get back?"

"No. I wanted you to meet them, but I want to get to know you better too."

I wondered if he could hear my heart beating, it felt loud to me. He asked if I was hungry, he hadn't eaten all day. I didn't feel hungry, I didn't care where we went. There was an Indian restaurant around the corner. It was quiet in there and easy to hear each other. Dan was hungry. He ate most of what I'd ordered as well as his own. He asked me lots of questions and by the end of the evening we knew much more about each other.

The following week I took him along to meet George and the others. After that, we spent as much time as possible together. I had fallen for him in a big way.

One evening when Dan was on duty, I was having dinner with Sarah, and she asked me how I felt about him.

"Is this a serious thing?"

"I'm not sure how he feels, I think he cares about me, neither of us have talked about the future. It doesn't seem important. Today is so good, tomorrow doesn't matter," I said.

My work was going well, we had lots of new data and Gareth was pleased with the suggestions I'd made for improvements. The weeks went by without me slipping into another time or body. Life seemed stable.

I'd found the papers I'd mentioned to Jules and Megan and taken copies with me when I'd met them. They struggled with the maths, but I explained the theory to them, and they were excited to think that someone seriously believed in what they called time travel. They asked me if I could persuade the prof to talk to their group. I rang his secretary to see if I could make an appointment to talk to him. I must admit I was surprised when he agreed to see me.

I walked into his office and waited for him to look up.

"Oh," I said. "You're not Professor Sinclair."

"No, I'm not. He had to retire due to ill health. I'm Duncan Grice. I'm continuing his work, and I was intrigued by your request. Take a seat my dear."

I looked at him, I recognised his voice.

"James?"

"My name is not James, although that was one of the aliases I used. They sent me to guide you while you were travelling. The head of the Royal Society - not usually a feeling fellow - was concerned that you were lost in time, and he had inadvertently caused it."

"Hang on, I'm confused."

"Hardly surprising in the circumstances."

"So, you weren't the person who summoned me."

"No, he made a hash of things."

"But I thought."

"Yes, we had to make sure that you would trust me, so I looked like him."

"So that I would trust the person that had caused my problems?"

"Not necessarily the best decision. However, would you have trusted me if you hadn't thought you recognised me?"

He had a point. I had trusted him. I had no choice. "Can you reassure me that it won't happen again? My life is good now and I don't want to spoil things."

He nodded, "I understand. You should be able to stay in this time now that you are firmly back. It was a mistake. You travelled too far forward at first instead of coming back here. We then had to bring you back in small jumps so that you didn't overstep the time again."

He waved his hands in a dismissive way, as if it was of small importance to him.

As if I'd spoken aloud, he said, "It is a small thing, only important to you. Now I understand you'd like me to talk to some friends of yours. Tell me more about them. How much do you want me to say?"

I explained my dilemma. I couldn't say that I had travelled back in time but wanted to explore the possibilities.

"I believe I can do that for you."

"You won't make it." I stopped.

"Personal, no I will theorise and as you say, explore possibilities."

I thanked him. He asked if there was anything else he could do for me.

"Well, I could do with some advice. I'm not sure how much to tell my boyfriend. He doesn't believe at all, but I feel I'm keeping a large part of me from him. What should I do?"

"I deal in facts, not advice. You must do what seems right to you. Now," he waved his hand again. "I must get on. Sort out a time for me to come and talk to your friends with my secretary."

I walked out of the building feeling strange. My mind was buzzing. I had begun to think I'd dreamed up some of my experiences. How could they be real? Now meeting Professor Grice had put me back in that strange place.

"Imogen." I looked up it was George. "You walked straight past me. I know you have a new boyfriend but..."

"Oh, George I was deep in thought."

"I saw that."

"Sorry. Have you time for a coffee?"

We went to our favourite little coffee bar. Good coffee and delicious cakes.

"How are you, Imo? We've hardly seen you. Not been off on one of your journeys, have you?"

"Journeys." I felt myself go red.

"You must admit you do seem to be absent sometimes. Even when you are here."

"Oh George." He reached over and took my hand.

"It's okay you don't have to explain, so long as you are okay. Is Dan treating you well?"

I said he was, and everything was going well with my degree too.

"I'm glad, but don't forget your old friends are still here and care about you."

We agreed to meet up when we both had time. His final year was difficult, and he was studying hard. As I walked away, I realised I had missed seeing him. He was a good friend.

Chapter 36

Dan was in the habit of coming round to my place whenever he had any time. I felt I'd known him forever, but realised I knew very little about him. I asked him if he had always wanted to be a doctor.

"My grandfather was the village GP, well respected, but he fell in love with a land girl in the war. His wife couldn't have children and when she found the girl was pregnant, she took an overdose and died. They said it was misadventure, she'd taken a double dose of pills when sleepy. But everyone knew. He joined up and worked with the war-wounded." He frowned, fiddled with the sugar spoon, spilling grains over my untidy table.

"I've never discussed this with anyone before. It's a sort of family skeleton in the cupboard thing. Grandma was much younger than him. They married in Southampton away from the village. When my mother was in her teens he retired, and they moved back to Wales. She hated it, always thought people were talking about her. Which they most probably were."

"Where in Wales? My dad lives there. He runs a camping village. It used to be a farm."

I knew the answer before he spoke. His grandfather had

loved a land girl, then married her. He was Robert's grandson, had to be. That's who he reminded me of. When he made the usual remarks about a small world I thought. *'Yes, but you don't know how small.'*

He knew of my dad's place. He said some of the older villagers didn't like what Dad had done. Resented what they called hordes of outsiders coming to what had been a quiet place.

"It's the only thing that's kept the village alive if you ask me. The village shop survives, and we still have a post office. Your dad has made a good business out of what would have been a failing farm."

I was pleased to hear him make such positive comments about my dad, but my mind was reeling. Was I in love with him because he was so like Robert? The attraction had been instantaneous. It felt like I was with the person that I was meant to be with. Magnetic, powerful and yet a niggle was there now. I was struggling with such powerful memories. I had felt the same about Robert, although I'd known I was in a time shift where I shouldn't have been. I had never stopped thinking about him until I met Dan. This was too confusing.

My head ached; I was frightened I'd find myself without warning, in another dimension. I had that same sense of unreality as if I could slip slide into another space. The walls of the room started to waver; the edges wobbled. I could feel myself going. Dan seemed to be fading. I could see someone else calling my name. Was it James/ Duncan? He'd promised me it wouldn't happen again. I tried to speak but it was difficult. What was he saying? I couldn't hear. I felt a wave of nausea, then, he faded.

Dan was speaking to me. "Imo are you okay, you've gone

dreadfully pale. I don't believe you've heard a word I've said. You look quite spaced out." He took my hand and felt my wrist. "Your pulse is too fast. You drink too much coffee."

"Sorry Dan, I do feel a bit weird." He got up and hugged me. "It's wonderful that we have the village in common. It might explain why we were so attracted to each other. It's exciting to think we might have met when we were little."

Possibly, I should have said something, but I didn't. I just smiled like an idiot. How could I say I knew your grandfather?

Another month had gone by, this evening Professor Grice was coming to talk to our group. They had hired the upstairs room in the pub and had a list of questions they wanted to ask him. When I arrived, the room was almost full, I had volunteered to wait at the door to greet him and get him a drink. He was early. He looked younger in his casual clothes, quite handsome I thought. I showed him upstairs and fetched pints of beer for both of us. When I introduced him to the room, there was instantly silence.

His talk was interesting. I'd not heard him lecture before. He was an improvement on the old prof, who was so dry. When he asked for questions at the end, hands shot up. He didn't just answer questions but encouraged conversation.

The evening was a great success. Dan appeared before the end, and we walked home together.

"Your Professor is interesting, not dull like so many of the ones that taught us. It will give Jules and co. fuel for a few weeks," he said.

I told him that Professor Grice had only recently joined the department and that I felt lucky to have persuaded him to come and talk to us.

"Yes, you are. You have a way of getting people to do what you want. Look at me, completely under your spell." I felt a bit uncomfortable when he said that, but he wouldn't say any more. Instead, he started to ask me about whether I believed in time travel and how did I think it worked. The evening's arguments had impressed him.

He interrupted my serious answers by kissing me, and saying he just wanted to travel to the bedroom with me.

Dan asked me if I could take a few days off at the end of the month when he had a break. He thought we could go to Wales together and see our families. I said I'd ask Gareth, but I knew it wouldn't be a problem.

When I met Sarah, I told her.

"We are going to Wales at the end of the month."

"Together?"

"Yes, it was his idea. He thought we could visit our families, as you know my dad and his parents are from the same village." I could feel my face burning.

"Sounds serious, Imogen. He wants you to meet his parents."

"I know, should I be excited or scared?"

"Silly, they'll love you, can't do anything else. Do we need to shop?"

I laughed, "I suppose I could do with a dress; I've only got jeans."

"Right, what day are you free to go shopping?"

After she'd gone, my mind was racing, I wished it was only a dress I needed to worry about. I had to talk to Dan, I must tell him about the past, not only the past. My period was late. Might be, because I was worrying, but I could be pregnant.

I'd wanted to talk to Sarah about it. The words had stuck in my throat, and she had been so excited about Dan wanting me to meet his parents. Next time Dan came round, I must tell him.

We were lying there on the bed, limbs untangled now. I felt relaxed. I was sure he would understand, and it was important that he knew. I'd argued with myself so many times that he didn't need to know. But now this relationship was serious, he had the right to know, didn't he? How could I have something so big in my life and not tell him? I wished that I had someone to help me decide.

Then I told him. Tried to, said it was meant to be we'd met in another lifetime, in other bodies. I saw his face change from love to horror. He opened his mouth, but no sound came out. I tried to make it okay. Explain.

"I need to explain." He stopped me, covered my mouth gently with his hand.

"Don't. Don't tell me anymore."

"But I must."

"No." He got up quickly, found his clothes on the floor. Pulled on his trousers. "It's too much."

"When will you be back?" No answer. He was at the door before I blurted out, "I may be pregnant." He didn't stop.

The door closed. It felt worse that he shut it carefully. A slam would show passion, but this felt cold. Dead. I've killed something wonderful. I wanted to scream, shout, cry. I tried to do the right thing and it's all gone wrong. I went over and over what happened when I was in Sally's body with Robert, his grandfather. But a little voice reminds me, it was your mind, your passion. We loved each other so completely and finding Dan it appeared everything was falling into place. We had travelled through time and found each other. Why couldn't he see it? All the anguish I had suffered before was nothing compared to how I felt now.

Chapter 37

The next morning, I couldn't face going to work. I phoned in sick. How could I work? I couldn't face seeing him. I found it hard to believe that everything had gone so horribly wrong. I was sick, was it morning sickness? I was only ten days late, surely the sickness was too soon. I had cried until I must have slept out of exhaustion. I wondered how he was feeling. He didn't ring. I kept looking at the phone, willing it to ring. When it rang, it was Gareth.

"Sorry you're feeling bad. Was it too much wine? Dan's not in either. Or are you really sick? By the way I saw Jules last night, she's still raving about your professor."

I told him that I had a bad head and would be in the next day. He asked again if I was okay.

"You've been working hard and doing all the stats in your own time. You need a break."

"Doctors work all hours."

"Yes, but you're not a doctor. You're entitled to a shorter working week than them."

I told him again; I'd be in the next day as I wanted to get the results finished before my tutorial with Dr Sutton. I spent the afternoon working on the graphs. My headache had responded to pills. I needed to stop thinking about Dan, I told myself that his reaction had been extreme, and he didn't care about me because he hadn't contacted me. He obviously didn't want to talk about it.

I needed some fresh air and a coffee that was high in caffeine. Before I left, the phone rang again, my mood instantly lifted, but it was Dad.

"Hello Dad."

"Thought I'd ring you while I have five minutes. You wrote about coming to see us, is that when the term finishes?"

"Oh yes, I did, but the master's doesn't stick to terms. I'm spending most of my time at the hospital."

"Okay love, no pressure but wanted you to know I was thinking of you. It will be lovely to see you anytime when you're not too busy. Don't want to lose you again."

"That would be lovely." I could feel the tears welling up.

"Are you alright? You don't sound that good to me."

"Think I may have a cold starting," I lied.

"Look after yourself, drink some hot lemon."

I promised I would, thinking it would take more than hot drinks to make me feel better.

I left the flat and walked, I didn't go to our usual place. It wasn't just that I was trying to avoid him. I couldn't bear the thought of sitting where I normally sat with him. I nearly bumped into George. I wasn't looking where I was going, my eyes were full of tears. He caught my arm.

"Steady there let a fellow have some pavement too." I looked up.

"George, I didn't see you. Sorry."

"Hey what's the matter? You look as if you need a coffee and a talk."

I agreed that I did need both. He turned around and walked beside me, when we got to the café, he told me to sit down. He ordered the drinks without asking me what I wanted. He knew of course a double shot Americano with milk on the side, and a chocolate cookie.

"Now tell me what's wrong. Is it about you and Dan?"

I nodded.

"Yes, we've split up. Well, I think we have."

"I have all the rest of the afternoon and evening so spill."

I tried to but it was so complicated, and my voice kept faltering.

After a while, George said, "Let me see if I understand. You have been having out of body experiences in several time zones. Is that right?"

"Yes, and I've had no choice, it's just happened to me."

"Right, so one of these times you were in the body of a young woman who loved and was loved by Dan's grandfather."

I nodded, blowing my nose, "but then I was transported, call it what you like, to another time where he didn't know me."

"Was that in a different body?"

"Yes, but I still loved him, it was painful." He gave my arm a squeeze and offered me a big cotton hankie.

"I met with Professor Grice, and he promised me that I didn't need to travel any more. He said, I was now securely in my correct time. He sort of apologised for messing me about."

"You needed your questions answered."

"I don't remember having questions."

"You know more about your family history now, don't you?"

"I suppose so."

"You were always bothered that you had lost track of where your dad lived."

"Was I?"

"I think so and you had such an air of sadness. Recently that hasn't been there. You have seemed happy. If I wasn't an old cynic, I'd be saying two lovers were parted and their spirits have been searching over time for each other."

I looked at him.

"If that's the case then one of us doesn't know."

"Imagine the shock of finding out."

"But you have listened to me and accepted what I'm saying."

"I have known you since the first year, I know you're truthful. I didn't say at the time, but I was worried about you last year. I came to your rooms several times when you were there, but not there. Often, you've looked at me but not seen me. It's a relief to hear your explanation. I thought you had something wrong with you and didn't know what it was."

I looked at George. He was such a good friend. "What can I do?" I asked him.

He shrugged, "Don't know, hopefully Dan will get his act together, if not he doesn't deserve you. Think you've got to wait."

I nodded, knowing he was right.

Chapter 38

I told Gareth that Dan and I had an argument, and we weren't seeing each other. I tried to be matter of fact about it but had to brush away tears. Gareth reached over and squeezed my hand.

"Hope it gets sorted, you two seem so good together. If you need a shoulder I'm here."

The next week I worked hard; evenings were empty. Thursday Sarah rang to say she was coming round. She arrived with a bottle.

"Just to let you know, you have friends," she said, going to the drawer to look for the bottle opener. George had told her Dan and I had rowed.

"But no details," she said. "Are you going to fill me in?"

"It's complicated."

"If you can't tell me it's okay but remember we are all here for you."

"Thanks, I do appreciate it. I'm a bit weepy, I think it's hormones. I thought I was pregnant but had the usual stomach cramps last night. I found out this morning that I'm not. So the wine is excellent timing."

"Oh, poor you, should you see a doctor?"

"No, I was just late, don't know if I was hopeful or not?"

"Was that what the row was about?"

"Oh no it was more basic than that. Anyway, let's drink to better times."

We finished the wine, opened another bottle from my cupboard then decided to go to get some chips. I was pleased to be with her, I had neglected my friends recently because I'd been so besotted with Dan. The smell of the chips was marvellous, and Sarah's arm linked through mine as we walked along felt good. I promised I'd introduce her to my new hospital friends in two weeks when we were due to meet.

Saturday evening Dan came round. He stood at my door looking uncomfortable.

"I'm so sorry I've been an idiot. I have missed you." I'd decided that when I saw him, I'd be cool and distant, I wasn't. I was so pleased to see him. In a short time, we were in each other's arms, me thinking it was the only place I ever wanted to be. His bleep went off just after midnight and he dashed off saying he loved me as he went. My world felt complete again. Except we hadn't discussed either what I had told him or how he'd felt. He didn't mention us going to Wales either.

The next morning, I left a note in his pigeonhole saying, *'we need to talk.'* He left one in Gareth's room for me. *'Monday evening.'* It was a long time to wait. I didn't sleep well. Sunday night my euphoria at seeing him had diminished and I started to have doubts about his feelings for me. By Monday evening he was there.

"I'm off duty thank goodness, so we have plenty of time," he said.

"You look serious," I said.

"I love you, but I can't deny I was very disturbed by what you said to me last week."

"It was the week before actually, you left me for nearly two weeks."

"Yes. I've been doing a lot of thinking."

"But you left me, I've never been so unhappy."

"Sorry, but that story you came out with, it blew me away."

"It wasn't a story, and it was difficult to tell you."

"Imo, I know you think it was real but it can't be. All this talk of being in two places at once. It's one thing to discuss it as a..." He paused.

"It *was* real."

He reached out and took my hand, I snatched it away.

"Look Imo, I've been talking to a good friend of mine. He's a psychiatrist, he studies mind disorders."

"You've talked to someone else but not to me."

"Please hear me out. He says the sort of thing you described might be due to a type of epilepsy. He would like to examine you."

"You think I'm mad now?"

"That's not what I'm saying. Please see Simon, you may have something that can be sorted." I started to cry. I didn't want to be sorted. I just wanted to be believed. Then I wondered if he was right, was there something wrong with me? Would it do any harm to see this man?

"I'm confused, I don't know what to say."

"Please say you'll see him. I am worried about you."

I reluctantly agreed, I didn't feel good about it though. Dan suggested that we go out for dinner, which we did. After copious amounts of food and alcohol I felt much better, and more than happy to be back in bed with him. In the morning my doubts returned, could he love me for who I was? Could he believe me as George had?

A week later Dan introduced me to his friend Simon, we sat and chatted about normal stuff, but I was ill at ease. After a while, Simon said Dan had told him about my 'time shifts' ; it wouldn't be ethical for him to see me as a patient. He could refer me to a Dr Edwards, a colleague who would be pleased to see me. He was doing some research and looking for volunteers.

"So long as you don't tell him I'm mad."

"I certainly won't, and I don't by the way, think you're mad, that is."

I agreed and wondered why he would see me, but I knew if someone were researching, they would always welcome volunteers. I realised when I was back in the flat, I hadn't asked what he was investigating.

I told Gareth that I needed an afternoon to help a friend of Dan's with his research. He said that it was always good to help fellow scientists.

I thought it might be a good idea to talk to Professor Grice to try to ground myself. But when I rang, he wasn't available, so I left a message with his secretary saying I'd like to talk to him when he was free.

Chapter 39

Doctor Edwards ushered me into his room. He was softly spoken and asked me questions about my family and myself. My nervousness evaporated as he listened to me. He laughed when I said I was relieved I didn't have to lie on a couch.

"I don't do hypnotherapy either, but I am interested in your belief that you have experienced time shifts. Please tell me how you feel before and after it happens."

I told him about the feeling of the walls moving, the unreality, slip-sliding from one dimension to another. Sometimes being a watcher on the side, sometimes being inside another body. I could feel myself relaxing, listening to him paraphrasing my answers. Nothing to be afraid of, it was getting dark. I tried to remember what the time was. The curtains behind him were moving. I could feel myself slipping. I think I called out for help. Everything went dark and my ears were full of a whooshing noise.

When I opened my eyes, the room was different. Where am I? I can't move, my hands are fastened down. I can feel straps biting into my wrists. Someone is talking to me, telling me to keep quiet. I can see Dr Edwards standing beside me.

"What's happening? What are you doing to me?"

"Don't worry my dear just testing a theory. You are very receptive, you know." He reached over and undid the shackles on my wrists.

"Thank you nurse that will be all."

I sat up rubbing my wrists and looked around me. The room was white tiled, there was a large sink in one corner. I had been tied down to what looked like a table. Beside the table was a trolley. It had some sort of electrical equipment on it, and wires and clamps.

"What are you doing to me?" I demanded, but as I spoke, I could see the white walls start to shimmer and move. I was sitting once more in his office. The dark red curtains were no longer moving. I was confused. My wrists hurt, I looked at them and red wheals were forming on the right one.

Dr Edwards came over to me. "Are you feeling okay? You seemed to go blank there for a while. Is that what happens to you?"

"You already know what happened you were there."

"Where? My dear I haven't left this room."

"I saw you. I think you had me strapped down. Then you undid the straps. What were you planning to do?"

"My dear," he said again, his voice calm and soothing. "I'm afraid your symptoms are typical of frontal lobe disturbance and unless you take medication you will get worse. Look how you've harmed your wrist. You were rubbing it very hard."

He started to write on a prescription pad. "Now take these morning and night, they will take time to make you feel better. They should help. I suggest you take some time off, working hard or being stressed only makes this condition worse." He handed me the prescription.

"Make an appointment to see me in ten days. You should be feeling the effect by then and feel much better. The ointment is for your wrist. You have made a mess of it." I looked at my arm. The wrist was swollen now and very painful.

"No alcohol for now and I will see you in ten days." He got up and opened the door, reaching out to shake my hand but remembered and squeezed my shoulder.

"Take care my dear." I stood in the outer office bemused.

"Shall I make you another appointment?" his secretary asked. I nodded.

"In ten days," I said, and she wrote it down for me.

When I reached the ground floor, I saw Dan.

"Thought I'd come and see how you got on," he said.

"Have you been waiting long?"

"Not long, how did it go?"

"I'm not sure. Dr Edwards thought I had a problem, which can be helped by pills."

"That's good then. Is that the prescription you have in your hand?" I nodded.

"Right then we can go to the pharmacy and pick them up. Simon said he was a good bloke."

Why was I not pleased? If a few pills sorted me out and kept our relationship sound I should be happy. Dan seemed to be, but I felt I was being controlled, manipulated. Which is strange, considering how previously I'd thrust from one place to another? I felt troubled about Dr Edwards, and yet initially he seemed kind and once calm I felt soothed. What had happened to me in that room? He insisted I'd rubbed my wrists to make them sore, but I distinctly remember being tied or strapped down. Was it a false memory like the others? My mind was in a muddle, had all I'd experienced been false?

I took the first pill when I got home and wondered how serious this might be. Was I ill? I decided to go to the library the next day and look up frontal lobe problems. Dan phoned me in the morning, asked how I felt and reminded me to take my morning pill, which I did. He said he would tell Gareth I needed some time off. I told him it wasn't necessary. I must have fallen asleep, because when I woke up it was dark, and Dan was there. I'd been asleep all day.

"One of the side effects of the pill is sleepiness for the first few days," he told me. He made me some supper and gave me another pill.

"You are not to worry about anything. I'll look after you and you'll soon be well."

I tried to tell him I wasn't ill, but it all seemed too much effort. He sat beside the bed and stroked my hair. The next few days passed in a daze. When I was awake, time seemed to drift by. I realised how stressed I had been.

It was pleasant not to worry about anything. Dan was there often, loving, and attentive. By the second week, I was more with it. I started to work on my thesis again, feeling pleased with the amount of material I'd gathered. Gareth called me a couple of times; I told him I was going to the library to do some research. He thought that a good idea. I didn't get there though. I had every intention but somehow the days drifted by.

Sarah came round to see me. This time I told her I couldn't drink the wine that she brought with her. She seemed concerned that I was so sleepy, saying I didn't seem myself. I told her I'd been having episodes where I thought I was somewhere else, sometimes someone else. She listened to me without interruption. I said that I was seeing someone about it. She started to question me then.

"Who are you seeing? Is he qualified?"

"He's a doctor in the hospital. Dan told his friend Simon he was worried about me. Simon couldn't work with me because it would be unethical as he's Dan's friend, so he recommended Doctor Edwards."

"And he gave you these tablets."

"Yes."

"What did he say they were for?"

"He said I had a frontal lobe disturbance. He said what has been happening to me is typical of that condition."

"He diagnosed without an x-ray, isn't that strange? I'm concerned how drowsy the tablets are making you."

"They are making me sleepy, but nothing seems to matter at the moment."

"You're not yourself. I hope this effect wears off soon. What does Dan think?"

"He's happy that I'm getting treatment."

"Has he queried anything? Why did he think you needed to see someone? More to the point, why did you agree?"

"I don't know, I was so unhappy, and Dan seemed convinced I must have something wrong. I'm not so sure now. I don't know what to think anymore. I'm so tired." My head throbbed. I wiped a tear away. "I can't think straight, Sarah."

She came over and hugged me. "Are you going to see this man again?"

"Yes, tomorrow. He seems very thorough. He hasn't just given me tablets and sent me away."

"Good, tell him your friend is concerned, they make you too sleepy to function properly."

"You would make a nice mother. I wish mine had been more caring." I closed my eyes.

"Imogen, you are drifting off again. Are you sure you are okay? Do you want me to come with you tomorrow?"

"I'll be fine, Dan said he'd meet me afterwards." Sarah made us another coffee and we chatted for a while. Before she went, she said again she could come with me and asked me the time of my appointment. I couldn't remember, but she found the card stuck in the corner of the mirror. I must have put it there, or perhaps Dan did.

"Right, 3.30pm. I'll be here just before." She gave me another hug and let herself out.

Chapter 40

George was at the door at two o'clock the next day.

"Come in, I'm about to have a shower, but it's good to see you."

"Sarah told me about this doctor you are seeing. I looked him up. He's a psychiatrist. What's going on? Sarah's worried about you but has a deadline so I said I'd come to see you."

I told George that there was nothing to worry about and got in the shower. The hot water felt good, I shampooed the greasiness out of my hair. As I wrapped the towel around myself, I could smell toast. I walked through to the kitchen where George was busy making poached eggs.

"Here at least if you're going to see this quack, have some food." He must have brought eggs with him. I hadn't been shopping.

"Your fridge is nearly empty, you need to eat," he said as he set two plates down on the table. I slipped my dressing gown on and sat down to eat with him. I was hungry. He made coffee while I dressed and came with me to the hospital. I was glad of his company.

I didn't have to wait long before I was ushered in to see

Dr Edwards. He asked me how I'd been. I told him the tablets were far too strong, and I'd slept for most of the time.

"But the headaches have they improved?"

"I didn't have headaches."

"You had a dreadful headache when you were here before."

"That's because I'd been," I paused. What had I been? I couldn't remember properly. "I remember my wrists being sore and bruised, but not a headache."

"Yes, problems with memory are common, so the brain fills in with false memories for us. I think that's what's happening for you. You have vacant periods due to a type of epilepsy and your brain compensates by giving you a false memory."

"Where do the memories come from?"

"Possibly the books you read; you said you were an avid reader. You had a disturbed childhood. Your unconscious is trying to make it better for you."

"But why now?"

"That I don't know, but I'd like you to have an x-ray so that we can see what is happening in there."

"I'm not so sure."

"It's not painful, you just have to lie still for a while. I've arranged one for you today, it's best to check that I'm not missing something important."

"I can see that. Do you think I could have a tumour on my brain?" The thought filled me with horror.

"I'm just being cautious, nothing to worry about. Now my secretary will show you the way. Keep taking the tablets, your system will get used to them and I'm sure they will help."

I stood up. The session was apparently over.

"This time next week then, we will have a little chat again to see how you are doing."

His secretary gave me instructions on how to get to the x-ray dept., and an envelope to give to the nurse when I got there.

"They are expecting you," she said.

I found it easily, a nurse came up to me, took the envelope and showed me to a cubicle, told me to get undressed and put on the gown that was hanging there.

"But I'm only having my head x-rayed."

"It's a precaution, just slip your things off and I'll take you into the room."

The room was dimly lit. I lay down as she told me and looked at the equipment above my head, the lights started to blink. I looked at her again and her uniform looked different, it must have been the lighting. I could hear male voices.

"Just a little prick in the arm dear." She came towards me with a syringe. I sat up. "Why do I need that? I haven't signed for anything. Don't I need to give my consent?"

I knew I was rambling. I needed time to think. Why would I need an injection to have an x-ray?

"Calm down dear, this is to give contrast to the brain." She picked up a larger syringe and showed me. "This first one is to relax you so that we have a good picture." It was as she said, just a tiny prick and I soon felt myself floating, not caring about anything. Even as they strapped my wrists down and started to put electrodes on my head, I didn't struggle. I tried to ask questions: would the metal interfere with the x-rays? The words didn't come out clearly though. I shut my eyes and when I opened them, I saw the white tiles of the room I'd been in before. I turned my head and saw the trolley with the electrical equipment. Some leads from it were joined to the electrodes that were connected to me. Despite the injection, I could feel panic climbing into my throat. All that came out of my mouth was a whimper.

Dr Edwards and another man in a white coat were standing beside me.

"Now Imogen you will feel a little discomfort, then hopefully your problems will be over."

"Are you going to kill me? Put me out of my misery? What are you saying?"

"Don't be silly, of course not, just a little treatment." His hands were on my shoulders keeping me still.

"I think we're all ready. Stand clear, everyone." The pain was awful in my head, I could feel my body twitching, jerking. It stopped.

I heard a door bang and the one to the room burst open. James's voice, loud, angry.

"What the hell are you doing?"

Dr Edwards voice soothing, calm, said, "Steady on old chap, we are removing her problem doing a bit of ECT."

"Get out of the way. She doesn't need that. Turn that equipment off." James bent over me. "Imogen, keep still, I'm getting you out of this." I closed my eyes. I was exhausted. He was there. I didn't know if it was past or present, but he was there.

He undid my wrists and removed the electrodes, gently massaging my scalp. I sat up and the room spun round, I definitely had a headache now.

"Gently does it." My knees buckled under me when I tried

to stand, but James caught me. He sat me back down and went out of the room, I looked around, what was going to happen now. He came back with a wheelchair,

"It's not a very comfortable one but the best I could find. I didn't want to leave you there on your own." We were alone, the others had gone. The whole place was strangely empty. He wheeled me down the long corridors, back to Dr Edward's room. I sat upright. I didn't want to be there.

"Don't worry," he said as if sensing my fears. "I won't leave you." He wheeled me past the secretary, who called out, "You can't go in there."

"I think you will see that I can."

Dr Edwards was sitting at his desk, he got to his feet as James wheeled me in.

"Do not presume," James's voice echoed around the room,

"Never interfere with anything to do with Imogen again."

"But," spluttered Dr Edwards.

"I said never, you nearly caused her some serious damage with your meddling."

"She is a very interesting subject; I'd like to include her in my research programme. I meant her no harm."

"Keep to the rats in cages, you are delving into things that you don't understand. Now write her a prescription for a lower dose of whatever pills you put her on so that she can slowly withdraw from them."

"I will." He scribbled furiously on the pad and handed a sheet over.

"Do not try to mess with time again. Take this warning seriously."

Dr Edwards picked up a tissue and wiped his face, I could

see his hand shaking. James turned my chair around and wheeled me out of the room.

"Now we are back in the present. I think you had better call me Duncan, or Professor Grice, it's simpler. Let's see where George has got to," he said.

"George? I think Dan is going to pick me up."

"How do you think I knew you were in danger? George and Sarah came to see me, insisted on seeing me, and wouldn't take no for an answer. They are your friends; they really care about you."

"Dan loves me, I know he does."

"I think you are both in love with an idea. Dan wants you to be what he calls normal, and you have an illusion from what happened many years ago. Perhaps you should let it go."

I stood up and I was still wobbly. He took my arm, steadied me. I didn't know what to say.

"I know it's hard. It's difficult for people like us. We tread a different path. I had hoped that you were securely in the present now, but what's happened shows that you can be pulled away again. You need a safe harbour. Someone who might not understand fully but loves you for who you are."

"You always seem to be there for me."

"I am, I always will be, and I do care about you, but the power shift is wrong."

I stretched up and kissed him.

"Thank you for always being there for me." He put his arms around me, and looked over my shoulder.

"Hello George. Here she is safe again but a bit wobbly on her feet." He waved the prescription at him. "Go to the pharmacy and get these and I'll take Imogen back to my office and see you there."

"Imogen, what are you doing, did you keep your appointment, sorry I'm late." It was Dan out of breath from running up the stairs.

"She did, I'm sorry to say and it did her no good." Duncan looked angrily at him.

"Sorry, what's it got to do with you? Why are you holding Imogen?"

"Your meddling psychiatrist friend almost caused her great harm."

"What, he was helping her, she has a problem."

"The problem young man is your belief system."

"Imogen." Dan turned to me. "What is going on, I met George on the stairs, and he just glared at me?"

I was still clinging on to Duncan's arm. It gave me strength to reply.

"The fact is. Well, the fact is, what I told you did happen. Dr Edwards tried to banish it from my brain, to please you."

He stared at me frowning, "Oh course it isn't true. You do need treatment. He told me how serious it is."

I was aware that we were on the top of the stairs in what was a public area. How could we be having this conversation here?

"If he discussed me with you, it's unethical. You know that. I don't need treatment Dan. I need you to believe me." The walls were melting. I could see grass, not stairs.

Duncan's voice was in my ears. "Imogen hold tight. This is the effect of the drugs they gave you." He had his arm tightly around me. I wasn't going anywhere alone, but I could hear the sea, waves pounding. I could faintly hear Dan's voice asking questions. The smell of the sea was very strong now.

"Come back Imogen, come back." I didn't want to. I wanted to stay in that beautiful place. The sun was warm on my arms, the sand soft beneath my bare toes. The top of the stairs and Dan's face came back into focus.

"Imo you faded out, you actually faded. The air shimmered around you." The waves were still pounding. I could smell the ozone. I had a strong desire to swim.

"My god she's fading again, do something."

I could only see the half of Duncan's arm that I was holding on to, where was the rest of him? I tried to walk towards the sea, but my legs wouldn't move.

"Stay here, you're not strong enough to go alone at the moment," Duncan's voice spelt safety and I relaxed into it, the sea would wait until another day.

"Imogen and I are going to my office. It's not far, are you coming? She needs someone with her. Those drugs have affected her badly." Duncan slowly guided me down the stairs.

"No, no-way, this is too weird for me. I'm sorry Imogen. I thought we could sort this out but..."

"Then go, she needs support not what you were offering."

Dan stood at the top of the stairs not moving. When my legs gave way on the half landing Duncan picked me up and carried me down the rest of the way. Once at the bottom, he sat me on a chair whilst he fetched his car. I felt so weak, but I needed to speak to Dan. I called up to him. He didn't answer me.

"Dan, please come down and talk to me," I called again, thinking, he hadn't heard me the first time. He looked down at me, shook his head and walked off along the corridor. I sat thinking, I'll love you forever, meant I'll love you so long as you conform. I could feel the hot tears running down my cheeks. I shuffled in my bag to find a tissue.

"Have this one." It was Duncan, handing me a large white hankie. I was grateful he didn't tell me, *he's not worth it*. I think I was crying more for what might have been.

"Are you able to get up?"

"Yes," I said, getting to my feet. I still felt wobbly, but I wanted to be strong.

Chapter 41

George was waiting in the office for us. He looked worried.

"I was beginning to wonder where you had got to," he said.

"Imogen was having difficulty holding on, then Dan turned up."

George frowned. "I'm not sure he's good news."

"I agree but I guess it's up to Imogen to decide that."

"Hey," I said. "I am here, you know. I think Dan has decided. Anyway, I think I am seeing things more clearly now. Thanks for being so supportive, George."

"I've got the other pills. Professor, are you sure, they are all right? The previous ones had a bad effect."

Duncan took them from George's hand and read the label.

"Yes, these are better." He turned to me. "Make sure you take them as directed, then after a week halve the dose. That should stop you from having any side effects."

"I want to stop taking them, they make me so sleepy."

"You can but it needs to be done gradually," said Duncan. After two weeks if you are feeling okay, we can reduce them further. We need to meet up as soon as you feel well enough to put some safeguards in place for you. In the meantime, make a note, if you can of what triggers your 'travelling'."

"I don't know how I managed to allow myself to trust him, Dr Edwards I mean."

"It wasn't your fault; he has an exceptional manner and is a good hypnotist."

"I still feel stupid, I put myself in danger because I wanted to please Dan. I guess it wasn't his fault that he couldn't cope with me being unusual."

"You're not unusual, you are exceptional and right now you are looking very pale. I think I should take you back to your place and you can come and see the professor when you feel better."

"George, you are completely correct. Take Imogen home. Call me at once if you are concerned about her."

"I can take myself," I protested. When I stood up, my legs proved otherwise. George took my arm, and we walked out of the office together.

A cab was waiting outside the building. I turned to George. "Did you order a taxi?"

"I did, you don't think you'll be able to walk do you?"

"I suppose not, can't believe how weak I feel."

"Have you felt like this when you travelled before?"

"No." We were in the taxi now. I leaned my head back, closed my eyes and gave in to exhaustion. I had no strength to question anything. We were soon at my address. George paid, helped me out and followed me up the stairs to my door.

"Here," he said. "Give me the key, I'll unlock it." I was struggling, it was all I could do to get in the room and fall on the sofa. I must have dozed; the smell of coffee woke me. I gratefully drank from the mug George offered me. My head cleared a little.

"The prof said they had tried to do a treatment on you in that place. That might be why you feel so groggy now."

"I agree, it was awful. I thought they were going to wipe my brain. I've read about how they used to use electric shock treatments on difficult patients." I struggled again to remember the name of the doctor. My mind wasn't working well. "The psychiatrist said I was to have an x-ray in case there was something wrong with my brain. The next thing I was strapped to that table with electrodes all over me. I don't understand why he did it."

"Had you travelled back in time?"

"Do you know I'm not sure. He was there so if I did, he came too. He was trying to cure me. He didn't believe me. Oh, George I'm so confused."

"You say this was different to other times."

"Definitely. I don't recall coming back, there was no clear distinction between then and now." I couldn't think straight. I was so glad George was there.

"Come on, I'll stop asking questions. I think you need your bed. I'll wait until you're undressed."

"George, please don't go. I feel safe when you're there."

"I'll stay until you are asleep."

I awoke just as it was getting light. There was a mug of cold coffee beside the bed and a glass of water with a note propped beside it. *Call me if you need me xx G.*

I had slept through the night. I sat up, the dizziness had gone, and my head felt clearer.

There was an envelope under my door. The note it contained was from Dan.

It was short.

Imogen. So confused, sorry it doesn't seem right. Can't do this. I really believed that Dr Edwards could help.

Sorry that it had to end like this, but I can only do 'normal'. This is way too weird for me. Hope we can stay friends.

Love Dan.

"Love Dan." Huh, if I'd still been yearning for him this would have cured me, but after his departure on the stairs it felt like I'd woken up. My passion had gone from ten to zero.

Stay friends? I didn't need a friend who ran when I was in need. The anger had given me strength. I felt clear headed now and ravenous. I ripped up the note and delved in my tin for a lemon drop. I'd missed my meal last night, the last time I'd eaten was with George. As if he knew I was thinking of him, the phone rang.

"Are you up for breakfast?" George asked.

"Sure, meet you at the Coffee Bean in half an hour." I replied.

I quickly had a shower and didn't hear the phone ring again. As I went out, I saw it flashing. There was a message from Duncan. "Hello Imogen. I hope you're feeling better, today. Call me, please when you see this."

"I'll have breakfast first," I thought.

George was at the table. "You look better," he said as I sat down. His smile turned into a big grin when I ordered a full English.

Chapter 42

"Duncan rang me this morning. I missed the call, but I think he wants me to go to see him. I'm not sure that I want to," I told George as I finished my last bit of toast. "I want to be normal, and he reminds me of everything that was so strange."

"Things aren't quite right yet though, are they? Yesterday proved that. He said he wants to talk to you about keeping safe. It's up to you of course, but I think he has your interests at heart. He certainly seemed concerned about you."

"I know, but I'm not sure. He was tangled up in what happened."

"Look, go and see what he wants. Do you want me to come with you?"

It was so sweet of him. All my life I'd had to sort things out for myself.

"Thanks, no I will go. I feel stronger now that I've eaten."

When I got in, I called Duncan's number. His secretary answered, saying he would be free at eleven o'clock.

When I arrived, there was no one at the outer desk so I knocked and walked into Duncan's office. He was sitting in his chair. Upright, staring ahead, he didn't speak. I looked at my watch two minutes past eleven. I stood feeling awkward, should I sit down. The room felt strange, the floorboards melted beneath my feet, and I was running, running away from something, what? Then, Duncan was beside me, he grabbed my hand.

"Come on, nearly there." He was breathing hard; how long had we been running? I could feel the air rasping in my chest, my knees were hurting. The shouting behind us was getting louder. They were getting closer, I could hear dogs barking, growling. We came up to a wall, he ran at it pulling me through with him.

I collapsed and found myself on the office floor. He was sitting at his desk, his face scratched, and my jeans were covered in brick dust.

"That was close."

"What happened? I came in here to see you and then I was there, running for my life it seemed."

"Sorry, somehow you were caught up in it."

"Is that all you're going to say?" I was angry, my voice loud. "That felt dangerous. How did I get there? How did you? You were sitting at your desk looking as if you were in a trance, then I was running beside you." He got up and sat down beside me on the floor.

"I was waiting for you, but I was summoned. A fellow traveller was in danger. I needed to be a decoy. You shouldn't have been involved. It wasn't meant. I'm not sure how or why you were there."

"But you were there in your chair."

"Was I? Perhaps my body was."

"Your body? Yes, there was an absence about you. Is that how I look when I'm elsewhere?"

"Maybe."

"But it was you I was running with, how were you in two places at the same time?"

"The same time? Time is not a straight-line Imogen. People treat it as it were. You know different though."

"Do I?"... I'm not sure if I know what is real or imagined any more."

"I believe it's all real, just happening on different levels. How did you know to come find me just now?"

"What, in that place where you were running?"

"Yes, how did you know I needed help?"

"I didn't. I saw you sitting there and wondered why you were so still. Before I knew it, I was running, and you were with me. I still don't understand how you could be here and there. Now I'm more confused than ever."

"Time is not..."

"I know it's not a straight line. I get it, things happen at different levels. When I'm sitting in my room, I could be milking cows on a different level."

"That's right. Did you know that I was in trouble?"

"No, you just didn't seem right. I wasn't sure what to do."

"You came to help me though."

"Did I?... I don't know. I didn't think about you needing help. Its usually me in trouble."

"I was sending out signals that I needed help, you were the one who came. No one else answered me."

"How did I help? I was just running."

"Your appearance threw them off balance and gave me a chance to catch my breath. You saved me."

"I think running through the wall saved you and me."

"I wouldn't have reached the wall. I took some of your strength. I think we should get up now if anyone came in, they would wonder what we were doing here on the floor."

I laughed and I think he saw the irony of what he said because he smiled at me. I got up and fetched a tissue, which I wetted with water from the glass on his desk. I bent down and wiped his face as gently as I could, he still flinched. It looked sore but at least the brick dust was wiped away. I could see he was in pain.

"We were in our own bodies but in a different time and place," I said.

"Yes, we were and that's so much more tiring." I looked at him. His colour wasn't good.

"Are you okay?"

"Yes, but hungry now. I need to work out how you knew I needed help and how you managed to transfer." He reached into a drawer and took out a packet of chocolate biscuits. The chocolate was thicker than the biscuit. It seemed to make him more ordinary somehow. He offered me the packet, but I refused, as desirable as they were, I'd had a huge breakfast. I was very thirsty though and offered to make some coffee. I went into the outer office and put fresh water in the machine, as I did so his secretary came in carrying boxes of paper.

"Oh, thanks for doing that. He does like his coffee." She took over from me, "I'll bring it through."

Duncan was sitting with an almost empty biscuit packet, writing out what looked like complicated calculations. He had beside him a book entitled, 'The Mathematics of Time Shifts'. He looked up,

"I've almost finished." In other words, I thought, keep quiet. I did and drank my coffee when it came. I watched him drink his without his eyes leaving the paper. I helped myself to another coffee and tried to make sense of one of the sheets of paper he passed over to me. Almost an hour later he finally looked up.

"You have passed another barrier. You are shifting in your own body, and you were answering a call for help. We need to work together to ensure you are safe and don't get lost in another dimension." He held up his hand as I started to speak.

"This is important, you must do this, otherwise the strains on your body and mind will be unbearable."

"I don't want to be in another dimension. I just want to live an ordinary life. I am grateful I've found my dad and understand about my family, but I don't want to carry on like this. It's too complicated."

"You are right in one sense. You didn't choose. For some reason you were chosen whether you continue or not you must learn control." He looked at me for what seemed like a long time.

"You have proved you make a good partner, your response is excellent, and you learn quickly. You say you want to be ordinary, somehow, I'm not convinced. If you really mean it, we must lock you out to keep you safe." He stood up from the desk, put both hands on my shoulders. I felt a shiver pass through me, not a shiver more like a current. Of what I didn't know, I didn't want to lose the connection I had with him.

"I don't know. I'm confused, I don't understand what happened today."

He took my hand. "I know, it's a great deal to take in and you had your psyche messed about by that Edwards idiot." He frowned and looked at his watch.

"I'll walk you back to your flat, you need to concentrate on getting your strength back."

"My work at the hospital, I'm enjoying it, would I have to stop?"

"No, definitely not. You carry on, this is an addition to your normal life. Think of it as an enhancement."

"But if I go spiralling off without warning?"

"This is what we need to work on. You would be a pupil initially."

"Whose pupil?"

"Mine of course."

Chapter 43

Locked in. Locked out. Which was the worst option? To be trapped, stuck in my present, or risk all. Not knowing what might lie ahead, where I might be. How could I choose? Rest, Duncan had said. I could rest my body, but my mind raced. When I slept, I had the wildest dreams, usually of being chased, falling into an abyss. When I was awake, I tried to make sense of what had happened to me over the summer. Mostly, it had just occurred. Sometimes there was a warning as the room or scenery began to melt, or waver before it disappeared. Changed, plunged me into another time. Duncan said I could learn control. I needed to go back and talk to him.

By the end of the week, I felt physically stronger. I stopped taking the tablets Dr Edwards had prescribed and my mind was clearer. I was still confused about the choice I had to make, but I was no longer feeling in a fog. I decided to go to the hospital to see Gareth before I went to Duncan's office. I was concerned I might bump into Dan; I knew I had to face him sometime.

Gareth was pleased to see me. He had some results he wanted me to analyse, and we talked about a plan of work for the next week.

"It's so good to see you, Imogen. Your algorithm is helping so much. I've missed having you around, everyone has been asking if you are better."

"I'm so much better thanks," I said. "I'm keen to get back to work."

I was, I'd nearly messed everything up by seeing Dr Edwards.

Chapter 44

"Why do I have to make a choice?" My voice was loud. Too loud, I could feel my face and neck getting hot. I bent my head and pulled my collar up hoping he wouldn't notice. I hated the way my body gave away my emotions.

When he spoke, his voice was quiet. "Life is full of choices. We rarely make the right ones."

"But I didn't choose this. It just happened."

"In some way everything is a choice. You didn't have to open the door, or step inside. A timid person would have left it shut. Someone without your ability wouldn't have been able to get over the threshold."

I thought back, although it was only a year ago in present time, that evening felt a lifetime away. I looked at his face. It had become so dear to me. When did that happen? I guess he'd been there for me in every time space. Quietly looking after me even when I wasn't aware of him. I saw he was looking at me, one eyebrow raised.

"Well?"

"I remember feeling compelled, there was no question in my mind. I had to open the door."

"Precisely. You were called and you answered. Your

perception and courage led you there. Your special powers allowed you through the time barrier."

I stared at him.

"Where does that leave me now? I don't understand any more now than I did then. I'm always out of control, never understanding what's happening to me. I find myself in these strange situations and just blindly do the best I can."

"This period has been fulfilling in two ways. It's been difficult for you, but it's shown us that you're able to adapt. The positive for you is, it's enabled you to find your past, mended the holes in your family story."

I nodded, "It has."

"The decision to make now is do you leave it there? Endeavour to be content or do you reach your potential and join us. I can't promise safety, but I don't believe you will be bored."

I was aware of the clock on the wall ticking loudly. I didn't know what to say.

"Explain to me again, how it happens please."

"Time is like a wheel with spokes sticking out of the rim. It's possible to jump from one spoke to another but beware, if you fall in between, you could be lost forever in oblivion. It's not something just anyone can safely practise. Only those with ability can do it. You do have to learn how to use and control those powers you have, so you're not destroyed, or destroy the lives of others."

"How do I do that?"

"I can't tell you how. What we can do is exercise your mind as if it were an Olympic athlete. I will do everything I can to help you. That's if you decide to join us."

I felt as if I had been here before. I could hear music. His voice became fainter. I dug my nails into the palms of my hand.

He pushed one of the heavy books over to me. "You need to read this and make notes. Underline anything which isn't clear so we can discuss it later."

We worked until late afternoon when both our stomachs were growling with hunger. It seemed natural to go for something to eat together.

He relaxed as we shared a large pizza, followed by Italian ice cream. He looked younger, the graze on his face reminding me he could be vulnerable too. I thought of what he'd said about the power shift between us. It seemed more balanced now to me. He would always know more than I would, but I no longer felt like a little girl in his presence.

I realised he's talking to me.

"This is good. I've not had the chance to try many eating places. The coffee is excellent too." He smiled at me. Less the professor, more, well more like someone I wanted to get to know.

"Steady on," I told myself. I'd just come out of a relationship I needed to...

I didn't know what I needed. Only time will tell, but I did know I was happy to be here with him.

Acknowledgements

My thanks to Mike whose belief in me and encouragement has kept me writing.

I am grateful to all my writing friends, particularly Will Sutton, from whom I have learnt so much.

Their support, friendship and insightful comments have been invaluable and helped to improve About Time.

I am indebted to Fiona Ballard who has edited my manuscript and turned it into the finished book.

Thank you.

Eileen lives in Southsea, she enjoys writing and performing short stories and poetry. She is a member of Portsmouth Writer's Hub, Portsmouth Poetry Party, and T'Articulation, where she takes part in spoken word events.

Eileen has written for projects across the city such as the 200th celebration of Dickens and the Gallipoli Centenary. Her poem the Dockyard Gate was made into a short film for the DarkSide PortSide trail.

She was one of the authors for the interactive trans media production Cursed City -Dark Tides, which was performed across Portsmouth in 2019.

TeaTray Creatives was formed by Eileen in 2019, it meets weekly for fellow writers to read their work, give and receive feedback in a friendly environment.

Eileen is an avid reader, books like Stephan Donaldson's The chronicles of Thomas Covenant and Time Traveller's wife by Audrey Niffeneggar fed her fascination with Time Travel.

During Covid Restrictions there was plenty of time to dream, to write and About Time was born.

Milton Keynes UK
Ingram Content Group UK Ltd.
UKHW021114021124
450589UK00014B/1156